HATE
AT FIRST
SIGHT

LIZZIE O'HAGAN studied Law and Australian Law before going into publishing, where she now works as a Publisher at an independent press. She writes and paints in her spare time and though she can usually be found drinking coffee near her flat in central London, Derbyshire will always be home.

Also by Lizzie O'Hagan:

What Are Friends For?
The Visa

Writing as Elizabeth Neep:

The Spare Bedroom
Never Say No
The New Me
Twelve Days to Save Christmas

HATE AT FIRST SIGHT

LIZZIE O'HAGAN

REVIEW

First published in Great Britain in 2023 by
HEADLINE REVIEW
An imprint of HEADLINE PUBLISHING GROUP

2

Cataloguing in Publication Data is available from the British Library

ISBN 978 1 4722 8635 2

Typeset in Bembo Std by CC Book Production
Printed and bound in Great Britain by Clays Ltd, Elcograf S.p.A.

HEADLINE PUBLISHING GROUP
An Hachette UK Company
Carmelite House
50 Victoria Embankment
London EC4Y 0DZ

www.headline.co.uk
www.hachette.co.uk

To Bex Nelson and Juliet Trickey –
once-work-wives and the best of friends

Prologue

'Don't you *dare* leave me,' I hiss into the dim room, which pulses with colour and chaos.

'But this is my song.'

'The last seven songs have been your song.'

I put my hands to my hips as my line-manager Amanda starts to shake hers in time to the monotonous bassline of the music. She's so much cooler than me it hurts.

'Come on, Kate. This is a *party*, not a prison.'

'At least in prison I'd get three square meals.'

I look down at the minuscule canapé in my hand with disdain and Amanda laughs. No wonder most of my colleagues here are paper-thin. I study the narrow slice of meat laid atop an open lettuce leaf that is trying to pass itself off as some sort of burger. I opt for another glug of wine. I know you shouldn't drink on an empty stomach but believe me, I've been trying to fill it ever since I scurried into the office summer party four hours ago.

'This is Poster. What did you expect?'

She grins, reaching for my rejected slider and gulfing it

down in one. The truth is, I'm not sure. Ever since I got my job as a data analyst here, it's been both everything and nothing like I expected. On the one hand, there are the creatives and fashionistas who have occupied the tenth floor for over a decade now, ever since this superior office with its outrageous views became available and the then-directors decided that, though it was floors apart from the company's existing office downstairs, at least *some* of the Poster staff should level up somehow. These are the ones whose scarily symmetrical faces I found on the company's website as soon as the recruitment agent told me there might be a suitable role for me at the 'luxury e-tailer that professes to give Net-A-Porter a run for its money'. Then, there are the rest of us. The ones left downstairs in the basement, who make the dreams of the 'creative' types become a reality: the website developers, the financial forecasters, the technological support staff, the data analysts. The people like me.

'Come on, Kate. I thought you wanted to see what tenth-floor life was all about.'

Amanda stumbles slightly as she thrusts her arms wide and spins around. The tenth floor would be decadent even without the forest of fresh flowers and temporary dance floor they've brought in for the annual summer bash, the one where everyone from the office is invited to drink more than is advisable with people responsible for their future promotions. I try to remind myself that Amanda is technically my boss, that three months is probably not enough time to be this playful or pugnacious towards her. And yet, her natural ease in who she is seems to have enticed her entire team into becoming scarily unfiltered around her.

'No, *you* told me it was mandatory,' I argue back. See: scarily unfiltered.

'And it is . . .'

'Everyone else from downstairs has left already.'

'. . . for you.'

'Why just for me?'

'Because you're the newbie. Everyone else has done their time at one of these.'

'It's sounding a lot like prison again.'

Amanda smiles, bridging the gap between us and the tenth floor in the way I've seen her do ever since I've been working here. 'The people upstairs are honestly not as bad as the guys downstairs make out.'

'One of the women made Toby cry last time he came to deliver reports up here.'

'In her defence, he did offer to show her his latest aquascape.'

'Is that so bad?'

'I think she thought it was some sort of manscaping situation.'

'Poor Toby.' I can't help but smile, the expletives he relayed to us just last week finally starting to make sense.

'But we digress . . .' Amanda says, shaking away the thought. 'All this to say, this is your first time to really mingle between departments. Get to know some people.'

She's your boss, Kate. Your *boss*. I try to bite my tongue, to muster some professionalism. But then Amanda's swinging hips shake it away, at least for this evening.

'So, you can come dance to *my* song,' she says. 'Or you can stand in the corner and—'

'Stand in the corner! Sold to the woman with two left feet.'

'Kate!'

3

'Well, you gave me the option.'

'I know,' she groans, trademark cheeky glint in her eye. 'And I would order you to dance with me . . .'

'You *are* the boss.'

'But I think that could be outside my powers as your manager.'

'Enforced dancing.' I grin over my glass. 'I could report you to HR.'

'Oh, babe. They're probably too busy processing Toby's manscaping accusation.'

It's only as I watch Amanda disappear onto the crowded dance floor that I realise how drunk I am. I wish I could tell you how many glasses I've had but it's the kind of party where as soon as you get to a glass-half-empty situation, someone is already topping you up. There was the one as soon as I walked into the decked-out tenth floor, where my hands were shaking from the sight of no less than a hundred people who could have just climbed out of a catalogue. Then there was the drink fifteen minutes later when the company's new CEO, Gareth Grey, waved across at me, only for me to realise as I raised my hand that he was signalling to someone else. And was it one or two glasses of champagne I grabbed from a passing waitress when my first attempt at interdepartmental small talk led to a five-foot-eight cold-hard stunner telling me she'd worn the exact same blouse I'm wearing to a family funeral fifteen years ago. I'm not usually a fan of work drinks. Of being overly chummy with 'contacts'. But in this crowd, with this number of drinks flowing, there is no semblance of sensibleness left to hold on to.

I try to count the glasses and soon find that I need to use the fingers on *both* hands.

'Working out when you can clock off?'

4

I look up to see a man standing in front of me, his square jaw set, his lips pursed into a nonchalant grin as the pulsing lights from the dance floor illuminate him more for a moment before fading once again.

'Eh?' I shout above the music.

'The counting on your hands. Thought you were trying to work out when your shift ends. Either that, or you prefer children's nursery rhymes to Jason bloody Derulo.'

'Nursery rhymes?'

'You know. One, two, three, four, five. Once I caught a fish alive . . .'

Is this beautiful man really standing in front of me singing nursery rhymes to a backdrop of *Want to Want Me* right now?

I look behind him to try and catch Amanda's eye, to send her a silent SOS - *Is this guy a model or a mirage?* - but it's futile; she's already getting down and dirty to Derulo. I look back to the guy, tipsy and tantalising; I'm not entirely sure how a self-respecting twenty-four-year-old is supposed to reply to a midnight nursery rhyme.

'My shift?'

'Yeah, clearly you don't want to be here.'

'Of course I do!'

'Which part of sitting in the corner and counting hours on your hands is meant to convince me of that?'

'I wasn't counting hours, I was counting . . .'

The stranger has taken a step closer, leaning on the wall beside me. He's wearing a t-shirt, one of those strong, simple cuts that you can tell is expensive without needing to look at the price tag. Everyone else is wearing lightweight shirts, something a little smarter; like me in my family-funeral blouse.

'Yes?' He cocks an eyebrow, folding his thick, toned arms, intrigue suitably piqued.

'I was counting drinks.'

'Drinks?'

'Yeah, I don't like to drink too many and . . .'

I hate feeling out of control. Not that I'm going to tell nonchalant t-shirt guy that. Or the fact that this conversation, him approaching me from across the room, is making me feel like a fish out of water too. He could chat to any person at this party he wants to. So why me?

'You've been drinking on the job?'

What is it with this guy and shifts and jobs?

'Hasn't everybody?'

'Well, yeah, *we* have, but I didn't think the . . .'

His unfinished sentence fades into the sultry sounds of Sisqó and I have a horrible suspicion he's about to insinuate that the drinks budget doesn't stretch to those from the basement, that he's coming over to tell me that I've had more than my fair share.

'Didn't think the *what?*'

'No, no, don't worry, forget about it.'

He shakes his pretty head, struggling to hold my eye, and it's at this moment that a waitress walks past us carrying a tray of drinks and wearing precisely the same outfit as I am: skinny black jeans, loose black blouse. The family-funeral favourites of circa fifteen years ago. Both of us see her. Both of us realise . . .

'You thought I was a waitress?'

'No, I . . .' His confusion is palpable. 'You're erm . . . you're not, are you?'

'Do I *look* like a waitress?'

6

His eyes dart to the doppelganger-dressed woman who has just passed us.

'Do you really want me to answer that?'

'Your dick—'

'Bit forward.' Another cocked eyebrow, a cheeky smile.

'I was going to say, "You're a dickhead."' I struggle to be heard over *Thong Song*.

'Bit *forceful*, then. What's wrong with being a waitress?'

'Absolutely nothing apart from the fact that I'm not one,' I say, becoming hyperaware of my Northern twang clashing with his Southern accent. 'I work here, for Poster.'

I gaze into his grey-blue eyes as he neatens his perfectly groomed hair. Toby and the others downstairs were right about the tenth-floor fashionistas. Clearly, if you aren't wearing this season's latest threads, you can forget about fitting in with them. I look around the room at the heels and the bags and the effortless way people are swanning around the space. It makes me feel precisely how I used to around the mean girls at secondary school. Except, years have passed since then and I don't have to put up with it now.

'Look, it's okay. I'm going to get another drink. Have a nice night.'

'Now, if only you knew someone who was serving them.'

I can tell from his tone that this is meant to be funny and maybe if I didn't feel like such a joke, I could take it as one. Instead, I move past him, cheeks burning, biting my lip.

'Wait—'

He reaches for my hand, electricity running through me as his fingertips touch mine.

'It's not my job to *wait* on anyone.'

'I know, I made a mistake. It's just someone . . . Please, can we start over?'

For a moment, he looks genuinely mortified. So much so, that against all my better judgement, I find myself nodding.

'Let me buy you a drink to make up for it?' He's still holding his hand on mine.

'It's a free bar.'

'You would know.'

'You wanker,' I mutter back to him, but between his hand on mine and his full and unreserved smile and the alcohol in my system, I can't help but feel any anger in me bow to something like affection.

'So, what do you *actually* do for Poster?' he slurs over a freshly opened beer as soon as we've found a vacant desk to perch on, a little away from the drama of the dance floor. Amanda is a slave to it now; my other colleagues from the downstairs office are long gone.

'I'm a data analyst.'

'Working in the basement?'

'Would you not have noticed me before now if I wasn't?' I flirt, regretting it instantly. This is why I don't drink wine. Why I rarely go to parties. Especially parties like this one.

'Oh, I definitely would have noticed you.' He shuffles a little closer to me, until the sides of our thighs are almost touching. 'It's my second week. Still finding my way around. Hey, the basement office is pretty big too. How did you know I'd be working up here?'

'Because you're stun—'

I stop the rest of my sentence; I *cannot* tell a man I've just

8

met that he's stunning, especially one that has managed to get under my skin already.

'Because I'm stun?'

'I was going to say stunted . . .'

'I'm six foot two.'

I get up from the desk to stand before him, all five foot three of me.

' . . . emotionally,' I add, for want of anything better to say.

'That's not very nice.'

'You managed to insult me within three minutes of me meeting you.'

'I know,' he says. 'And that's the last thing I wanted to do.'

He reaches for my hand again, and I take a step closer toward him.

'Oh yeah?' I whisper.

'Yeah,' he echoes, taking a slightly stumbly step to close the sliver of space between us, my breath catching in my mouth; I can't believe this is the turn tonight is taking.

'Why?' I cast my blurry eyes to his, which are set firmly on my own.

'Because the first thing I wanted to do was . . .'

He allows the rest of his sentence to fade away as he leans in closer, reaching a hand to my face and gently pulling me towards him. I linger there, my lips inches from him, the model or mirage who has managed to approach me, serenade me with nursery rhymes, mistake me for a waitress and somehow still make me want to kiss him, all before telling me his name. Of course, I blame the booze but, in this moment, I'm not mad about it. In this moment, I want to be out of control, to lose myself in kissing someone I don't know for the first time in my carefully calculated life. I move to close the remaining gap between us, his lips grazing mine ever so softly as my mind drifts away from my body completely.

Then, someone turns the office lights on, and the room is filled with a collective groan as it dawns on people that this midsummer night's party is about to be murdered. His eyes are still on mine, my face held in his hands, until a voice hurtles through our moment.

'Hey, H. After-party at mine.'

Suddenly, he stiffens, inches from my face, jolting back so that my already puckered lips are kissing the canyon of air between us. I follow his unsteady gaze to the gaggle of women behind me, some looking down at me, others giggling to one another, some simply confused by my presence and particularly my proximity to *him*. Behind them, Amanda is standing there, staring in our direction, expression caught somewhere between shock and concern. And though I can't work out why exactly, the sinking stone in my stomach tells me that this is one of those rare occasions where the employer-employee strand of our dynamic is straining to be heard. Sadly, the young woman who has just caught his attention – who *must* be a model – is stepping forward from the fashionable fray to drown any silent warnings out.

'Come on, H. You coming with us, or have you got better things to do?'

I watch as his cheeks turn the colour of her plunging red dress, her blazing green eyes fixed on him as he stands, stepping forward, stalling for a second even though we all know her question is rhetorical. I sit there next to his discarded beer can, my stomach flipping over as the back of my neck starts to prickle with sweat.

If I thought being mistaken for a waitress or a funeral attendee was bad, this is a thousand times worse. Because this time I'm unmistakably me and I'm unmistakably hearing that I really don't belong here. Out of the corner of my eye, I see Amanda walking towards me, but then she is cornered by Poster's CEO, his broad frame eclipsing her from my gaze.

'There's taxis downstairs for the eight of us,' the woman in the red dress continues.

I don't need to count on my fingers to see that I'm unlucky number nine, that any after-party invites are clearly not for me. I look at my mystery man, morphing into a little boy right before my eyes. One that doesn't want to miss the after-party, and especially not for me. He holds my gaze for a moment longer, the same intensity I felt when he touched me still seeming to spark between us, but it's no power for the seven perfect Poster People who are laughing a little louder behind him now.

'Told you he wouldn't go through with it.'

I hear a whisper somewhere from the crowd of colleagues. Wouldn't go through with what? With kissing me? Like it was some sort of bet?

I force my legs to leave, to head towards the lifts, all the while hating the fact that tears are starting to prickle in my eyes and make their way down my burning hot cheeks. I don't even know him, I don't even know them, but they are looking at me like they've got my number down and it turns out, it's not a number worth knowing.

One, two, three, four, five. I rush towards the lifts, hitting the down button at least ten times in quick succession. *Once I caught a fish alive.* Stumbling inside, head still hazy from drink, I see the shape of someone approaching and from where I'm standing, it looks a whole lot like him. But if he thinks I'm going to give him another chance to embarrass me, he's got another think coming. I hit the button again, his broad frame gaining ground, his grey-blue eyes catching mine for the briefest of moments as the tall, silver doors close in front of me, the lift mirrors reflecting the shame on my face. *Six, seven, eight, nine, ten.* I watch the floor numbers descend, trying to forget the faces of the women looking back at me as the stranger left me suspended mid-kiss.

Then I let it go again. The doors open into the lobby, and I run out of Poster House, circling the grandiose building until I come to the shabby-looking stone stairs down to the back door into the basement office, all the while vowing never to go swimming with the tenth-floor sharks again.

Chapter One

Five Years Later

My stomach sinks as soon as I see Poster House coming into view. Well, the back of it. I've made a point of walking the extra twelve minutes from Tottenham Court Road, even on a cool March morning like this one, just to avoid the melee of models flocking into the glamourous front entrance. But then I remind myself of what lies at the bottom of it: a job I love, with colleagues I adore who are physically ten floors and ideologically *worlds* apart from our upstairs counterparts. Sure, after five years of working here some might say I've outstayed my welcome, but my time here feels a bit like running a large report: I've waited too long for the outcome to refresh the page now.

'Kate. Kate. Kate!'

I hear my name getting increasingly louder, cutting through the husky sound of Meatloaf telling me that he would do anything for love that is blasting through my headphones. I fumble to find my phone, longing to switch the track to something more age-appropriate and, well, cooler than the classic rock that me and my dad used to sing in the car together when I was young, but then I look up to see Blair beaming back at me.

'Meatloaf again?' She grins. The tinny music is still echoing through my earpieces, now hanging around my neck. If only I could justify buying AirPods.

'I'm going through a phase.'

'Two decades and counting.'

'I didn't say it was a *short* phase.'

Blair throws an arm around my shoulder, which at several inches below her own causes her hand to hit my backpack and almost knock my battered KeepCup out of my clutches. Even so, we manage to fall into step beside each other, one hand on our coffees, the others stashed in coat pockets and both of us chatting about the sheer number of reports we need to produce for the senior management team upstairs by the 'end of play' today.

'I hate that phrase,' she says, as we descend the spiral stone steps down to the basement office entrance, the 'Enter at your own risk' sign a semi-ironic relic of a departmental pirate-themed party we held shortly after the annual office mixer; we should probably begin planning the next one for in a few months' time.

'Which phrase?'

Blair loves the word *hate*, adding a good dose of dramatics to absolutely everything. Deep down, under the long, black hair and dark, gothic trench coat, she's a complete softie.

'End of play. Like, what part of work feels like a game to them?'

'As someone who has seen their monthly expenses, I can assure you they're winning.'

'But all work and no play for us?'

'Speak for yourself,' I grin as she rolls her eyes. Poster might personify everything I hate about the corporate world, capitalising on the latest 'trends' of cultural angst and social media induced comparison. But my actual job, the thing I do down here every day, taking seemingly random data and turning it into something useful, something that makes sense? That part I love; that part is play for me.

Blair pushes the door into the basement open and no fewer than ten faces glance at us from computer screens scattered around the back entrance, colleagues further afield already sat behind their monitors, headphones on and plugged into the task at hand. Some will have been here since seven this morning. Charlie lifts his messy, blond mop to look up to us with dark circles around his eyes that make me wonder whether he even went home last night. Still, he waves a hand, eyes reorienting to his screen before him as he does.

'Good morning, ladies!' He beams.

'Good morning, Charlie,' we echo back in perfect *Charlie's Angels* unison. It's the same greeting we've given each other almost every day for the three years since he started working here. Like everything else down in the basement, it's routine, orderly, comfortable, like a pair of worn slippers waiting for you to sink your feet into as soon as you arrive home.

'Whatsauppppp?' Toby asks as soon as I sit down at my usual desk next to him, ditching my phone face-up on the tabletop and proceeding to pull my laptop out of my bag. I feel his comfortable presence next to me; the bold orange hue of his shirt seeming even brighter next to his dark-chocolate skin.

'Hello. The nineties called. They want their greeting back.'

'That's a coincidence. The seventies called for you. They're really missing Meatloaf.'

I look down at my phone, my Spotify page still trying its best to expose me. Somehow being exposed here doesn't lead to embarrassment like it does upstairs.

'Good weekend?'

'*Great* weekend. I discovered fly fishing . . .' Toby hums with enthusiasm; he always does. Only, his enthusiasm flits between different hobbies quicker than his callused fingertips are writing code on his laptop keyboard as he speaks right now.

'Yeah?' I say, only half-listening, firing up the wizard I was working on before the weekend. 'Didn't have you down as the outdoors type.'

'I'm not.'

'But you said—'

'Fishing Sim World. It's a game on the Xbox.'

He says this as if I know nothing, when before this weekend he wouldn't have known the game existed. And once he moves on to the next thing, he'll forget that it does.

I smile back at my screen, reading over my latest report, still open from the last time I looked at it: the one that is meant to show the conversion rates between social media click-throughs and real-life purchases. I've tried not to work over the weekends ever since I realised, early on in my London life, that this city will never slow down for you, so you have to pace things yourself. Still, with my housemate Lucy working remotely for a digital start-up, it's hard for the hustle mentality not to spill out at home; especially when she's working for the employer I want, the very employer I foolishly turned down just over five years ago.

16

'Got much on this week?' Toby asks absent-mindedly. He's probably googling expansion packs or fan memorabilia for his latest fad.

'The usual. Need to get my annual review in the diary with Amanda though.'

'Has it been four years since you started here already?'

'Try five.'

When I first turned down the next-to-unpaid start-up position alongside Lucy in favour of the well-paid graduate package at Poster, I promised myself I'd stick it out for a year, hone those all-important 'transferable skills', and then move on to something more meaningful. And, despite the two years between graduation and *finally* securing my first salaried position seeming to unfold in a slow-motion montage of zero-hour contracts, unpaid internships and mounting insecurity, the years I have spent at Poster have racked up far quicker than I would have liked. But every time I've tried to leave, they've found another way to make me stay. It's a bit like trying to switch from EE: you only get the good deals once you start flirting with Vodaphone.

'Surely due another promotion?'

'Toby, I've been due another promotion ever since I became a senior analyst two years ago. It's the carrot they've been dangling that never quite comes.'

This time last year I swore I'd leave Poster if I hadn't become a director by my next annual review. After all, I wanted to get into data to help people, not just help them become better dressed. And yet, here I am, twenty-nine, stuck in the same role and too cowardly to remind Amanda that my review was due two weeks ago, because then I'll have to finally admit to myself that I've failed to stick to my own director-or-new-direction

17

ultimatum. There was once a time when the goal of becoming a director before turning thirty was unheard of, but now the idea of achieving something monumental before that milestone feels like an expectation, sometimes even an entitlement. And I know it's my next strategic step.

'Anyway, I think Amanda may have forgotten about it,' I say, mentally trying to work out my next ten-point plan. Then the sound of my name beckons me from my scheming.

'Kate?'

Amanda pops her head out of her office; she's cornered off from the open-plan space now that she's running with the big dogs upstairs. Thankfully her feet are still firmly on the ground – metaphorically and physically, after she turned down the offer of a room on tenth.

'She knows everything,' Toby whispers under his breath before swinging around to look at her, as we all do.

'Can I see you in my office for a sec?'

The same collective 'Ooo' you might hear when a teacher asks a student to stay after class echoes around the basement floor. I might cringe if it wasn't laced with comradery, and might even feel fearful, if Amanda wasn't still one of the best things about being here.

'Reel that role in, tiger,' Toby whispers as I get to my feet. I'm pretty sure it's a fly-fishing pun and I do *not* feel good about Toby calling me *tiger* but I'm too excited right now to care. Surely this is about my annual review, my overdue promotion, taking on the Data Analytics Director role I've pretty much been doing for over a year now. Sure, if I get it, it'll mean staying at Poster that little bit longer, maybe just another year, but then I'll be able to make that all-important sideways step

18

into a director role at another company, maybe even a charity or start-up like Lucy's now that I won't have to live off their slim entry-level salaries.

'Kate. How are you doing? Take a seat.'

Amanda beams, swivelling around in her chair. She suits this office; she suits this role. I knew that once she had set her sights on Operations Director, she was going to get it. It's part of the reason we get on so well. Not that I've held up my side of the bargain. Yet.

'Good, thanks. Lovely weekend. Board games with Lucy, gym, walks in the park.'

'Sounds wild.'

'Shut up.'

Probably shouldn't be saying that to someone about to give me a promotion, but Amanda has no qualms about being my friend as well my boss. She's a chameleon like that, always has been, flipping between roles effortlessly. As opposed to someone like me, who knows what they're good at, what environments bring out their best, and who actively enjoys staying in their lane.

'So, there's something I need to talk to you about.'

I sit straighter in my seat, feeling the shift from sarcasm to seriousness, the one she always makes when she's going to talk about something completely work-related. My promotion. To director. I smile back at her, willing her to give me a knowing wink.

'Is this about my annual review?' I can't take her silence any longer.

'Oh, crap. We need to book that in, don't we?'

So, not about the promotion then. Unless it's mine already, no need for debate?

'Yes ... my work anniversary was actually a fortnight ago ...'

'Congratulations,' she says, failing to look me in the eye.

'No, that's not what I was ...'

It's only then that I realise how tired she looks. And Amanda never looks tired. She's thirty-six with the skin of a twenty-six-year-old and though she refuses to get Botox out of principle, she does claim her skincare bill is twice what a little nip-tuck would cost her.

'Amanda, is everything okay?'

'Yes and no.'

'Okay ...' I say slowly, my heart picking up pace.

'Do you want the good news or the bad news first?'

I gulp. What does she mean? What is she on about? From the way she's looking at me, I'd think I'm about to get fired. But of all the things I know about myself – the good, the bad and the downright ugly – I know I'm good at my job. I've made sure of it.

'The bad news, always the bad news.'

That way you can control the situation, prepare for the worst.

'Poster is losing money.'

'How? We charge three thousand pounds for a cardigan.'

'Not *all* our cardigans.'

'My nan could knit them.'

'Okay, but your nan can't market them to fancy people with disposable incomes.'

'I've heard her friend Margery is minted.'

She smiles, but then her face falls again, worry knitting her brows together. 'But in all seriousness, our key clients buy clothes for status, not just for style. And there were only so many cashmere sweatsuits one could justify in a global pandemic. Zoom meant people only had to impress from the waist up.'

I bite my lip; now doesn't feel like the time to joke.

'Anyway, I know it's a good while now but the lockdowns obviously had an adverse impact and as a company, we need to tighten our belts.'

'What are you saying? Are people going to lose their jobs again?'

There was a company-wide reshuffle shortly after Gareth Grey became CEO that I'm pretty confident saw our downstairs team reduced by half, the internship scheme scrapped, new recruitments halted and anyone over ten stone axed from the tenth floor.

'No, not if I can help it, not yet. But we've had to think outside of the box in terms of cost-cutting and in developing new revenue streams for the company.'

'Okay,' I say slowly, not sure where she's going with this, why she'd need my help.

'And that leads me to the good news,' she beams.

'My promotion?' I ask, ashamedly hopeful.

Amanda shakes her head slowly. 'There's a companywide freeze on promotions for the next six months.'

'How is that *good* news?'

'Look, we both know you're performing at the level of director, but the other members of the management team don't . . . well . . . they don't really know who you are.'

'How can they not know who I am?' I allow myself this one Mariah Carey moment. 'My name is on every report that is sent to the tenth floor.'

'That's the thing. They know your *name*, but they don't know your face.'

'Why should that matter? I'm good at my job.'

'It shouldn't matter, but this is Poster, so it does.'

'So, what are you saying?' I force the question; not sure I want to hear the answer.

'I'm saying there is a new opportunity for you to work on a high-profile project, one that will secure your promotion to director the moment the freeze is lifted. And if that's not good news at a time when many of our colleagues could have lost their jobs then I'm not sure what is.' She breathes, begging for me to not make this more stressful than it already is.

'So, I work on this new cost-cutting project and then I get my—'

'Who said it was a cost-cutting project?'

'You said that there was cost-cutting and—'

'No, the project is a new revenue stream thing. The cost-cutting has been sorted.'

'You've not actually hired my nan to make the cardigans, have you? Because—'

'We're moving upstairs.'

'. . . she's dead.'

My words cut across Amanda's.

'Sorry, what did you say?' My heart is now galloping in my chest.

'Now don't freak out . . .' She holds her hands up like I'm a horse about to bolt. 'But the senior management team have decided to merge the two offices.'

'WHAT?!'

'I said don't freak out.'

'I know, but back-office has been in the basement for ages.'

'Not anymore.' She looks deadly serious. 'They're getting rid of it.'

'But we don't have anything to do with upstairs. It's like two different companies.'

'They think it will be a good time to develop a more integrated approach.'

'But we're like chalk and cheese,' I argue.

'Yes, but chalk and cheese both cost money and we can only afford one pantry.'

'Who keeps chalk in a pantry?'

'You know what I mean.' Amanda sighs, shaking her head. 'Look, Kate, I've spent weeks trying to work out whether there's another way, but this is happening. This is it.'

'But there's people down here that wouldn't *want* to work for Poster if we didn't sit separately. The people, the ethos . . . that's as much a part of our jobs as anything nowadays.'

'Either we merge offices and lose some people who don't think they can stomach working up there, or we don't and lose even more. There's been more than enough room to merge the teams since Gareth's initial reshuffle and that was *years* ago.'

I want to ask why he didn't merge the offices back then and put us out of our misery sooner, but I already know that Gareth takes great pride in the tenth floor being used for the 'outward facing roles' of Poster only: aka the employees he wants external people to see. Clearly, he's held on to this dream for as long as physically – and financially – possible.

'Why can't they move back into *our* office, then?'

'The tenth floor is bigger.'

'Not by much.'

'The tenth floor is *nicer.*'

'Beauty is in the eye and all that,' I argue lamely.

'Okay, they heard about the mouse problem.'

'Maurice is not a mouse problem. He's *one* mouse.'

'Kate . . . ' She says my name like a mother might to her child. 'This is happening.'

'When?'

'Two weeks today.'

'Okay, and I'm supposed to just go back to my desk and pretend that it isn't?' I ask, feeling sick to my stomach. Toby will lose his shit. So will Blair.

I've tried to give the Poster People a chance. We all have. So many times. And each time we've been met with the same cold, judgemental, arrogant responses.

'No, there'll be a company-wide announcement that goes around this afternoon.'

'Okay.'

'And no, you're not going back to your desk right now.'

'Okay?'

'You're coming up to tenth with me.'

'Okay,' I echo, though right now, *nothing* about this feels okay.

Chapter Two

'You ready?' Amanda turns around to face me as models and wannabe models swarm into the front entrance of Poster House.

No, I'm not ready, I silently reply with narrowed eyes, my heart racing in time to the hurried click-clack of Manolos and Moschinos surrounding me on all sides. I imagine this is what it feels like to be a mouse trapped within a herd of giraffes.

'Kate?'

She repeats my name again, reaching to pull the scrunchy holding her red hair high on her head so that it cascades down one side effortlessly, her chameleon-like tendencies transforming her into front-of-house material in an instant. It would take a lot more than a hair-flick for me to transform the boxy, black M&S pant suit and six-year-old ballet pumps that I decided to wear today. I pull my coat further around myself. Looking about me, I take in the open jackets of the Poster People passing by, the ones that clearly don't feel the cold; underneath them, I catch flashes of fuchsia blouses and simple white t-shirts tucked into jeans so ripped that they should be sold half-price and wonder why I still feel like the one who hasn't made any effort. Dressing smart helps me think smart.

'Are you sure this is necessary?' I ask, as a bony elbow juts into my side. The woman who has just bumped into me doesn't even look up from her phone, her cortado-sized take-away coffee cup managing to make her look even more like a giant blessed by the gods.

'As necessary as keeping your job?'

Amanda makes a persuasive point.

'No, I mean . . . me coming upstairs now . . . Can't it wait until . . . ?'

I look down at my outfit, hating the fact that just standing outside the front of the ornate ten-storey building is making me feel like I need to level up somehow. It has been ages since I've been up there, always managing to avoid trips to the tenth floor like the plague, sending reports via email or simply sending Blair or Toby or someone else. Each time they return to the basement, the reviews are the same. *Treated like a foreigner or overlooked completely. Hostile environment. Would not recommend to a friend.*

'I really had to stick my neck out,' Amanda begins, as another gorgeous, giraffe-like creature strides past us, 'to get you onto this new project. And Georgina wanted to meet you today, just to make sure you're the right fit.'

'Unlikely,' I mutter, feeling more childlike with every passing moment.

'Come on, Kate. You know someone up there has seen something in you before.'

The guy from my first summer mixer flashes through my mind for the first time in ages, as if after all this time the embarrassment of that moment is entrapped on the tenth floor, refusing to be released. And the conversation Amanda had with me shortly afterwards? The memory of it has become a bit like a bruise: something you forget about until someone gives it a poke. How was I supposed to know that my mystery man was an intern? That romance in the office is not forbidden, but it is frowned upon? And yet, for some reason, telling Amanda that the kiss she *thinks* she drunkenly saw didn't actually happen, in that particularly awkward moment, felt more embarrassing than her warning not to get romantically entangled with anyone from work in the first place. Either way, any entanglements had come undone.

'Who? Who saw something in me?' I push the memory to the basement of my mind.

'Well, they gave you the job in the first place, didn't they?'

'*You* gave me the job,' I laugh, forcing my legs towards the entrance.

'No,' she smiles, buoyed by the fact I'm finally moving forwards. 'I convinced them to give you the job, but you needed four yeses to make the cut.'

'Like *X Factor*.'

'You had it, baby,' she laughs, pressing both hands to the revolving door, which I know spins incessantly throughout the day as we can hear the heel-clacks downstairs. I step into the same compartment as her, feeling like my whole world is spinning as we head inside.

'Floor three?' A man in the lift takes one look at me. I scan the logos printed against each floor number, highlighting the external offices that exist between the two sides of Poster: three is a kitchenware marketing firm. First time I've been typecast for that role.

27

'Ten, please,' Amanda corrects him, as I notice that the Poster logo isn't even listed next to the basement floor, our offices simply afforded a big non-descript 'B'. I guess the days of being out of sight and out of mind are soon to become a thing of the past.

One, two, three, four, five. I watch the floor numbers ascend, trying my best not to think about that mixer, that guy, the way the laughter of the staff upstairs had played on my mind all weekend before Lucy finally convinced me it was no big deal. The only good thing about Amanda's warning – *I've seen countless colleagues held back from rising through the ranks by getting down and dirty in the office* – was learning that his internship had come to an end. Not that he was ever the issue. The issue is that I'm still here, still not a director, simply 'earning my keep', when I'm part of the team keeping this place in business.

'You ready?'

I wish Amanda would stop asking me that. Even so, the lift doors are opening and I'm stepping out onto the tenth floor of Poster House for the first time in weeks, maybe even months. The ceiling-to-floor windows flood the open space with light, the hubbub of Oxford Street down below mirrored by the goings-on inside the room: long legs striding the length of the office with purpose, other people gathering in groups, laughing into freshly bought lattes. Every time I come up here, I'm surprised to see it set out as a proper office. Long gone are the flower arches and dance floor of the summer party, but the room feels no less decadent for it, with long glass tables spanning from window to wall, state-of-the-art MacBook Pros lined up along them for as far as the eye can see. Each time I begrudgingly visit it manages to be both exactly as I remember it and yet completely different, like an ageing woman who is constantly modifying herself to look precisely as she always has. I recall it instantly, but every time it feels fresh and shiny and new.

'Told you this floor is nicer,' she whispers.

'Nicer looking, at least.'

'Now, *you* be nice. It's been ages since you were up here. Things change.'

Following Amanda across the open-plan space in the direction of the cornered-off offices and meeting rooms at the back of the floor, I find myself subconsciously holding my breath, waiting to work out whether today is an imposter or invisible day. Not one person looks up from their newly delivered avocado on toast or freshly baked pastries.

'Mandy!' A young woman pops her head out of a meeting-room door as soon as we come into her sight through the tall glass windows. *Mandy?* I crinkle my nose in Amanda's direction and she narrows her eyes in response, as if to say, *Don't you start.*

'George.' Amanda smiles in return, opening her arms for a half-hearted hug.

'Now, Mandy, you know I prefer Georgina,' she says playfully. Amanda stiffens at my side, making me think that she's said the same thing about her own full name a time or two. 'I'm so glad you could make it; this office merger is going to be really . . . something.'

Something sounds about right.

'Come in.' She beckons Amanda into the room, where four velvet office chairs, each a different shade of green, are pulled around a mahogany table. 'And where is Catherine?'

Amanda and I look at each other. Clearly, today I am invisible.

'Oh, *this* is Catherine.' Georgina beams, pulling a chair out for me with arms so slim that I am surprised she's able to move the office furniture at all. Who did she think I was? Amanda's shadow? 'I'm Georgina, I'm the Managing Director here.'

I know exactly who she is. For starters, I sit next to the person who uploads the directors' photos and bios to the website downstairs (updated regularly lest anyone changes a hairstyle), and then there's the fact that she's met me before, more than once in the past two years she's been working here. Amanda may want me to be more visible, but at this rate I'm not quite sure what that's going to take: twenty meetings, a candle-lit dinner, a full-on snog?

'I'm *Kate*, Senior Data Analyst.' I re-introduce myself.

'Kate is the best data analyst we have working downstairs,' Amanda chips in. I'm not sure whether to feel pleased or patronised; she's looking at me like she's one step away from sticking my latest report on her fridge.

'Wow,' Georgina replies, without an ounce of *wow* in her voice, before sitting down in a chair across from us, her loose-fitting silk dress revealing more of her fashionably flat chest. She looks young: really young, younger than me. And yet, here she is, Managing Director at Poster, when I can't manage to get promoted or leave or even upgrade my M&S suit.

'I'm so pleased that you were able to make it up here today.'

Georgina makes it sound as if ascending to the tenth floor is akin to climbing Everest. Right now, I think I'd rather be sweating it out in the snow.

'We're really excited by the prospect of working alongside our support staff . . .' Her sentence trails off and for a moment I think she's self-correcting, that she's realising just how preposterous calling the people who build and maintain our website

30

'support staff' is, when selling products via our site is what we do. Then, I see what she's looking at. Gareth Grey, CEO, walking towards us, his oversized suit jacket billowing behind him and layered over a tight black polo neck tucked into perfectly tailored trousers. He looks like Poster personified, as does the woman walking behind him: curly blonde hair tied up into a bouncy ponytail that falls down her exposed, bronzed back, her backless blouse paired down with dark, ripped jeans. Is she not *freezing*? She's so vivacious that she makes Georgina look like a fuddy-duddy grandma.

'Georgina?' Amanda pulls her attention back into the room. If Georgina is perturbed by the gorgeous creature that has just swanned past us with the CEO, there's no hope for the rest of us. I may as well pack up and go home. I *want* to pack up and go home.

'Yes, yes.' Georgina is flustered and yet still manages to look flawless. 'What was I saying? That's right – we're really excited to have you all on board.'

We've always been on board. We're keeping the ship afloat.

'And we can't wait to use the office merger as an opportunity to really mix things up around here, to develop a more integrated and interdepartmental approach to our work.'

This sounds like a spiel, one that wasn't written by her.

'Kate . . .' She turns her full attention to me, bony elbows pressed into the wooden tabletop. 'We'd love for you to help develop a new microsite.'

'A new microsite? But that's not what I do.'

Amanda crosses her legs, kicking me under the table. I suspect it's intentional.

'Oh, I know what you *do*.'

31

Does she, though? Ten minutes ago, she didn't even know who I was.

'But we want real user data to feed into every decision we make, from how the site looks to the items that are listed. We've been working in silos for far too long.'

Sure, what she's saying makes sense, but our silos are comfortable, cosy, safe.

'Amanda and I have joined together to highlight small inter-departmental groups that can work closely together to really create something . . .'

What is it with Georgina and her nondescript *somethings*? Then I see what she's looking at: Gareth Grey closing the automatic blinds around his office, seeking privacy.

'. . . something magical.' She finally forces the words out.

'So, who will I be working with?' It feels like I'm asking on someone else's behalf, like my body is here but my brain has already left the building.

'Our new Innovation Executive,' Georgina explains, eyes oscillating between me, Amanda, and the CEO's closed office blinds.

'Innovation Executive?' I echo back to her. Is that even a job?

'It's a new role.'

'I thought you said there was a freeze on new roles?' I turn to Amanda, a pained smile pinned to my face.

'Gareth Grey can make exceptions,' she replies, her own teeth gritted into a grin. I can tell that she doesn't agree with Gareth's 'one rule for them and one rule for me' way of doing things around here and it momentarily makes me hate this place even more.

'So, me and this innovation person develop a new microsite?'

'Along with one of our creative managers,' she nods. 'And if it is successful—'

'*When* it is successful,' Amanda corrects, always having my back.

'We'll set the website live and you can really make your mark on Poster.' Georgina smiles. 'And if it doesn't work—'

'Which it *will*,' Amanda chips in again.

'. . . we'll have to make some more cuts.'

No pressure, then.

'I'll brief you fully on the project when the office merger is complete, but for now I'd love to introduce you to the colleagues you'll be working more closely with.'

'It's okay, I can wait,' I begin, mentally planning my exit strategy from this place, from this organisation, for the umpteenth time since I first started working here. But almost immediately the logical side of my brain begins to pipe up: *You've worked too hard for too long to give up on the plan now.*

Amanda coughs loudly.

'I mean, I *can't* wait,' I correct.

'Good, because here's one of them now.'

Together, Amanda and I follow Georgina's gaze behind us and out through the sheets of glass into the open-plan space to see a statuesque figure striding towards us.

No, no, no. I double-take, my pulse starting to race. It *can't* be. I look from his broad shoulders to his glossy brown hair, higher on the top, shorter at the sides, and then to his strong, square jaw; he looks an awful lot like the intern from the summer mixer all those years ago. I force my eyes to focus, praying with every step he takes towards us that he morphs into someone other than the once-mystery man who rejected me in the most public of ways. But he's looking more and more like him . . . devastatingly gorgeous, like *him*.

A stupidly handsome half-smile turns up the corners of his mouth as he nods at a triplet of pretty women gathered around a computer and then turns back to a now-standing Georgina as he raises a large open palm in her direction, following her signal to step into her office. The office that I am in. The office that I now desperately want to get out of.

'Are you okay?' Amanda whispers, eyeing up my shaking hand as it tries its best to smooth down my suit, as if the laying of hands will miraculously turn me into a model. The fact she doesn't twig that this is the man from the mixer shows just how long ago it was, perhaps how tipsy we all were as well.

'I'm actually not feeling so good,' I say, forcing myself to stand precariously on my now-shaking legs, the room spinning around me. This shouldn't matter; he shouldn't matter. But the way he looked at me back then, the way *they* looked at me, like I would never measure up, like I would never make the cut, makes me really want to prove him wrong. And I've never known anyone show someone up whilst wearing a tired, ill-fitting suit, worn black ballet pumps and not a scrap of makeup on their face.

'You look awful,' she goes on, as if I need the confirmation. 'Georgina, can we leave the introductions to another day?'

'Sure thing, but . . .'

I turn to race out of the office but instead hit something hard, strong.

'Oh crap, sorry . . .' He begins to mumble as my cheek accidentally makes contact with his chest. 'I didn't see you

34

there . . .' He pulls away to look down at me, my now exposed cheeks burning bright red.

'It's okay, I . . .' I begin, daring to look into his big blue-grey eyes.

I see them widen in recognition, his dimples deepening as he looks me up and down, only inches away from him.

'You've *got* to be kidding me.' My whisper escapes between us.

His smile vanishes instantly and he stalls for a moment before taking a decisive step back, as if the Poster People were sniggering at him for fraternising with the 'help' all over again.

'Catherine, allow me to introduce you to . . .'

Georgina's voice trails into silence as she clocks the intensity of our stand-off.

'Sorry, do, erm . . . do you guys know each other?'

'No—'

'Yes.' My answer cuts over his. Great, so he doesn't even remember me? 'Well, erm . . . not really.' I continue, his eyes widening even further at the awkwardness of it all.

'But you have met?' She tries to understand the increasing frostiness between us.

'Once,' he says.

'Briefly,' I add.

'Okay, well, in that case, perhaps a refresher would be helpful.' Georgina's already relentless positivity shoots into overdrive as she tries to steer our introduction back on track. She probably thinks we've brushed shoulders in the lifts or something. She has no idea that this isn't the first time that my mystery man has looked at me like a stranger, or an alien, like the way he seems to be sizing me up and finding me wanting now.

But I don't want him. I can't, I *won't*.

'This is Harry, one of our leading creative managers.' She's practically singing the words over the quiet hum of hate seemingly searing between us now. I look him up and down, his body still squared up to mine like we're in some unspoken staring match. He's wearing dark jeans, turned up at the cuffs, his exposed too-white socks signalling that he's the kind of man who wears and disposes of a new pack every day rather than bother himself with looking after them; I don't need to imagine that he'll be the same way with women.

'And this is Catherine; she's a data analyst from the basement.'

Catherine? Mandy? Is taking it upon herself to lengthen and shorten people's names at will some sort of Poster People power move?

'*Senior* data analyst.' I make a lame power play of my own.

'Nice to meet you.' He thrusts his hand into the space between us. Nice to meet me? So, now he's backtracking on his admission that we've met before?

'Charmed,' I force through my clenched jaw. I reach my hand out and he takes my fingers in his, shaking them in a firm handshake that manages to send shivers up my spine, transporting me to the moment when he first drunkenly laced his fingers through mine.

'Sure,' he shrugs, reclaiming his hand and any electricity that sparks between us.

'You guys will be working closely together after the merger,' Georgina goes on.

'Excellent,' Harry says, deadpan.

'Can't wait.' I force a smile, my words dripping with sarcasm.

Amanda's head jolts between us like she's watching the Wimbledon finals.

'This isn't going to . . . erm . . .' Georgina struggles to retain her shininess as I shuffle from foot to foot and Harry stares into my soul. '. . . be a problem? This will be fun, right?'

'No.'

'Yes.' Harry's answer cuts over mine this time as he folds his arms in front of him.

'No, this isn't going to be a problem,' I correct, my feist finally consuming my carefully crafted career plans. I repeat it to myself: this is *not* going to be a problem. Because in two weeks' time, when the office merger happens, I'm going to be long gone. Working somewhere else, for something that matters. Working a long way away from people like him.

'Yes.' Harry looks to Georgina, dismissing me again. 'This is going to be fun.'

His blazing eyes turn back to me, narrowed in suspicion, lingering over the clenched fist that is pressed against my slightly popped hip. Then, they turn away. They're looking past me, gazing out of the room to the bouncy-haired backless-blouse-wearing blonde who has just emerged from Gareth Grey's office. And I find myself invisible all over again.

Chapter Three

It's still freakishly light outside by the time I escape from the tenth floor and plant my pumps safely on the pavement of Oxford Street. Hordes of colourfully dressed tourists pass me on all sides, clutching shopping bags so full that they manage to make the street feel even busier, coats slung over their folded arms as they marvel at how the crisp morning has mellowed into a mild afternoon despite it only being mid-March. I wish I could join them in enjoying it. But all I can think is that it's probably due to global warming and that this whole world is going to burn, and I'll *still* be stuck at Poster.

'Cheer up, love.'

I'm walking too fast to detect the unhelpful person who said the words. Because since when has 'Cheer up, love' ever made anyone actually cheer up? But maybe he has a point? Maybe it's not so bad. Perhaps I could work alongside this Harry guy, and we could create something amazing together and I'd finally get the recognition I deserve?

'Ouch!'

I come cheek to chest for the second time today as I

accidentally bash into someone coming out of Tottenham Court Road tube station in a hurry. Everybody is in a hurry.

'Wake up, would you?' A man, grizzly in every sense of the word, looks down at me as I scurry past him as fast as I can. But maybe he has a point too? Maybe I do need to wake up. To the fact that I've been trying to make something of myself at Poster for far too long, that they are never going to affirm or celebrate or promote a person like me. That their world is designed for people like Harry who win repeatedly without even knowingly competing.

As soon as I'm underground, I plug in my headphones, just trying to drown out the voice that has been repeating on a loop in my brain – *You need to leave, you need to leave* – Meatloaf's *Bat Out of Hell* confirming that I have to find a way to be gone before the morning comes. By the time I emerge at Kentish Town, the sky has grown dark, and my resolve has grown even stronger: I must quit my job before the office merger takes place.

The further I walk from the station, the more the melee of passers-by peters out and I can finally think straight. Okay, so I quit Poster . . . then what? I have no savings to speak of. No family able to help me out with anything other than warm hugs and hot cooked meals. The job market sucks. And I have rent to pay. The data of this dilemma does *not* look good.

But . . . I almost heave with relief at the optimism of my own subconscious. But . . . maybe I'll get a new job sooner than I think? But . . . maybe they'll take me on as a director at a higher salary? But . . . maybe some long-lost relative somewhere has an inheritance with my name on it that will arrive in my bank account at the optimum time to keep a roof over my head until the director job of my dreams falls into my lap? Just maybe.

I arrive at the slightly battered red door to the flat I share with Lucy and know that I've got that lucky at least once before: the moment I moved in with her. We hit it off during a week-long internship at Cancer Research and we were both looking to move to the city. And it just so happened that her incredibly cool film-producer parents wanted to invest in a property in London, albeit a modest one.

'*Hola, chica*,' Lucy says as soon as I've stepped a foot inside, a semi-ironic nod to her Mexican roots. She looks up immediately from her laptop, set open amid a smattering of reports strewn across the wooden dining-room table at the back of the open-plan space.

'Hey,' I reply.

'Woah, no semi-racially inappropriate *Hola, niña bonita* today?'

'How is that racially inappropriate?' I'm powerless not to take the bait.

'It's not what you say, it's the way you say it,' she says mockingly, pretending – not for the first time – that we're living here as wife and wife.

'You try speaking Spanish with a Yorkshire accent,' I quip back, ditching my backpack and proceeding to slump into the structureless sofa.

Lucy closes her laptop, coming to join me on the other side of the small space. It's only just gone six thirty, hours before she usually clocks off for what's left of the evening, which means she's probably noticed my on-edge energy, that I'm about to laugh or cry or quit my job. Or work with a guy that has unknowingly unearthed hang-ups I didn't even know I had. Either that, or she's about to tell me her parents are coming to visit. That, as well as finding a new job, I'm going to have to top and tail with her in her double bed whilst they cruise the city 'on business' again. I knew their visits were part of the mate's-rates rent deal, but for a *niña bonita* she sure does snore a lot.

'So, how was your day?' She says this in a super-chipper voice that makes me confident she can detect the smoke coming out of my ears.

'It was . . .' I begin, but my too-busy mind is already stalling on the thought of her parents, about the fact that they own this place, that they don't even *need* my rent, that maybe, just maybe, if I explained the situation to them, they'd accept even less whilst I found a job.

'That good, *ey*?' Lucy shuffles in her seat and I notice that she hasn't tucked her slender legs under her body like she usually does, curling into the corner so intently that you'd think she wanted to be a part of the furniture. She's perched on the edge woodenly.

'I think I need to quit my job.'

'You *think*? You've been thinking that since the first day you started there.'

The way she says it makes me sure she thinks I'm the girl who cried wolf.

'I've had good days too.'

I don't know why I feel the need to defend myself.

'I know that.' She smooths her long dark hair behind her heavily studded ears. 'I know you love the *job*, and the people.'

'Some of them.' Harry's deadpan face when he said he barely knew me lunges to the forefront of my mind. The fact he's been working up on tenth and never thought to ask about me is something I find deeply annoying; and the fact it annoys me is even more irritating.

'But you've never loved the *place*.'

'Preaching to the choir, *hermana*.'

Lucy doesn't laugh at my feigned attempt to speak her mother tongue.

'What's up?' I ask, as she crosses her long legs in front of her, too formal for home.

'Nothing's up, not really . . .' She smiles softly.

'Good, because there's something I want to ask you.'

'There's something I need to tell you . . .'

Lucy and I hold each other's gaze, giggling slightly as our sentences collide.

'You go first—'

'Shoot—' We both speak at the same time again. I don't know why I feel so nervous. It's not like I'm asking *Lucy* to pay my rent. I'm asking her to ask her parents to waive it for a bit, or maybe just postpone it. If I get a job that pays more than peanuts, I may be able to save something, pay them back with interest. Lord knows, they understand that living in London on anything less than twenty thousand pounds a year is hard work if you want to actually *live* in London, not just exist here. It's part of the reason they bought this place, so that Lucy could start on the year-long internship wage at the start-up. It's entirely the reason I had to take a job at Poster rather than join her at Do Good Data in the first place.

'I've got a new job,' she says, her grin wavering momentarily.

'Oh, Luce. That's amazing!' I move to throw my arms around her, but she still feels a bit stiff. 'But wait . . . Don't you love Do Good?'

42

'I do and I'm not leaving.'

'You got promoted?' I say, my joy for her genuine but my words still forced. In five years, she's gone from intern to director of her department. In five years, she's gone from earning less than the minimum wage to earning the same as me working for Poster.

'Kind of. I got a secondment.'

'Amazing.'

'It'll just be for a year.'

'It's still amazing.'

'For the San Francisco office.'

'*Luce*, that's incredible. Will you get to visit?'

'No, not exactly . . .'

'That's okay, I guess it's to be expected with how much cheaper remote working is for companies. It's still amazing though, the experience you'll get working for—'

'Kate . . .' She cuts over my nervous chatter. It's just that between Lucy's news and my day at work and the question I'm about to ask her, I think I'm one more shock away from exploding. 'I won't be visiting San Francisco, because I'll be *living* in San Francisco.'

A silence stretches between us as I try to process what she's saying.

'You're leaving?'

'Only for a year.'

'Then you'll be back?' I hate that I sound so needy. It's just, she's family.

'Maybe,' she says, reaching to hold my hand in hers. 'They've said that if the role suits me and I like living there, there may be a chance to make it permanent.'

'Is that what you want?'

'Maybe. I don't know. I guess I'll cross that bridge when I come to it.'

I know being closer to her parents again will be at least part of the draw.

'I'm so proud of you,' I say, willing my voice not to crack as I do.

'Really?'

'Of course. I mean, I'll miss you like crazy, but you've got to take the opportunities when they come.'

Unlike me, taking the wrong path five years ago and still trying to get back on track.

'I'll miss you too.' She looks like she's going to cry. 'But you can come visit.'

'I can,' I nod, even though what I really want to say is 'With what money?' But this *could* act in my favour? Lucy's parents could charge whoever takes her room double and reduce my rent to next to nothing whilst I plan my next move. I imagine they'll be so happy about Lucy's job and her moving closer to home that they might just say yes.

'And when you guys visit me, we'll just have to turf out the new girl for the week or invite your parents to our top-and-tail party and have four in a bed like we're in *Charlie and the Chocolate Factory* or something . . .'

'Kate—'

'Fine, I'll sleep on the sofa.'

'Kate . . .' She says my name again, squeezing my hand a little tighter. 'My parents are selling the apartment.'

Eh? They're doing what? My mind races. My mouth hangs open, mute.

'They're selling the apartment,' she repeats as I reclaim my hand. Not because I don't want Lucy to hold it but because it's starting to prickle with sweat, and I somehow feel like I need to use it to steady myself on the sofa beneath. 'They've been thinking about it for some time, ever since the pandemic. You know, like, we were working from home, and we could be working from anywhere and then, yeah, with me getting this secondment and moving to San Francisco, they just wanted to sell it and—'

'So, I have to move out?'

'Unless some unsuspecting family wants a two-bedroom apartment complete with twenty-nine-year-old millennial.' She tests the water with a softly spoken joke.

'Get your parents to tell them I make a really good spag bol.'

'I will,' she says, a stray tear escaping from her big brown eyes. 'End of an era, *ey*?'

'You can say that again. When do we need to move out by?'

'Well, don't freak out but . . .'

Why do people keep saying that to me today?

'. . . they want to get the ball rolling quickly and have found some contractors who can start doing some work to the house in . . . well . . . two weeks today . . .'

Lucy's sentence continues but I don't really hear it. Two weeks today. The same two weeks that will see the back-office basement intermingled with the front-of-house Poster People. That will see me wrestling with Harry and some silly 'Innov-ation Executive' over a microsite that doesn't even matter. Now I have to find somewhere to live too?

'Obviously, if that doesn't work for you, I'm sure I could chat to my parents, and they can find another contractor and . . .'

45

'No, no,' I say quickly. Lucy's parents have already been too good to me. And I refuse to be an inconvenience, someone they need to take care of. Kate the charity case. 'Tell them that will be fine. I will be fine.'

I'm not sure which one of us I'm trying to convince.

'You're the best.' She gives me a sad little smile. 'So, what did you want to ask me?'

'It doesn't matter.' I choose to celebrate her amid the confusion that is clouding my mind.

'Come on, Kate, it always matters.'

'This time, *niña*, it really doesn't.'

I make my way to my bedroom for the umpteenth time, except now it feels different. Now my days here are numbered. Unlike my days at Poster. How is it that when you're in your early twenties you feel like some sort of time millionaire and yet towards the end of the very same decade you feel time is slipping away? I look around my bedroom, the multiple houseplants I've managed to keep alive popping against the plain cream walls, the ones me and Lucy donned overalls to paint together. Quitting my job and finding a new one on reduced rent was risky enough, never mind having to find somewhere affordable to live without the luxury of mate's rates.

Reaching for my phone, I am tempted to call my parents, but I don't even know what time zone they'll be in right now, their post-retirement gap year set to rival even the most wanderlusting of millennials. And if they do pick up, I know exactly how it'll play out. They'll be full of empathy and encouragement as they listen to me process an angst that they can't quite get their heads around. And then, as soon as I've hung up the call, I'll feel haunted by guilt that I've made them

46

feel helpless when it comes to helping me financially. They've given me everything a woman could wish for, but you can't pay your rent with love. Instead, I swipe to LinkedIn and try my best to search for a lifeline. I'm either too qualified or not qualified enough. And now I feel like every moment I spend on applications is a moment when I should be finding somewhere else to live. Somewhere to live without Lucy.

'Kate, can I come in?'

'Just getting changed,' I lie, only then realising that I've been crying this whole time.

'Liar,' Lucy says, thrusting her way into the room.

'Hey! What if I was naked?'

'Nothing I've not seen before, baby. Oh, Kate.' Her face falls when she sees mine.

'It's okay; honestly it's okay,' I lie again. I refuse to turn her brilliant secondment news into the final nail in my thrive-before-thirty coffin.

'I've just spoken to my parents,' she begins.

'They've changed their minds?' There's too much excitement in my voice.

''Fraid not. But they know of someone renting a room.'

'In London?'

'No, in Saudi Arabia. Of course, in London, you donut.'

'How do your parents know everyone?'

'Just people in the biz, *darling*.' She elongates her vowels, mocking the creative industry her parents inhabit, the one she's never wanted to be a part of.

'Tell me more.'

'All I know is it's a two-bedroom apartment owned by some eccentric actor they worked with on a film in the seventies.

One of their tenants has gone on tour supporting some band and they need someone else to take his room for five months or so. So, it'll be temporary, but maybe that's a good thing?'

A good thing? I look to my housemate of more than half a decade, my best friend of even longer. Right now, nothing about this feels good.

'The rent is three fifty a month.'

'Three fifty what?'

'Three hundred and fifty pounds,' she beams. This is my lifeline.

'But that's so cheap . . . cheaper than here.' I narrow my eyes suspiciously.

'He doesn't want to move all of his stuff into storage. So, you'd be living with his things. Some of them. The rest, he'll move into friends' houses and whatnot.'

'So, I put up with living with some of his stuff. That's the only catch?'

'And his housemate.'

'His housemate is a catch?'

'Don't know anything about him, I'm afraid.' Lucy shrugs. 'Reckon you can put up with some stuff and a stranger for three hundred and fifty pounds a month?'

'For three hundred and fifty? I'd throw in a daily backrub for the housemate.'

'You've not seen him yet. He could have a hairy back or something.'

'I thought you were trying to make me feel better?'

'Well, I have some more good news.'

'Oh yeah?'

'If they offer me a permanent job in San Fran . . .' Of course they will. Lucy already sounds like a local. '. . . then my director role will be available. And they recruit via referral.'

Scrap the apartment thing. *This* is my lifeline.

'You'll need experience at directorship level,' she adds.

'Easy. I've been operating as a director for years.'

'Official experience. Like on-your-CV experience.'

Damn you, six-month promotion freeze.

'Might be worth waiting around for one more ride on the Poster-coaster.'

I groan out loud, knowing what this really means is one more ride with *him*.

Chapter Four

Two Weeks Later

I wedge my mouse mat down the side of my already over-flowing cardboard box, the one that I'm moments away from lugging over to the lifts, past the other offices and all the way up to the tenth floor. Yes, I know mouse mats are pretty much redundant since the days of the mechanical roller mouse but if the merger thinks it can take my retro Art Attack one – a gift from Toby and the best coaster I have ever known – it's got another think coming. Plus, Toby's assurance that Neil Buchanan's smiling face will perpetually remind me that 'it doesn't take much to make something beautiful' might be exactly what I need up there. Not that I imagine anyone upstairs will think the same thing. About anything.

'Woah, an expertly packed box if ever I saw one.'

Blair has materialised beside me. I thought she might tamp down the gothic attire for our first day upstairs but if anything, she's applied even more eyeliner. It's like she's digging her heels in, an act of protest for all that's to come. I love her even more for it.

'I wish I hadn't had so much practice lately.'

'You and Lucy moved out of the apartment?'

'Lucy's moved out of the flipping country.' I have to say the words out loud, if only to remind myself they are real. The last two weeks have flown by in a blur of separating books and cooking appliances and reminiscing on the last five years before packing it all into boxes.

'And you?'

'Still here.' Still ashamedly here, even though I swore I wouldn't be around to see our basement staff mixed into the upstairs culture like oil and bloody water.

'I meant have you moved into your new place?'

'Yes and no,' I say, bending my legs before lifting the box, which wobbles in my hands. Blair comes to my rescue, grabbing the other side until my stuff becomes stable. 'I moved my boxes in this morning; my first night sleeping there is tonight.'

'Big day.'

She can say that again. My personal life is in boxes in some teeny flat in Greenwich, awaiting my mystery housemate's arrival home. And now that the movers have gutted out Poster's belongings from the basement, what's left of my professional life is in boxes about to be moved upstairs so that I can 'work closely' with a man who publicly humiliated me on that same floor. I know it shouldn't matter, that it was a long time ago, that people won't remember, that everyone's moved on. But *we* haven't. I'm still here. He's still here. And, if our second encounter is anything to go by, he still thinks he's far superior to me.

'Why does it surprise me that you guys are the last ones standing?'

Amanda arrives behind us, her red hair falling in Hollywood waves; she looks even more stunning than usual, and I worry that we've lost her to the dark side already.

She takes one look at Blair's raging face. 'Come on, it's not going to be that bad.'

'No.' Blair smiles her sweetest smile. 'It's going to be worse.'

Together, we walk towards the exit of the basement and out of the heavy industrial door to find Toby and Charlie standing at the bottom of the stone spiral stairs, boxes clutched in their arms too, fear written on their sorry expressions.

'You didn't think we were heading up there without you?' Toby looks incredulous.

'Come on, Angels.' Charlie winks. 'We got this.'

'Guys, you're moving offices, not going off to war.' Amanda laughs, shaking her luscious locks as she begins to stride up the stairs. Charlie and Toby follow her. As Blair and I fall into line behind them, balancing my box between us, she looks at me intently.

'That's what *she* thinks.'

The lift opens onto the tenth-floor reception area, which is lined with low white sofas whilst its plain walls play backdrop to three large photographs taken from Poster's new summer campaign. Four female models are captured dancing around an idyllic meadow packed with pretty flowers that seemingly don't need soil to survive as there's not one grass stain or mud mark on any of the floaty cream and pale-blue garments they are wearing. As we shuffle through the room with our boxes – me in a grey suit, Blair in all black – we couldn't look more out of place if we tried. And, as we enter the main office floor, it dawns on us that not only are we out of place but there is physically no place for us to sit.

'Of course there is!' Amanda objects as one ludicrously tall lady double-takes as she swans past the five of us. 'There's a hot desk over there.'

She points across the busy office to an empty desk wedged between two gorgeous-looking creatures who are leaning so far into one another to flirt that there's barely any desk space left to sit at.

'And there's one there.'

She points in the opposite direction to a desk that would be empty if there wasn't a guy sat nonchalantly on top of it, twisting his buff body slightly to look at the desktop of the equally hot man sat next to him.

'There's one here.'

Amanda pivots again to point in the direction of another desk that must be on the other side of the five colleagues stood around laughing and joking like they've only just arrived at work, even though it's already gone eleven. My stomach jolts and I don't need the broad, tall figure of one of them to turn around to know that it belongs to Harry. He's leaning a hand on a messy-looking desk that I assume must belong to him, and each of the young women around him are quite literally swooning. If there's a thin line between confidence and arrogance, Harry's nonchalant stance screams that he's crossing it and doesn't even care.

'And there's one over there.' Amanda points all the way to the far side of the office and Toby, Charlie, Blair and I all squint to try and make out the tiny desk in the distance.

'I'll take that one,' I say quickly as the others groan. I may

53

have to 'work closely' with Harry, but at least I can retreat to the desk furthest away from him.

'Damn you, Kate.' I'm sure Toby means for me to hear him as we disperse from our 'safety in numbers' formation and he beelines for the desk that is the next furthest away from the group of five colleagues and the woman he tried to show his aquascape to.

bph@poster: How long are we expected to put up with this?

Blair's email arrives in my inbox almost as soon as I am back at my desk, which tells you just how blissfully far away it is from the area where most of the upstairs staff are now congregating. Blair is right in the middle of it, sitting in the thin sliver of space between the two could-be catalogue models who are flirting across the top of her.

cc@poster: I'm staying six months and if I'm not made a director the second the promotion freeze is lifted, I'm out of here.

My new ludicrously cheap rent would galvanise this kind of threat if it wasn't going to come to an end around the same time as the freeze is lifted. It's director or back to Yorkshire. Not that I have a home to go back to, now that my parents have retired into their second adolescence, selling our family home to go travelling before planning to downsize on their return. Then, there's the niggle in my stomach which tells me that until I get 'director' on my CV, there's no way leaving Poster wouldn't mean a monumental step back in my career. I watch as Blair plugs in her headphones, the colleagues on either side of her practically kissing each of her cheeks in their bid to get to one another. She catches my eye.

bhp@poster: The worst part is they're pretending not to like each other.

'Woah, Kate. Could you have picked a desk further away?' Amanda is standing by me, looking a little out of puff having just walked the entire length of the office floor.

'Nope.' I beam back at her. The one thing I've done right today.

'Well, get your walking boots on.' She casts a sharp look to my footwear, like she wouldn't put it past me to be wearing walking boots to work. '*Gina* wants you in her office.'

I follow her gaze all the way to the other side of the floor. If I thought Georgina was a rake before, from here she looks like a single, black line. Harry, on the other hand, looks as solid as ever as he stands to make his way towards her, and I realise that I'm now going to have to do the walk of shame past the entire office floor to meet them inside.

Harry, Georgina and the bouncy blonde I had seen disappearing into the CEO's office a fortnight ago are all sitting around Georgina's mahogany table by the time I walk in, a slight sweat forming on my upper lip from the journey and the sheer stress of having them each look me up and down right now. While the blonde woman – who looks closer to her teens than to her thirties – takes one look at me and then turns her attention back to her freshly painted fingernails, Harry's gaze fixes on mine for longer than is comfortable.

I'll admit, he looks as gorgeous today as the first time we met, maybe even more so. His brown hair is pushed up high in a way that makes it look like he's only just run his hands through it, and he's grown a bit of stubble which somehow makes his jaw look even more defined. I look to his ripped jeans, exposing thin slivers of his tanned skin below, to his green t-shirt, which is so tight that I can just glimpse the outline of his nipples. He clears his throat. I force my eyes away from him, my cheeks burning at the thought that he's just caught me checking him out. But I wasn't checking him out. I wasn't. I catch his eye once more and he gives me a knowing smile that reminds me he's just a cocky jock all over again.

'Thanks for joining us, Catherine,' Georgina says.

'I was just getting settled at my new desk.'

I look over my shoulder to show just how far I've had to travel to be here, like they should be honoured or something. I can see from the look on her face that she feels the honour should be all mine.

'Can I see you for a sec?'

All four of us look up to see Gareth Grey hanging his head around the door into Georgina's side office, trying to feign inconspicuousness, a move that is largely redundant given that his whole imposing body is visible through the office's glass walls. That, and the fact that he's the man in charge of the entire company.

'Yes,' both Georgina and the blonde chime in unison.

'Oh, I think he meant me.' Georgina turns to her younger counterpart, somewhere between beaming with pride and pretending to look sheepish. It's a pretty hard look to pull off, but as with everything else she chooses to wear, she does it to perfection.

'I actually meant both of you,' Gareth corrects.

The young(er) woman sits up straighter and squares her shoulders a bit broader, whilst Georgina seems to shrink before us.

'Hazza, I'll return these lovely ladies to you in five minutes.'

Gareth Grey winks at Harry; I try not to be sick in my mouth. Then, I realise that it's just me and Harry left alone in the room and even though I know it's all in my head, I suddenly feel the burn of a thousand eyes on me from the other side of the glass. He looks at me. I gaze down at my phone. I look to him and he starts staring at his own.

'Look, I think we—' he begins, looking startled by the sound of his own voice.

'Hazza?' I crinkle my nose at the pet name, at the awful way Gareth Grey insinuated that Georgina and the other woman were somehow his, to be 'returned' to him. 'Bit familiar.'

'We've known each other for years.'

He shuffles in his seat, making himself look bigger somehow, unable to hold my eye one second and then fixing his gaze on me so intently that it feels like he's staring the next.

'Yes, so I've heard. I've worked here longer than you.'

I actually don't know how long he's worked here. All I know is that after his internship five years back, we haven't crossed paths once until a fortnight ago.

'Calm down, mate. It's not a competition.' He smiles again, halting my mental calculations, and I feel like he knows that if it was a competition, he'd be winning.

'I'm not your *mate*.'

I hate it when guys call women 'mate' generally. Even more when the guy saying it is someone you are interested in. Correction: *was* interested in, for like a second.

'Noted.'

His eyes scan over my face, as if he's searching for something . . . perhaps my admiration? That was shot the second he thought he could use me in whatever initiation game he was playing with his new colleagues back then. *Told you he wouldn't go through with it.* I had almost forgotten the sound of that whisper before I was forced to come back to the scene of the crime with him again. I guess the universe is giving me another opportunity to show him that I'm not the kind of woman you can toy with.

'What's in the bag?' He grins, moving to place his right foot to rest on his left knee, forming a perfect triangle with his strong thighs, exposing his bright white socks as he does. He's leaning back in his chair nonchalantly, bothering himself only slightly to nod down at my tote bag, oversized, and overflowing with everything I could need for the meeting. His full lips twist into a smirk and I know he's read the slogan written across it: *Wanna data me?*

'Laptop, notebook, pens, refills—' I begin defensively as he folds his arms.

'No wonder you were sweating on your way over.'

'I was *not* sweating.'

He laughs, exposing his big toothy grin as he leans back even further in his chair. 'Tell me, wise one, why would you need a laptop *and* a notebook?' His expression is one of genuine curiosity, even though I suspect it's a front for another chance to tease me.

'What if there's nowhere to charge it?'

'And the pen refills?' He laughs again, leaning even further back in his chair.

'Better for the environment. We can't all wear single-use socks.'

'Who said anything about single-use socks?' He sees me glancing at his. 'You think I wear a pair of socks *once* before ditching them?'

'I don't know. Maybe.'

'These cost twenty pounds a pair!'

'That's obscene!'

'Not as obscene as single-use socks.'

Harry looks offended now, his arms folded as he leans on his chair again. It tilts further and further back, his laissez-faire attitude putting me more and more on edge.

'Can you not just keep six feet on the floor?'

The words fall from my mouth and his mild offence turns into amused curiosity. 'What did you just say?'

'It's just . . . I mean . . . your chair,' I begin, feeling embarrassed by the intensity of our conversation. But then, I did try to kiss him within an hour of meeting him. 'If you keep leaning back like that you're going to fall and go straight through this glass wall.'

He leans forward so that his feet and the chair legs are all on the ground again.

'Better?' He's chuckling to himself as he clocks my obvious relief. 'Six feet?'

'It's something my dad used to say to me.'

His expression changes from one of surprise to something more pensive. He studies his shoes and for a moment I can tell his mind is somewhere else. Then he's back. And his disdain for me feels even more resolute. But he's the one who left *me* hanging all those years ago – so maybe he doesn't just not

59

fancy me, he doesn't *like* my personality at all. 'Man, you're bossy, aren't you?'

'Some would say *assertive*.'

'Yes, *some* might.' The way he says it makes it clear that he's not one of them.

'Well, if you want to fall, be my guest.' I gesture to his chair.

'There'll be no falling here.'

'Fine.' I match his defensive expression before he seems to soften somewhat.

'Six feet? Never heard of that one before.'

'What did you think I meant?'

'I don't know.' He shakes his head; there's the tiniest hint of warmth in his voice. 'I was too busy thinking about how many single-use socks I'd need.'

Georgina slips back into the room, with the other young woman following in her ever-so-slight shadow. Today she's wearing her bouncy blonde hair down, which she keeps sweeping to one side to reveal the cold shoulder of her one-sided pale-blue blouse. If I wore that to work, I'd look unprofessional, my breast just visible where the top scoops under the arm, the pale skin between my arm and my chest puckering just enough to make you believe I was showing too much skin. On her, however, it looks tasteful and on point, her bronzed shoulder leading the eye to her flawless clavicle and just hinting of what's underneath enough to make you unable to look away. Just like Harry isn't looking away from her now.

'Right, now that *that's* over,' Georgina says, her tone suggesting that whatever interruption Gareth Grey has sent their way wasn't exactly fun – for her, at least – 'let's get down to it. You should all know by now that you are one of a handful of interdepartmental groups that we're putting together to work on some new income leads for the organisation.'

Georgina looks to each of us in turn. As I do the same, I catch Harry's eye for a moment before he fixes his stare safely back on our new blonde friend.

'The purpose for the new microsite is to try and target a younger buyer,' Georgina goes on, and I hate that at twenty-nine I feel encouraged that they'd still see my insights as representative of that demographic. 'Obviously, millennials are buying from our main site.'

'No, they're not,' I hear my voice saying before my mind can recall the words. 'Sixty-four per cent of our buyers are over forty.'

And I imagine ninety-nine point nine per cent of millennials can't afford a £3,000 cardi.

'That can't be right.'

'It can . . . I have it all right here. I . . . '

I reach into my tote bag to pull out my laptop or notebook or something else to help me back up my facts, but then I catch Harry's widening eyes. He shakes his head from side to side, leaning back again. I stop shuffling.

'As I was saying,' Georgina goes on. 'That is why Gareth decided to bring Caroline on board, to offer us insights into the wants and needs of the centennial generation.'

'It's Cally.' She loses all her bounciness when it comes to correcting her name.

'But your file says—'

'No-one calls me Caroline anymore.'

'Perhaps you should introduce yourself?' Georgina's clipped voice stands at odds with the pleasant expression on her face.

'Gladly.' Caroline – or *Cally* – beams once again, and from the way she is looking at Harry right now, I can tell it's mostly for his benefit. 'Well, I'm Cally, and I've been working in fashion since I was twelve.'

Two years, then? I might berate myself for my bitchiness if I wasn't too busy feeling foolish for thinking I could ever have been called on for a 'younger perspective' with her in the room.

'Isn't that, like, child labour?' Harry asks, a deep crease forming between his knitted brows. Why is it that every line on a man makes him looks wiser, but on a woman, it apparently looks 'weathered'?

'Well, by working, I mean my social media platform. I've been posting @CallyforniaDreamin for eight long years.'

'When did you spend time in California?' He leans a little closer towards her, no doubt imagining her straddling a surfboard.

'Never been,' she smiles, unperturbed. 'Just liked the name.'

'And so do two million other followers,' Georgina adds. *Two million?*

'Yes, when my uncle told Gareth how many followers I had, he said he just *had* to get me involved in this new project.'

Nepotism, then. Go figure.

'I'm *so* excited to really get under the skin of the Gen Z buyer.'

'Yeah, it should be really good,' Harry says with more enthusiasm than I've heard him speak with before. For some reason I find it infuriating. 'We have loads of data on the Gen Z buyer already. They want cheap, cheerful, disposable.' Harry catches my eye, then rolls his, and I know he's thinking about our sock chat. 'Or they want second-hand, vintage. They aren't buying so-called "affordable" luxury.'

'Some are,' Cally objects. '*I* don't want cheap.' A preposterous thought, clearly.

'Will we be sourcing new items to sell to them?' Harry asks.

'No, same great Poster stockists, same great prices,' Georgina chimes. 'Just a new digital shop front and marketing campaign to reel a new buyer in.'

'The new buyer doesn't want what we're selling, or they'd be buying it already.'

If Amanda was here now, she'd be squeezing my leg under the table.

'Some do,' Cally says, pointedly. 'I think it sounds like a really exciting challenge.'

'Great, thanks Carol— *Cally*,' Georgina corrects herself. 'How about you?'

She looks at Harry, who steals another quick glance to me. 'I'm up for the challenge.'

If they think this is really going to work, they must both be dreamin'.

'Besides,' he adds, looking directly at me. 'There's more to people than just data.'

As I walk back to my desk, my blood is boiling. It goes up a degree as I pass no less than seven upstairs colleagues mingling around where Charlie is sitting, with no regard for the fact he needs silence as he studies Poster's eye-watering pricing structures. It cranks up another notch as I pass Blair, sitting in the middle of the two lovers with her fingers physically clutched over her headphones to muffle their flirting so that she can get on with assisting Amanda in keeping this place operating. And it positively boils over as I see a 'send to all' email from Gareth Grey as soon as I open my laptop again.

gg@poster: Hello and welcome to all our new colleagues today, and a special shout out to Cally who is going to be working with Harry on an exciting new project.

Amanda said they wanted my input as a senior data analysist, that this could be the visibility I need to finally get my promotion. But I've been used or overlooked every single time I've stepped foot on tenth-floor territory. Why did I think today would be any different?

ha@poster: Do you want to send over your initial thoughts on the microsite?

I look at my screen to see an unexpected message sitting at the top of my inbox.

ha@poster: P.S. You look really nice today. What are you up to tonight?

I expected to see this one even less.

ha@poster: P.P.S. It's Harry, btw.

I study the words, wondering why he would send them when he could just come over to chat. Is this his attempt at an apology or his latest means to mess with me? I look down at my grey suit, slightly more tapered than my boxy black one, but still far from Poster material. Next to Cally's this-season spring attire, I look like I'm running for a seat on the local council. I refuse to entertain whatever game he's trying to play.

cc@poster: I just need to finalise them. I'll send the PowerPoint over first
thing.

The afternoon passes much slower than it would in the basement office. Up here, there is no lunchtime gathering, complete with card games and Scrabble. Up here, I don't have Toby next to me showing me YouTube videos related to his lasted craze; he's across the room with his head down trying his best to keep himself to himself, lest he accidentally cause another HR inquiry. And up here, Harry appears to send one rogue email asking how I am and what I've got planned for the evening and then ignores me for the next *seven* hours whilst he sits across the room, entertaining one gorgeous colleague who perches coquettishly on the edge of his desk after another.

It's only when I arrive outside the draughty-looking door to my new temporary accommodation that my work phone vibrates in my hand.

ha@poster: Didn't have you down as a PowerPoint person.

What part of my '*Wanna data me?*' tote bag and incessant need to overprepare makes him think I'm *not* a PowerPoint person? My heart races as another two emails come through.

ha@poster: And I thought you would be better at taking compliments.

ha@poster: You always seem so sure of yourself.

It's not that I wasn't expecting the dig from him after our accidental altercations today, but does he really need to send messages outside of office hours? I pocket my phone and push my way into the foreign apartment, longing for something familiar to hold on to. Because after today, after my interactions in the office and the way that the mystery man from my past is managing to force his way into my present, everything feels strange, everything feels *new*.

Chapter Five

I count to three at least six times before finally pushing the door open into my new apartment. Between the barrage of boxes that I dropped off here first thing this morning and the mystery housemate waiting to be met, somehow I feel the need to mentally prepare myself.

'*Grrrrr.*'

But nothing could prepare me for *this*. Because there, in the middle of the box-scattered front room, is a seventy-pound boxer dog. It's leaning forward on its front legs and baring every one of its front teeth. And I know better than to think it's smiling.

'*Shit.*'

I leap backwards, pressing the full length of my body against the closed front door. The dog leaps forward, growling even more aggressively.

'Go away,' I hiss, waving my hands in front of me with as much authority as one can when one is terrified of losing a finger. I reach into my tote bag, looking for some sort of ammunition to throw at him. The laptop feels a bit extreme.

Instead, I tear out a page of my notebook, scrunching it into a ball and throwing it to the far corner of the room. Except, before the makeshift ball can even get to the other side of the room, the dog is jumping in mid-air, grabbing the paper in his teeth, and gulfing it down in one gulp. I guess 'my dog ate my homework' is a valid excuse after all. The boxer licks his lips before turning his attention back to me. Oh crap. I reach into my tote to pull out the pen refills, throwing them haphazardly around the room. The dog goes mental, running round in circles as I make a beeline for the sofa, not thinking twice about standing on top of it.

'Nice to see you've made yourself at home.'

I jump out of my skin at the sound of the gruff voice behind me, turning around slowly to see the shape of a stocky man, tattooed arms folded, his floppy dark hair framing his raised eyebrows. He looks one second away from calling the police.

'I couldn't . . . the dog, it . . . growling . . . and violent . . .' I try to explain through pants. The stranger raises one eyebrow even further as the light catches the delicate ring in his nose. He's either my new housemate or a really lost unofficial fourth member of Biffy Clyro.

'Violent?' he asks, taking a step towards me. I'm still standing on his sofa.

'Yes, you should warn people about him. Or keep him on a lead.'

I brush my hands down the sides of my suit, unsure whether I'm checking if the fabric or my femurs are unscathed.

'Violent?' he repeats again, this time an octave higher. He bends his knees as the dog flops onto his back, begging for a belly rub. 'You think this guy is violent?'

The boxer rolls from side to side, tongue lolling as if butter wouldn't melt.

'He was growling at me,' I say, trying to reclaim some decorum.

'He's not used to—'

'Strangers?'

'I was going to say strange women standing on our sofas.'

'I'm not strange, I'm . . .' I decide this argument would carry more weight with my feet back on the floor. 'I'm your new housemate. I'm Kate.'

I sit perched on the edge of the sofa, offering him my palm cautiously.

'Wolf,' he replies, too busy rubbing the dog's belly to take my hand. I style my outstretched arm into some sort of over-dramatic yawn.

'It suits him,' I say, only just catching my breath.

'No, *I'm* Wolf.' The man looks to me now, his eyes almost as dark as his hair. Wolf? I guess that suits him too, in a dark, brooding, could-turn-into-a-werewolf-at-midnight-type way. 'This violent guy . . .' he says as the boxer licks his face with so much affection that I almost wish he was still snarling at me, if only to prove my point, '. . . is called Boner.'

'You called your dog *Boner*?'

'And?'

'Why?'

'Why do you think?' Wolf laughs, baring his teeth; not a fang in sight.

'Wish I never asked.'

'Fancy a tour?' He stands, Boner staying so closely to his side that I begin to suspect he has *trained* the dog to snarl at strangers.

From behind them, I can see the door to my soon-to-be bedroom creaking ajar and I suddenly feel overcome with exhaustion; exhaustion at the thought of the office merger and now having to live in some stranger's house rather than be able to debrief every detail with Lucy at home. Then, any tiredness leaves me as I see an all too familiar frame exiting the bedroom, what I thought was *my* bedroom. He's holding a cardboard box in his hands and looking for all the world like he's moving in too.

'No!'

The exclamation escapes as Harry looks past Wolf and Boner in my direction.

'No tour, got it.' Wolf's eyes widen as he mentally moves me from his 'crazy' to 'certifiably insane' category.

'What are *you* doing here?' Harry asks, stepping forward whilst simultaneously trying to pick his pretty jaw from off the floor. 'You're not dating Wolf, are you?'

'She would be so lucky, mate.' My housemate swings around to stare at him too. My cheeks flush red and I'm not sure whether to blame Wolf's comment or the fact Harry is here, in my apartment, to witness it all. At least, this better still be my apartment.

'I thought this was a two-bed place?' My eyes plead with Wolf to confirm this fact.

'That's right,' he nods, looking between me and Harry, trying to work out our dynamic, a silly half-smile forming on his bearded face. 'And seeing as you and Anderson already seem to know each other, I thought you wouldn't mind bunking in together?'

'No way in hell.'

'Chill out, Kate, he's joking,' Harry says, deadpan, evidently not finding this funny. 'You're moving in here?'

'And you're, what, moving out?'

I look from Harry to Wolf and back again. How is this even happening right now?

'No, my *friend* is. Sam.'

'Sam . . . Sam, the guy in the band . . . going on tour. He's your . . . friend?'

'Yes, he's my friend.' He's looking at me like: *Is it so hard to believe that I have any?*

'Well, he ain't my friend,' Wolf mutters under his breath.

Harry's eyes dart to Wolf in a disdain that is so momentary that if my entire attention wasn't solely fixed on him right now, I would have missed it.

'He didn't have time to move everything he wanted to before he had to leave,' he says rapidly, trying to make sense of this ridiculous situation. 'So I told him I'd pick up some more of his things, create as much space as possible for the person renting his room . . .'

This might be the first nice thing Harry has done for me, and he didn't even know he was doing it for me. Well, apart from sending me a rogue email saying that I looked nice today.

'Oh, erm . . . thanks . . . I guess?'

'You're . . . welcome?'

I don't know why we're speaking in questions now.

'And thanks for your email earlier.' I decide to break the question-thing.

'My email?' Clearly, Harry didn't get the memo. Confusion clings to his face for a beat too long before he shakes his head again, coming to. 'Oh, my email.' He looks embarrassed about it. 'You're welcome.'

An awkward silence sneaks up on us, expanding and

expanding until it's all any of us can feel. Harry's eyes are still searing into my soul; I can't seem to look anywhere but at him.

'Anyway, mate, you better be going.' Wolf appears a bit too pleased about this.

'Yeah . . . I . . .' His eyes linger on me a moment longer. 'Yeah, I should go home.'

Which is importantly not *my* new home. I watch as Harry moves through the living room, stalling slightly as he gets to the front door. He moves the weight of the box into one hand with ease and looks over his shoulder in my direction.

'See you around, Kate.'

Around? Or, you know, *tomorrow, at work*, because we work together now.

'Sure,' I nod, before he disappears out of sight and the room finally stops spinning.

'Let me guess, you guys used to date?' Wolf asks as soon as we're alone.

'We're just colleagues.'

'But doesn't that dude work at Poster now?'

The fact that Wolf is calling Harry 'that dude' tells me they don't know each other that well. That, and the frost between them just now, which didn't scream BFFs.

'Yeah, and so does this gal.' I point both thumbs to my chest and instantly regret it.

'You don't look like the Poster type.'

'Thank you?'

'It's a compliment.'

Apart from the fact that everyone at Poster is aesthetically outstanding.

'So, about that tour?' There's a genuine smile on his face

now, and though getting to know my new housemate is something I would usually want to do, the momentary horror that
Harry was going to be *that* dude seems to have stolen any last
shred of my energy.

'Don't worry, I had a quick poke around when I dropped
my stuff off earlier. You must have left early?'

'Or stayed out late,' he grins, seemingly proud of himself.

One by one I pick up the pen refills from the floor, wondering whether Harry clocked them too, that familiar feeling
of shame rushing through me. All I want after the day I've
had is to be left alone to unpack my boxes into my temporary
box room.

'I think I'm going to go and get settled in.'

'Okay, but before you do,' he says, his gravelly voice
softening somewhat. 'There's coffee in the cupboard here.'
He points past the fridge to above the cooker in the little
kitchenette in the corner of the room. 'The TV is broken,
so it only plays ITV.' He lifts the remote control before
setting it back on the coffee table with an apologetic smile.
'I'm pretty much nocturnal, so the bathroom's all yours in
the morning.' He points towards the door leading to the
bathroom. 'And I'm over here.' He gestures to another door
I haven't opened yet. 'Call me if you need anything. Well,
provided it's after midday.'

Okay, I can live with this. For three hundred and fifty
pounds a month, I can do this.

'Oh, and Vera likes to sleep on your bed sometimes.'

Strike that. I absolutely *cannot* do this.

'Who the hell is Vera?'

'The neighbour's cat.' I don't know whether to be relieved.

'Lets herself in through the window. Acts like she owns the place. Never stands on the sofa, mind.'

'You should have seen him; I swear he was . . .' I begin, trying to muster my indignation from before, but Boner is chasing his tale so joyfully right now that I give up.

'I'm glad you lived to tell the tale.'

'Maybe he was just angry that his owner gave him such a ridiculous name?'

Deep down I know the source of my anger has just left the building.

'You have a lot of opinions for someone who has only just moved in.'

'I know, I'm sorry, it's just . . .' It's just today. Poster. The merger. *Harry.*

'No, don't apologise,' he smiles, retreating to his room. 'I like it.'

At least that's one person who appreciates my opinions today.

Chapter Six

'Shall we have a quick debrief?' I ask Harry and Cally as soon as we're released from Georgina's office, where she's just identified our next steps for developing the microsite.

'Good idea.' Harry nods. 'First deadline is a fortnight away. Regroup next week?'

Clearly, he has decided not to mention our run-in last night, to just pretend that he doesn't know where I live now, that he *maybe, could have, definitely, I hope to God didn't* see my pen refills scattered all around the living room.

'Wow, that was quick.' Cally laughs, giving a playful push to his arm.

I have to look around the room to avoid rolling my eyes. The early spring sunshine is illuminating the open-plan space, but Blair's latest outfit is almost oversized enough to cast a shadow across the tenth floor. Well, that and her mood. It's only the second day of our office merger and I suspect that half of the basement staff are already subtly scouring LinkedIn on their laptops. I should be doing the same.

'I think the two weeks are to actually *do* the work.'

'Okay, so regroup in a couple of *days*?' he asks hopefully, not so subtly stifling a yawn.

'I don't think we need to *regroup* at all,' I object again.

'Kate, I'm too hungover for your cryptic crosswords.'

How does he know I like cryptic crosswords? I have one on my person right now. I pull my bag closer to my chest, sure that Harry has some sort of X-ray vision.

'What I mean is,' I begin, purposefully slowing my voice down so that he can keep up. 'Why don't we just take five minutes now to divvy up the jobs. Divide and conquer?'

'Can we divide and conquer when I'm less hungover?'

It's only then that I notice that his seemingly perma-tanned skin is a queasy shade of grey. He swallows another yawn as I tighten my grip on my tote before me, my armour.

'It's not my fault that you went out on a school night.'

As soon as I've said the words, I regret them.

'Sorry, *Mum*.' He grins, looking me dead in the eye.

'Well, sorry for actually *caring* about my job.'

'I'll have you know, I was *doing* my job last night.'

'Crayoning under the influence?'

'Oh, the old "creatives just crayon for a living". *That's* original.'

He looks genuinely offended now. For a moment, I feel terrible. Then I remember his email yesterday about me always being sure of myself, the way he looked at me last night.

'I was at a networking event,' he confirms, arms crossing before him.

'Flirt with any waitresses?'

He looks confused by my question for a second, scrambling for a reference that he's clearly stored far deeper in his mind than

76

I have. Then he finds it, instantly mortified by the memory. And now I feel mortified too, for bringing it up in the first place.

'I mean . . .' I rally. Cally looks confused as well, confused but a little bit interested, like she wants to find out whether he was flirting with anybody too. 'Did you make any connections? Business ones. For the microsite?'

'I did.' He puffs out his chest slightly. 'I met an illustrator who may be good for the website design, real hand-drawn, fluid lines—'

'A crayoner, then?'

'A *professional* crayoner,' he bites back.

'So, are we debriefing, regrouping or dividing and conquering?' Cally demands.

'I will gladly do any of the above provided it's with coffee.'

'I have some instant in my bag—'

'Stop right there, Mary.' Harry holds up a hand. He can't seriously have forgotten my name? Then, I clock what he's looking at: my hand, busy reaching into my apparently bottomless tote, and I know he means *Mary Poppins*. He grins. 'I mean a *real* coffee.'

If stepping into the front entrance of Poster House feels wrong, stepping *out* of it only an hour later feels even stranger. I can count the days I have left the office in daylight in the past six months on two hands. Sure, spring is finally starting to bloom, lulling us into a false sense of security that there are no dark days left to come. But striding out of the office for a coffee before midday, unabashed and unashamed, feels completely foreign to me.

'There's a great place around the corner.' Harry looks over his shoulder to me, Cally keeping in step by his side.

'What's wrong with Pret?'

His expression tells me he's not going to dignify my question with a response. And I don't need him to tell me that he thinks he's too cool for coffee-shop chains.

I follow two or three strides behind the two of them as we mingle into the madness of Oxford Street, trying not to lose one another in the process.

'Keep up.' He turns back to me again as someone's bag bashes into my middle.

'We don't all have swift legs.' I scurry to keep up.

'Swift-fast or Swift-Taylor?'

'Does it matter?'

'When it comes to Swifty it always matters.' His face is deadpan as he turns back to navigate his way through the crowds towards his chosen coffee shop. I never had Harry down as a Taylor Swift man. Though I already know he has the capacity to blindside me completely.

Very soon the chaos of the main street peters out and we're closing in on a café complete with a chunky wooden bench outside and a simple black sign brandishing its name.

'*Kaffeine?* It's spelt wrong.'

'I think it's Dutch,' he says, as he leads us into the small coffee shop, its exposed brickwork and low-hanging lights bringing a thousand Instagram photos to life.

'It says here that it's inspired by Australasian coffee culture.'

'Must you be right about everything?' he asks as he approaches the counter, nodding at a pretty woman behind it who seems to glow with familiarity.

'No, I just googled it. It's not that hard.'

'It's also not necessary.' He turns to look at me, hungover

and dishevelled and yet still managing to look handsome with it. Every inch of him seems to know it.

'So, you're happy to go through life thinking white is black and black is white?'

'Can't it all just be shades of grey?'

'Not when the facts are *right* here,' I say, holding up my phone to show him their website, which states what they were inspired by, as clear as day.

'I prefer feelings,' he says dismissively. 'Three soy flat whites, extra hot.'

'Hey!' I don't even try to hide my disgruntlement at his ordering on our behalf. 'I'll take a hot chocolate, please.'

'A hot chocolate? It's not nine pm yet, grandma.'

'I've already had a coffee this morning.'

'And heaven forbid you go over your limits?'

'Not limits, just *boundaries*.' My cheeks blush at the speed at which he has managed to bring them down before.

Harry shakes his head, pursing his lips as if to swallow a smirk. 'The coffee here is *really* good. You're going to want to try it.'

'No,' I object, feeling more and more riled. 'I'm going to want *my* order.'

'Trust me.' He puts a hand to my arm. It feels warm and surprising and *unwelcome*. I shrug it off quickly. 'I'm right about this.'

Harry grins as soon as we sit down at a high table. I take my first sip.

'Good, right?'

I shrug and say nothing, even though it's *gorgeous*.

'It's gorgeous.' Cally steals the thought right from my mind.

79

Harry looks vindicated.

'Just what the hangover ordered.'

'You're hungover too?' I ask, once again feeling on the outside of the party.

'Oh no, I don't drink,' she says, like the thought of consuming that many empty calories is preposterous. 'I meant Harry's hangover.'

'Nice to know someone is thinking of me.'

Another dig.

'I'm *nice* like that,' Cally says, leaning a little further into him.

And I'm not?

'So, let's get this over with,' I begin, reaching into my bag for my notebook.

'Woah, way to boost the team morale.' He laughs over his raised flat white.

'Some of us have work to get back to.' I shut down his banter. I need this promotion. And, if launching the best damn zoomer shop front is the way to do it, so be it.

'In two weeks' time we need to present which products we're choosing for the microsite and why.' I reiterate our first task, as Harry and Cally struggle to focus; they are both scanning around the small coffee shop, looking at each of the customers inside. 'Let's identify actions to work on independently and then—'

'Gareth said we should work collaboratively,' Cally interrupts, reminding us she has the inside track, that she's been privy to the goings-on of Gareth Grey's mind ever since her uncle started playing golf with him at 'the Club'. Well, according to Blair, who seemingly knows how to find out everything here. She's wasted at this place.

'Yes, but surely playing to each of our strengths. I'll dig into the data we have—'

'And you'll get the answers you already know,' Harry says.

'What do you mean?'

'Well, if all you have is the data from our site, you'll only have part of the picture.'

'A pretty good picture,' I say, stopping myself from mentioning crayons again. 'We'll know how many Gen Z users we have, what they click on, what they actually buy.'

'And that means you have them all figured out?' He says this like the idea of drilling down on data and forming conclusions is preposterous. Somehow it feels like a challenge. 'What about the ones who aren't coming to our site at all? They're the ones we want.'

'Okay, so I can see whether there's any big data from our competitors to purchase.'

'What about qualitative data?' he asks, a silly smile forming on his face.

'Surprised you even know what that is.' I manage to wipe it out just as quickly.

'Let's go and talk to our target audience,' Cally suggests boldly.

'I'm talking about purchasing the data of hundreds of thousands of users.'

'And Cally's suggesting we actually *talk* to them – well, some of them.' He is defending her but leaning into me.

He turns to her now. 'You're talking about a focus group?'

'Maybe, but just getting out there, being where our buyer is.'

'I can tell you where they are, where they are shopping,' I promise, before the two of them can get carried away on something as flimsy as a feeling.

'You can tell us *what* they are doing.' He turns to me. 'You can't tell us *why*.'

'I've been invited to the Boo Babes' Influencer Breakfast next Tuesday,' Cally continues, looking pretty proud of herself. 'Some of our main competitors in this space will be represented there; we can chat to the attendees, the influencers, see what they're wearing, what's hot right now.'

'I don't think that's necessary,' I begin, already imagining a hoard of Gen-Z stars snapping my ancient M&S suit and uploading it as a 'what not to wear'.

'I think it's a great idea,' Harry says, looking directly at me.

'Really?'

'You do?' Cally adds. I'm not sure who out of the two of us is more surprised. 'I mean, of course you do. It's a great opportunity.' Her confidence is completely restored.

'It'll be a nice way for us to get a feel for the end user.'

'We don't need to *feel* the end user; we need to know what they are buying.'

'People get a tonne of products at these events,' Cally says, like I know nothing.

'Yes, but for free. They're not parting with their hard-earned cash.'

'Maybe not the influencers,' she confirms. 'But once we post one of our old Poster products from a Gen-Z-minded account, you better believe the purchases come.'

'So, that's decided then.' Harry nods. 'First stop, Cally's influencer breakfast?'

'How about you guys go without me, and I'll concentrate on the data and—'

'Cally's right,' he confirms as she grins like a Cheshire cat. 'I think interdepartmental means doing stuff *together*.' He says this like 'interdepartmental' is the first six syllable word I've heard.

'Maybe it's not black and white; maybe it's one of those shades of grey things?'

'This one feels pretty black and white to me.'

'Me too.' Cally beams, putting a hand to Harry's arm. 'And it's two against one.'

So much for female solidarity.

'Time to get ready for your first ever networking hangover, Carter.'

bph@poster: First week on the tenth floor, done. We made it, friend.

cc@poster: Only just.

bph@poster: That bad?

cc@poster: There's just so much to do and the pace up here is frustratingly slow.

cc@poster: I can see why every piece of information we asked them for was delivered late. Everyone's too busy lolling around and drinking cappuccinos.

bph@poster: Or flirting.

cc@poster: They still not asked each other out yet?

bph@poster: Relationships in the office are *frowned upon*, remember?

cc@poster: Do you really think I can forget?

bph@poster: I never imagined that Harry Anderson guy would come back here.

bph@poster: He was just an intern, wasn't he?

cc@poster: Screw Poster for only listing directors on their website.

bph@power: Guess 'minions' are frowned upon as well.

bph@poster: Well, frowned upon or advised against or whatever new rules this place churns out, if one of these guys doesn't make a move soon,

I'm going to make it for them. Anyway, it's Friday. We can forget about Poster for the weekend. Any plans?

cc@poster: Applying for new jobs?

bph@poster: Oh, so it's *that* bad?

bph@poster: Remember you love the job almost as much as you hate Poster.

cc@poster: I know but I have to go to some sort of influencer breakfast next week.

bph@poster: Why? To eat an overly frosted cupcake and get a goodie bag?

cc@poster: To get into the mind of the Gen-Z buyer.

bph@poster: I thought you did some research into our centennial users last month?

cc@poster: Apparently, it's not enough.

bph@poster: At least your date isn't bad to look at.

cc@poster: If there's one thing I know for sure, it's that Harry Anderson is *not* my date.

Chapter Seven

'Got a big date?'

'Coming back from one?'

Wolf has just walked into the living room, clothes ruffled and bed hair even more so. He's either just snuck out of some unsuspecting woman's house or he got mugged on the way home. I can tell from his grin that it's unlikely to be the latter. He studies my attire as he kicks off his chunky biker boots. I have no idea what one is supposed to wear to an influencers' breakfast, but I thought skinny black jeans and a tighter-than-normal long-sleeved t-shirt was a safe choice. I even ran Lucy's old straighteners through my already straight hair, which I'm surprised to find has made a difference. As has applying a lick of mascara.

'Wouldn't you like to know?' he teases.

'Not really.' I smile.

As much as I miss living with Lucy, there's something refreshing about becoming housemates before you become anything else. It's like you get to set the parameters of your friendship or lack thereof from the get-go: no expectations, no disappointments. Though I've spent a grand total of an hour 'passing ships' with Wolf this past weekend, I get the impression that when it comes to him, what you get is what you see.

'Where are you off to? You look nice.'

'I've got a meeting. At work.'

'Sure.'

'Well, sort of, it's an influencers' brunch or something. A promotional thing.'

'You really don't look like the Poster type.' He looks surprised all over again.

'As you've made quite clear already.'

'It's not an insult.' He throws up both palms in defence. 'You're just not the pretty-boy, acoustic-guitar-playing type that I've come to associate with that place.'

Given that Blair's insane investigative skills have confirmed that my bedroom predecessor has never worked for Poster, I can deduce that he's talking about Harry. And though the majority of my mind is now occupied with trying to work out what kind of beef the two of them could possibly have with one another, I can't for the life of me stop an image of Harry sat atop a rusty bar stool strumming said acoustic guitar from flitting through it too.

'I don't look like a pretty boy? Good to know.'

'You know what I mean.' Wolf laughs warmly. 'You just look a bit *neat* is all.' I watch as he peels off his leather jacket, discarding it on the back of the sofa. Boner jumps on top of him as soon as he sits down. 'Like you're trying too hard.'

'I spent fifteen minutes getting ready.'

'And I'm sure the models at Poster spend hours, but they *look* like they took five.'

'The kind of talents that might one day save humanity,' I joke sarcastically and Wolf laughs again, giving Boner another belly rub before he comes bounding over to me – the dog, not the man – and begins gnawing at the bottom of my jeans.

'Can you control your hound?' I shake my leg to the side and Wolf laughs harder.

'He just knows ripped jeans are *in*. Hey, that's not a bad idea. Rip your jeans at the knee, cut off three inches from the bottom of your t-shirt and you'll fit right in.'

'And tell the fashion journos at the breakfast that I'm "styled by Boner"? No, thanks.'

It takes me no less than three seconds upon arriving at the venue to realise that I've somehow managed to underdress and overdress at the same time. That I would have been better off being styled by the dog after all. Flower arrangements tower at either side of the entrance to The Ivy, their wine-red and blush-pink petals popping against the white stone building. More than fifty brightly dressed, zero-fat demi-gods mingle around the patio space outside, their bare shoulders and legs safely warmed by the outdoor heaters that are turned up full whack, despite the fact we're experiencing an unusually warm spring. I wonder whether it's too late to go to the bathrooms and cut some ventilation into my jeans?

Cally walks towards me, towering an extra four inches in her thin-strapped sandals, her hair once again pulled to the side to reveal the flawless lines of her collarbone, her skin even bronzer next to her bright orange off-the-shoulder number.

'You made it, then?' I'm not sure if she sounds happy about it.

'I did.' It's not like I really had a choice. But now that I'm here, I could really do with an ally by my side. I have no idea how I am going to get into the minds of the late teens and early twenties who are swanning around the outdoor space and spilling inside but Cally looks entirely at home. These are her people.

'Have you seen Harry?' she asks, surveying the space nervously. There must be a nine-to-one ratio of women to males here, so he shouldn't be hard to find.

I shake my head.

'Let's go inside anyway. I'm sure he'll be here soon.'

Given his patchy time-keeping and ability to change his mind at will, I'm not so sure.

'Ready?'

I turn to smile at Cally but she's already striding confidently into the room.

If I thought the outside area of the venue was luxurious, it is nothing compared to what's waiting inside. Mirrors and picture frames adorn the high walls, each of the tables covered in crisp, white tablecloths and loaded with enough cutlery per place that I'm not entirely sure the Boo Babes' breakfast isn't expecting an influx of octopuses. For all the pastries and waffles and berries and fritters that are piled high in the centre of each table, there are very few people who are actually eating. I wouldn't usually drink at work, but this is an exception. I reach for a mimosa and begin to load up my plate.

'I wouldn't do that if I were you.'

Harry's voice from behind me makes me tense up in places I didn't think could. I turn around to see him looking at the three mini pastries on my plate, the pancakes that I'm forking two crispy rashes of bacon on top of now. How *dare* he tell me what I can and can't eat? Though, given his athletic physique, I doubt he's enjoyed many pastries in his time.

'Watch me,' I say, shovelling one into my mouth, regretting it instantly.

He shakes his head, a smug smile on his face. 'No, I just meant—'

'Hi, I'm Janette.' A tall, blonde-haired lady appears between us, holding a hand out in Harry's direction. He shakes it, putting his spare hand over their touching ones gently, as if to show the genuineness of their new connection.

'Harry.'

I must admit, his confidence is pretty sexy – when he's not erring on the side of irritatingly sure of himself. Janette turns to offer me her open palm and it's only then that she realises that my hands are occupied: my piled plate in one hand, glass of mimosa in the other. I go to introduce myself and then realise my mouth is full of pastry.

'And *this* is Kate Carter, Senior Data Analyst at Poster,' he says on my behalf. I narrow my eyes, telepathically trying to tell him that I don't need him to speak for me, even though if I were to introduce myself, I'd be covering her in crumbs.

'Lovely to meet you both,' she says as I finally swallow my bite, cheeks blushing.

'I did try to warn you,' he says, reaching to relieve me of my plate as soon as Janette has disappeared into the crowded room. I clutch on to it for dear life. 'Come on, Kate, you can pocket the pastries for later, but we're here to chat to some Gen-Z influencers.'

'Kill me now,' I mutter, deadpan.

'I would but the murder would be on a hundred TikTok accounts in no time.' He grins. Gosh, I hate that his smile is so lovely. I hate even more that he knows it.

'Come on, what have you got against Gen Z?' He looks beyond me, targeting who he should talk to next. That's why I hate these things: they turn people into projects.

'Absolutely nothing against Gen Z. It's the influencer part I struggle with.'

'Why's that?'

'They make their living off telling people what they should have, making them feel without. Social media claims to be about connection but is increasing loneliness ten-fold.'

'Okay, well, how many influencers do you actually *know*?'

'Erm . . .'

None? No, that's not right. I know Cally. Ish.

'One?' I don't mean for my reply to sound like a question.

'Fine, so maybe gather a bit more *data* on them before reaching that conclusion?'

'I *have* data. I . . .'

He's already turned his back to me, moving his way into the room, the waves of women parting before him as he does. The rage at not getting the last word in surges through me. It's easy for him to say that. I bet he's never been taken aback by how rude colleagues who know nothing about you can be to your face, or been landed with ten additional reports to produce within minutes, as if the job you are actually being paid for doesn't matter at all.

I follow in his footsteps, but he's already been stopped by a rare male on the far side of the room, the two of them chatting to one another animatedly. Brushing through the small groups of people, I long for one of the social semicircles to make space for me but find myself arriving at the far corner of the room with neither a pal nor a pastry in sight. From my new vantage point, I can see that the way the room is dressed, the way it heaves with colourful activity, is not too dissimilar from the Poster summer mixer, from everything I've been trying my best to avoid for the past five years. But I'm here now, with a chance to prove I deserve my promotion, and I am not going to see that go to waste.

I pin on a smile and move back into the centre of the room.

'Hi, erm . . . excuse me . . . I . . .' I try to infiltrate a tight-knit circle clutching mimosas or green smoothies in their hands. Not one of them moves. The background music – played by some low-fi DJ who I imagine rarely sees this time of day – masks the noise of chatter and it's hard to get a word in edgeways.

I look around me and see Cally to the left, holding court with about eight people who perfectly represent our target audience for the new website. Then, I look the other way and see Harry surrounded by petite women who only accentuate his height. He's looking at his phone, held open before them, so he's either getting someone's number or noting down his research. And I'll be damned if I'm the only one left without data.

'Hello?' I move to another group gathered around the centre of the room, this time three people standing beside one of the heavily laden tables: a tall woman with long auburn hair, a shorter woman wearing a chocolate silk slip that blends effort-lessly with her flawless ebony skin, and another jet-black-haired woman who I think is wearing nothing but Kim Kardashian SKIMS. I don't know where to look, but thankfully, they are smiling in my direction.

'Hey, how you going?' the tall one asks, baring her perfectly straight teeth, her thick Australian accent making her appear even more like a young Elle Macpherson.

'I'm okay, thanks. I'm—' I begin, before the SKIMS lady begins introducing herself and I realise that 'How you going?' is just a greeting, not a genuine question.

'I'm Barbie.' She thrusts a hand towards me and – thanks to Harry – I have a hand free enough to shake it. *Barbie?* Wait until I tell Blair and Toby about this one. Even as the thought crosses my mind, her broad smile silences me. Unlike the tenth-floor people back in the office, Barbie is not looking past me or down on me.

'I'm Kate.'

'Kate, this is Angela, who is a buyer at Boohoo, and Chloe, who is a fashion features intern at *Grazia*.' Barbie opens her well-groomed hand to signal her introductions.

'Nice to meet you,' I say woodenly. 'I'm at Poster.'

'You don't look like you work at Poster.'

'I know. I'm . . .' I begin, the room starting to feel hotter, the voice in my head growing louder: imposter, imposter, you're an *imposter*. 'In the back office.'

Well, I used to be. Back when the basement office still existed.

'So, what do you *do*?' she continues.

The classic question that tries to put everyone in a box.

'I'm a data analyst. I essentially help the company understand their consumers and drive traffic to the site.'

'Basically, keeping the place in business?' Barbie says, with a knowing smile.

'I'm not sure about that.' I'm sometimes not sure I even *want* to keep Poster in business, but I feel buoyed by her compliment, nonetheless. 'What is it you do for work?'

'I'm a content creator,' she explains. 'I get paid to post other people's products on my own account and get commissions to do photography and digital engagement work for other big brands. And then, of course, there's the networking element, coming to things like this and highlighting brands and . . . I've worked for Poster before.'

She is speaking so fast that I struggle to keep up, but her smile never wavers. She's moving her weight from one miraculously white trainer to the other and clutching her mimosa with both hands now, her long lime nails tapping on the stem of the glass.

'Really?' I ask, trying to work out why she's making me feel on edge.

'Yes. I mean, it was a while ago so you may not remember the campaign, but . . .'

She's nervous. But what on earth does she have to feel nervous about?

'I post at *Barbie Is Real*.'

'I've . . . I've heard of that.'

I don't know which one of us is more surprised. I'm still trying to comprehend why someone like her would be nervous when speaking to someone like me.

'I have two hundred thousand followers,' she says, a meek smile on her face.

'Your campaign for Poster . . .'

I remember coming across it, being asked to review the company spend on influencers that season and whether the return on investment would justify a repeat commission. I had laughed at the account name before showing the report line to Blair, but I had never clicked through to it. Blair was too busy telling me that if Barbie *was* real, her legs would be too thin and her head and boobs too big to be able to walk on anything but all fours.

'It didn't do well.' Barbie studies her mimosa more closely. She looks so sad, and a pang of empathy washes over me.

'That's okay. Yours wasn't the only one.'

In fact, we started using older influencers after that, cementing our standing with the late thirties and over forties. Somehow, Poster always returns to wanting what it can't have.

'I tried to tell the Chief Marketing Officer that Gen Z . . . oh, it doesn't matter.'

Part of me doesn't want to hear about the plights of the social media influencer. I've heard from Blair just how awful they can be, how they are part of the reason she requested to be transferred to a role in the office downstairs, but something about Harry's challenge, about me never having met and listened to one in person, keeps my feet firmly stuck to the ground. That, and the fact that we're here to really understand this demographic.

'No, no. Go on.'

'It's just . . . I mean . . . I'm honestly the biggest critic of my own work – *believe me* – but I don't think the failure of that campaign was on me. I told the person who commissioned me that my followers would never go for the aesthetic they were after. I wanted to style the garments they'd asked me to post differently, but they just sucked any creativity out of it.'

In my periphery, I see Harry making his way through the crowded room in our direction as if one mention of the word 'creativity' has alerted him to the fact we need him close by.

'The post was okay,' she goes on. 'I really liked it, actually,

94

but it just wasn't right for the audience they were looking to target. Poster sells great luxury basics, but we don't want basic. We want to take a quality silk slip and add an overweight, distressed denim jacket to it. We want to take a perfect grey knit and pair it with cut-offs and trainers. Poster wants perfect, and we want real. The insights on my post showed that the impressions were high but the conversion rate of people who clicked through to Poster's site was really, really low.'

Barbie flicks through her phone to show me the insights she's referring to and together we lean into the screen. From my vantage point beside her now, I feel like I can see every single goosebump underneath her SKIMS, whilst not even a suggestion of my knee is showing. As she swipes to show me the data behind a different post and I reach for my own phone to take notes, her long lime fingernails clash against my gnawed and naked ones. We couldn't look more different and yet, for a moment, our similarities shine between us.

'Hey, do you have a business card?' she asks and it only just occurs to me that I do. That buried in my trusty tote is an entire box of business cards that I've barely had reason to use. I am reaching to find them when Harry finally arrives beside me.

'You and that bloody bag,' he whispers, just loud enough for me to hear.

'Shut up. I'm *networking*,' I hiss back to him, our faces momentarily a hair's breadth apart.

I swing back to Barbie. 'Here you go.' I hand her a card, trying to stay cool, even though Harry's presence is making me feel flustered again.

'And here's mine.' She hands me her card in return, which I pocket quickly.

'Woah, don't want to give her your pin number as well?' Harry says as soon as my new contact is out of earshot. I turn to look at him; he has that big stupid grin on his face.

'What?'

He's looking down at the box of business cards I am holding, one of the pristine white cards I designed facing up from the pile.

'Give me one of those things.'

'No, why?' I say, defensively. He's already grabbing one before I can stash them.

'I've never seen so much writing on one card before.'

'Managing to sound out all the words?'

'Ouch,' he says, ungluing his gaze from the card to narrow his eyes at me. 'Your name, work mobile, personal mobile . . . This isn't a business card . . . this is a novel,' he laughs, and it suddenly feels like we're the only ones in the room.

'Well, let's see yours.'

'Gladly.'

He reaches into his back chino pocket to pull out a black business card, crumpled at each corner, with a single white half-sentence on it: *H. Anderson. Creative.*

'Well, this is ridiculous.' I look up from the card to him, his expression seeming to say, *Well, why am I not surprised you think so?* 'This doesn't tell me anything.'

'It says enough.'

'But how do people *contact* you?'

'If it's fate, they'll find a way.'

'You can't *possibly* believe that.'

Sure, Harry would be so laid back that he doesn't even care if people can reach him.

'Of course I don't,' he laughs. 'My social media handles are on the other side.'

'What if someone isn't *on* social media?'

'Then they're probably not someone I want to network with,' he says. 'Either that, or they're *way* too creative to want to work with me.'

Some sort of humility darts across his features; it's gone just as quick. He takes a small step back from me, as if he's worried that I've just seen it. Then we just stand there, in some sort of unspoken staring match. It makes me nervous that I can't work him out.

'I think I'm going to get out of here.' I look to my watch, then around the room.

'Well, I know where you live.' He winks, waving my business card in his hand.

'Creep,' I say, about to add that my home address isn't even on there, but then I remember that on this rare occasion he isn't full of shit: he *does* know where I live.

'Can't wait to read the sequel.' He's still holding up the card, studying it closer.

'Very nice,' I mutter, just loud enough for him to hear.

'Learning from the best.' He narrows his eyes in return.

'You think I'm the best?'

'No – I—' Harry begins.

'Ah thanks, Harry, that means the world.' My words are soaked in sarcasm.

'No, I was *about* to say that—'

I turn to leave his half-sentence hanging in mid-air.

'Do you not want to know what I was going to say?' I hear him ask from behind me. I bet men like Harry aren't used to being overlooked.

I turn to stare over my shoulder at him. 'Nah, don't worry. If it's fate, I'll work it out.'

'How was the thing?'

Wolf is splayed across the sofa, an open beer can in his hand, Boner by his feet. I bridge the small space between us to flop into the misshapen armchair, which, like the sofa, is pointed towards a tired-looking television which is currently playing some sitcom rerun. Compared to an incredibly busy afternoon stuck behind my laptop – Harry safely on the other side of the office but still frustratingly visible from across it – the breakfast wasn't bad.

'It was okay.'

He crinkles his pierced nose at the thought, taking another swig of his beer. Boner lifts his chin to acknowledge my presence before resting his heavy head back down on his two front paws. Vera the cat is sat in the windowsill, breaking from her intensive grooming regime momentarily to look at all three of us with disdain. She must have let herself in through the impossibly thin gap in the window again, but I am starting to like her visits. It makes me feel like I have another female to help balance out all the Boner-energy. I settle into the somewhat companionable silence and reach for my phone.

> I was going to ask if you made any good connections at breakfast. For the microsite. You know, before you rudely walked away.

I look down at the message that has just lit up my screen, mobile number unknown.

> It's Harry, btw.

I reread his next message again.

> How do you have my . . .

I type the words and then delete them just as fast. That stupid, over-crowded business card. I reach for Harry's black one, pretentious in its simplicity. I save his number in my phone, glancing up to see that Wolf and Boner are still fixated on the TV.

> Me: Why?

> Harry: What do you mean 'why'?

I look down at his text, demanding information from me. He's clearly just messaging me because I cut him off earlier. Is the male ego really that fragile?

> Me: Why do you need to know about my connections?

> Harry: Last time I checked we were on the same team.

> Me: Couldn't it have waited until tomorrow?

> Harry: Okay, sure.

I read his words before studying the three dots that show he's typing something else. And then they stop. And maybe it's because Wolf and Boner are seemingly occupied, and Lucy is thousands of miles away, but I kind of want them to start again.

Harry: You and your bloody boundaries.

Okay, strike that. Now I wish he'd stopped at 'sure'.

Me: Last time I checked, boundaries were a good thing.

Harry: Kate, it's just gone 6pm.

Harry: It's arguably still within working hours.

Harry: Particularly for keenos.

Me: So I'm a keeno now?

Harry: Did I say you were a keeno?

Me: It was *implied*.

I could just stop messaging, join Wolf and his dog in watching low-budget gameshow reruns. But maybe because that sentence is *really* depressing, I find myself typing again.

Me: But to answer your question, I did make some good contacts today. Got some really great insights from an influencer called @BarbieIsReal.

Harry: I know who @BarbieIsReal is.

Harry: But good job, Carter.

Me: Thanks, but I don't need you to tell me that.

Me: You're not my boss.

Harry: Something you've made abundantly clear.

Harry: But at least now you know influencers aren't that scary after all.

Me: I wasn't scared.

Harry: You sure looked it.

Clearly, winding me up in the office isn't enough for him.

Harry: Well, at the beginning at least.

Harry: Towards the end you looked like you were getting the hang of things.

Me: Are you trying to patronise me?

Harry: I think I'm trying to compliment you.

But I've been fooled into thinking that he was trying to compliment me before.

Harry: If it's any consolation, I get nervous at those things too.

Me: Nervous? You?

Harry: Yeah, why wouldn't I?

Me: Because every single person in that room wants to talk to you?

Harry: Not *every* person.

He evidently means me.

Harry: Besides, it's easy to feel like the odd one out in those places.

Me: Are you asking me to feel sorry for you being a rare white male?

Harry: No, I'm just saying I can find those things nerve-wracking too.

Me: Could have fooled me.

Harry: Ever heard of the phrase 'fake it 'til you make it'?

Chapter Eight

'Oh wow, no way, it's *her*.'

Blair holds her hand to her heart as soon as I walk into the tiny kitchenette at the back of the tenth floor, becoming an overly dramatic Jane Austen character swooning before me.

I look around the small space, the one Toby stumbled upon late last week and has since claimed as our own. If the tenth-floor staff were using this kitchen before – which is unlikely, seeing as every coffee craving seems to call for something as decadent as Kaffeine – they certainly aren't now. I look to Toby, who is dressed in a yellow and green football shirt, even though I had *no idea* he was into sport, and wonder when I missed his latest craze.

'Do our eyes deceive us?' Charlie laughs between them, clutching his battered old KeepCup in one hand, his mobile phone swiped open on the other.

'Okay, so I've been busy lately.' Busy juggling my usual role with the new microsite development project. 'Plus, my desk is miles away.'

'It *is* her,' Blair says again, leaning in to look at Charlie's screen then up at me.

'What?' I say, coming to stand behind the three of them.

'You're *famous*.' Charlie hands me the phone.

It's then that I realise what they're on about. Because there, in front of me, is a photo of me and Barbie, candid and chatting at the Boo Babes' breakfast event. The light hits Barbie's bodycon shapewear in all the right places, her jet-black hair almost reflecting the flash. I look more understated – an understatement in itself – but still, I look quite nice.

'Congratulations,' Toby adds. 'You've made it onto the Poster Instagram account.'

I scroll down to look at the grid that the photo has been added to, the caption reading: *One week since the Boo Babes' Breakfast and we're still dreaming about the pastries.* Before I can contemplate whether my photo has been posted because I'm the only one at the event who actually *ate* the pastries, I see the likes, all three hundred thousand of them. If I wasn't surrounded by my friends, I might smile, because even though it shouldn't matter, for a moment I feel validated, *seen*.

'I thought you said you hated every second?' Blair narrows her eyes at me.

'Not *every* second. I said it was okay.'

'Looks better than okay to me.'

I don't know why this feels like a betrayal. I hand back the phone to Charlie. If only Blair knew about the sporadic messages Harry and I have exchanged since he messaged me after the breakfast, the ones that began with work chat – me telling him which products will work well for our new site; him telling me that our presentation will likely happen a couple days later than planned – but have since gone from feeling completely foreign to something like familiar in the space of a week. The ones that despite my better judgement, I've found myself returning to and ruminating over until I annoyingly almost know them by heart . . .

Me: I thought your ego would be too big to feel insecure about anything.

Harry: Has anyone ever told you how charming you are, Carter?

Me: Often.

Harry: Unlikely.

Harry: And is it ego or just thick skin?

Me: Ego. Definitely.

Harry: How about if I told you that I got bullied by my dormmates as a kid?

Me: Then I would bully you for having dormmates as a kid.

Harry: Because I went to boarding school? Closed-minded much?

Me: *cough* privileged *cough*

Harry: Sure, but no amount of privilege will protect you from the 'lads' when they find your cuddly toy lion in your bed and proceed to throw it around the room.

Me: HA!

Harry: Wow. Thought I'd at least get some sympathy for that.

Me: Oh, I'm sorry. Let me try again.

Me: Kids can be so cruel.

Harry: We were sixteen.

Me: Oh, Harry. And you were still sleeping with your snuggly?

Harry: I was away from my parents. There was no way I was leaving him too.

Me: Him? Doesn't the lion have a name?

Harry: Naturally.

Me: Let me guess. It's called something generic like Leo?

Harry: Give me some credit, Carter. I am a creative, after all.

Me: I know, I still have your pretentiously simple business card.

Harry: You kept it? Cute.

Me: Burning it as we speak.

Harry: Any more guesses, all-knowing one?

Me: Maybe your creativity could stretch to adding an 'n'. Leon?

Harry: Wrong again.

Me: Damn. You know how much I like being right.

Harry: More than anything in the world ever?

Harry: 'Fraid you're going to lose this one though, Carter.

Me: Rory?

106

Harry: I think I'll just keep you guessing.

Me: Simba?

Harry: Getting colder.

Me: Tell me or I'm going to send a companywide email about your cuddly called . . .

Harry: Colin.

Harry: My cuddly was called Colin.

'What are you grinning at?' Blair asks, as I pour some average-to-poor instant coffee into my KeepCup. She's readying herself to go back to her desk, out into the lion's den. I think of Colin and laugh out loud.

'Nothing,' I say, looping my free arm through hers. She shrugs me off playfully.

'Doesn't look like nothing.' She narrows her kohl-rimmed eyes again.

'Oh, there you are.'

A male voice interrupts her questioning and both of us look up to see Harry standing there, a thin, white woollen jumper pulled taut across his toned chest, the diagonal pattern of the wool drawing our gaze downward. I force my eyes to focus on his bronzed face and smile.

He doesn't smile back.

'Gareth wants to see us in his office,' he says, struggling to hold my eye, even more so to look directly at Blair. He scans the room like he's never seen this kitchen before in his life. If Blair, Toby and Charlie have their way, the Poster People won't see it again.

'Why?' I ask. I'm also trying to work out why, when our messages have seemed to bring us at least a little bit closer, he's acting so very distant now.

'How am I supposed to know?' he mumbles, eyes everywhere but on me. 'Maybe to present back on our product selection for the site?'

'What product selection? You said the presentation was at the *end* of the week.'

'Gareth's emails to me suggested he was busy, I assumed that meant that—'

'You just assumed?'

I begin to panic, whereas he looks characteristically chilled. Cold, even.

'Calm down, mate.'

'I'm not your—'

'Well, as fun as this sounds . . .' Blair interrupts as my blood begins to boil, looking between me and Harry like she's trying to work out our weird dynamic. That makes two of us. He may be calling me *mate*, but the fact that he's rolling his eyes at my professional dread now tells me we're still far from friends. 'I think I'll leave you to it.'

'Take me with you,' I mouth back to her, and she grins fully, my forever-ally, but this time I know I have to take this one alone. Well, not entirely alone.

'You said the presentation was going to be moved back,' I hiss behind him, as he walks a beat in front of me in the direction of Gareth Grey's daunting office. Today, his automatic blinds are open for the entire floor to see what will surely become a bollocking.

'I guess I got it wrong. Plus, I'm not really a diary man.'

'Yes, but you should be a *deadline* man.'

'Provided I'm not a *dead* man.'

'*You* may be able to wing it, but some of us like to prepare.'

I'm not even sure he's listening, but then he turns over his shoulder to look down at me like I'm an angry terrier snapping at his ankles.

'I bet you can wing it too.'

'No, I can't, I—'

'Have you ever let yourself try?'

His smug smile and my stunned silence show that both of us already know the answer.

Harry brushes a hand through his hair as we near the side office – if you can refer to an office as ostentatious as Gareth's as being on the 'side' of anything. I watch for any hint of nerves from Harry, but there is none. Is he 'faking it 'til he makes it' or was his flash of vulnerability over the weekend merely him faking it with me?

'Just play it cool, Carter.'

'How can I play it cool when we've missed our first deadline and—'

He is too far ahead of me now to hear my hissed whisper. As he steps into the room, Gareth, Georgina and Cally look up, and I have no choice but to follow him inside.

'Hazza.' Gareth nods and it makes any remaining affection I feel for Harry fade away.

'Gazza.'

Oh *please*. Harry catches my disgruntled expression, his jaw stiffening as he does.

'So, this microsite . . . the new buyer . . .' Gareth begins, in a manner that sounds so blasé that I'm pretty confident that

Georgina has only just briefed him that we are working on it. Maybe he won't care about our missed deadline after all. 'Who's your girl?'

Our girl? Sure, Gen Z aren't weeks away from turning thirty like me, but they are not girls: they are *women*. I open my mouth to tell him as much but feel Harry's finger jabbing into the side of my leg beneath the table. I know he's warning me to be quiet, like Amanda did during our first meeting with Georgina, but it still manages to send sparks through my skin, followed by throbs of rage. Who is he to warn me or tell me to do anything?

'We're still working on that.' Harry speaks before I can stand up to the man indirectly responsible for paying our salaries.

'We did some great research at the Boo Influencer Breakfast.'

'That's wonderful, Cally. There's no replacement for putting yourself out there.' Gareth beams at his young protégée. I take this as my cue to try harder to chip in.

'I met a good contact in *Barbie Is Real*, who has been sharing some insights with—'

'I hope you don't think that one influencer is a suitable research pool?' Georgina turns to me, reminding me of everything I hate about this place; if people aren't for you, they're against you.

'No, of course not . . . I—'

'I suggested we go to the influencer breakfast . . .' Cally fills in my blanks proudly. 'To really engage with our desired audience and find out what they want.'

'A great idea.' Gareth nods. Something tells me he'd think burping in our target market's face would be a great idea, provided it came from her.

'I thought so too,' Harry adds, straightening out his shoulders.

'Wonderful,' Gareth grins, as I sink back into my seat. 'And did you?'

'Find out what they want? Yes,' Harry says.

Did we? All I found out was that some influencers have style *and* substance and no longer want to work with Poster.

'Unlike the older demo' – Cally shortens the word 'demographic' with the kind of confidence that tells me she's only months away from stepping into Georgina's shoes – 'they don't aspire to "be" Poster; they want to buy our garments and then style them their own way.'

'So, we're thinking of developing a feature whereby people can upload their favourite items from home and see what they'd look like mixed-and-matched with our pieces.'

I look to Harry like he's an alien speaking Mandarin. Either they're both bluffing their way through this meeting or they have been discussing things behind my back. So much for working together. I could have told them how ridiculous the plan was.

'Another great idea.' Gareth smiles at them both, his polo neck and jacket combination making him look smarter than I now suspect he is.

'Who is going to make that?' I finally speak up. Harry jabs my leg under the table again. I don't know if he's trying to protect me or silence me, but either way it's *infuriating*.

'Well, you are.' Gareth looks surprised. 'You're working on this microsite, no?'

'No, I meant . . .' I begin, realising I'm about to go toe-to-toe with the CEO. Maybe this is why I'm yet to get promoted?

But no: I've barely said a word to the upstairs staff before this merger, my so-called chance to become more *visible*. 'Who will be responsible for the functionality?'

'Oh, the devs,' Gareth says dismissively. I bet he couldn't even tell me their names.

The website development team used to sit in the far-right corner of the basement office. I look out of the glass room to try to spot where each of them is working now. I see Olive perched in a hot-desking space beside Poster's beauty buyer, lotions and potions surrounding her on all sides. Sebastian's a stone's throw away from her, head literally inches from his screen and hands clutched over his ears in an attempt to focus. I can't see Richard, Yolanda, Lauren and Alexander, who have probably propped up their makeshift workstations near the company's servers, seeking a quiet space to get on with some of the biggest and most important workloads in the whole e-tailer industry.

'The development team need to be briefed months in advance,' I say.

'The development team work for *me*.'

'Sure, but in order to do the work you pay them for they need much longer to—'

'We're going to be launching the microsite in mid-May.'

Clearly, the upstairs staff aren't going to stop demanding miracles anytime soon.

'But we're already in *April*.'

'Barely,' Harry says.

'What month we're in is not a "grey thing". It's pretty black and white.'

'You know what I mean,' he mutters, leaning closer into me.

'I promise you I don't.'

'We're only a few days into the month.'

He's so close to me that I can feel the breath of his objections kissing my cheek.

'We feel the market is ready for it,' Cally chimes in, breaking me from the thought.

I sit on my hands, trying not to make a scene, but this is ridiculous. Gareth Grey could ask the devs to make pigs fly and he'd still expect them to have worked it out within the week. And Harry and Cally are just nodding their heads, agreeing with everything he says.

'And you've selected your products for the site?' Gareth continues, remembering why he called us in here in the first place. 'We're starting with one hundred products?'

'That's right,' Cally nods.

'But in different colourways,' Harry adds.

I look between them. When did the two of them decide this?

'We want the buyer to feel like they can collect the whole capsule,' Cally goes on.

Since when has one hundred products constituted a capsule wardrobe?

'And where are they?'

'They need to be finessed,' Harry says, calm as anything, as I begin to sweat.

They need to be *finished*. Or, you know, properly started.

'We want to do a bit more digging into the data,' he goes on. No, I did. *I do.*

'And a bit more qualitative research too,' Cally adds, beaming at her teammate.

'Another influencer event?' Gareth asks.

Oh, please *no.*

'I think we need to look a little further than the influencer events,' I say, feeling the incessant need to compete with my colleagues, or at least keep myself in the ring. 'The influencer scene attracts a certain *type* of person—'

'Our girl,' Harry interrupts, stealing Gareth's lingo.

'Our *woman*,' I clip back. 'Still, maybe looking outside of the box to really understand what the public perception of our brand is might offer some wider insights.'

'Great idea,' Gareth says, and I'm not sure which one of us is most shocked by this. 'So, you'll get out onto the street and interview members of the public . . .'

'Well, that's not exactly what I—'

'. . . And you'll film it too,' Gareth muses, as if he's even surprising himself with his own brilliance. 'See if there's any good clips for social media. It'll be good for our investors to see that we're more than just fashion, that we're impacting real lives.'

Impacting people's bank accounts, more like.

'I'm a data analyst,' I begin, regretting not adding *senior*. 'It's not really my domain.'

'I thought you said it was good to look outside of the box.' Harry looks smug as he says the words, making me feel like a fool.

'That's settled then,' Gareth says, thrusting a fist onto the tabletop like a judge crashing their gavel. 'Harry and erm . . .'

'*Kate*.'

If looks could kill, I would have just murdered Poster's CEO.

'Harry and Kate will go record interviews on Oxford Street,' he continues, unperturbed. 'And Cally, if you could stay behind, I've got a special job for you.'

'Of course,' she beams back at the boss, looking coy, like butter wouldn't melt.

As Harry and I walk out of the office, my skin is simmering. This place is ridiculous. I need to get out of here. And not to interview any Tom, Dick or Harry on Oxford Street.

Chapter Nine

'This is a joke,' I exhale as soon as we're out of earshot.

'It was *your* idea,' Harry reminds me.

'Recording interviews on Oxford Street was *not* my idea.'

Nor was working my arse off here only to see someone like Cally get my promotion.

'Well, thanks to you and your big . . . brain . . .'

We both know he was about to say 'mouth'.

'. . . I'm afraid we have no other choice, because once Gareth sets his sights on something, he rarely changes his mind.'

I follow his gaze back to the CEO's office, back to where Gareth and Cally are sat laughing inside, and resolve to apply for new jobs, *any jobs*, the very second I get home.

'Right, do you want to head towards Bond Street?' I gesture in front of me as soon as we're standing on the overpopulated pavement. 'And I'll go Tottenham Court Road way.'

People swarm out of Oxford Circus station and into the heavy flow of foot traffic filling up one of the city's most famous streets. Famously hectic, at least. Where the busyness crashes over me like waves, passers-by pushing me this way and that,

Harry stands tall above it all, his bold stature like some sort of lighthouse that people can't help but stare up at.

'Who made you the director?' He folds his broad arms, stifling a smile.

'No-one, but they *will*.' This assurance might carry more weight if Gareth wasn't currently fawning over his new favourite, and I wasn't planning to look for a new job tonight.

'I meant of today's interviews, but nice to know you're content in your work,' he says sarcastically.

What's left of my dogged determination leaves me feeling exposed. 'So, I want a promotion? Don't tell me you're scared by a bit of female ambition?'

'It's more the evil-genius-raised-fist that bothers me.'

I follow his gaze to my clenched fingers suspended between us and blush.

'So, yes . . .' I lower my subconscious power-pump slowly. 'I'll head this way.'

'Shouldn't we stay together?'

'Do you *want* to stay together?'

An almost-bored expression washes over his face. Our messaging last night seems to have had little impact on our working dynamic today.

'Who will record your interviews if we split up?'

'I can voice-record them.'

'But what about social media? That needs to be visual.'

'Look, Harry . . .'

I'm still glued to our spot as people deviate from their bee-lines to avoid us. To anyone who doesn't know us this must look like a lovers' tiff.

'I'm a data analyst—'

'A very *senior* data analyst,' he grins.

'I'm not that old.'

'I never said you were. You're what, thirty-four, thirty-five?'

'I'm twenty-nine, you pleb.'

And about to risk starting over. I force the thought from my mind.

'Chill out.' He raises his hands in defence. 'I was joking. I just mean you usually make a point of adding the "senior" part to your job.'

I ignore his jabs. 'It always seems to slip people's minds – and, well, I think social media content is a little below my paygrade.'

'*You're* on more than sixty thousand?'

'Is that so hard to believe?' I say, before his words register. 'Our social staff are on more than sixty k?'

'The directors are.' He nods. Clearly, the salaries go up with every floor. And despite my fears, my resolve to apply for new jobs as soon as I get home cranks up even further. 'It's a big jump between managers and directors. So, let's stick together and nail this thing.' He smiles, striding into the crowd in the direction of Bond Street and leaving me no choice but to follow in his wake.

'How about her?' He points to a young woman walking in our direction as soon as we've come to a standstill just to the left of Selfridges' main entrance.

'Oh, because she's pretty?'

Ergh, I hate that I sound jealous.

'No, because she looks like she's in our target demographic.'

'Don't you mean *demo*?'

'Be nice, Kate. Cally knows what she's doing.'

Now I hate that I *feel* jealous.

'Okay, well, who would *you* suggest?' he asks as we watch potential interviewee after potential interviewee passing us on all sides.

'How about him?' I gesture towards a man who appears to be in his seventies who is moving at a stable pace towards us. Against the purposeful speed of tourists and professionals surrounding him, he looks like someone has switched him into slow motion.

'I don't mean to alarm you.' Harry lowers his voice. 'But I'm not sure he's a zoomer.'

'I'm not sure he's zooming *anywhere*. But isn't that the point?'

'I'm not entirely sure what the point of any of this is.'

'Couldn't you have had this existential crisis before we left the office?'

Harry's expression is hanging somewhere between amusement and insecurity. I don't know what to make of it. I'm not sure what to make of him full stop.

'I could have it in that nice coffee shop over there?' He nods across the road.

'And go back to the office empty-handed?'

'Man, you're a nerd.' He looks wistfully in the direction of his beloved soy flat white.

'Look, Harry, some of us can't fake it 'til we make it.'

He looks down at his feet; it's the first time either one of us has referenced any of our messages, or the fact we've been messaging at all. I wait for him to take the bait, to soften and start sharing more of himself, but his walls visibly go up before me.

'I know we're trying to explore the wider public perception, but . . .'

'Harry, don't be such an ageist.'

'I'm being a *realist*.'

'Excuse me, sir.' I approach the man before Harry can stop me.

'At least ask him if he knows what Poster is,' he hisses behind me.

I cast a sharp glare in his direction before turning my attention back to the man.

'Fine,' he relents. 'You clearly know what you're doing.'

'Excuse me? Sir?' Okay, this guy's seeming lack of hearing doesn't exactly fill me with confidence, but there's no way I'm backing out of this interview in front of Harry now.

'Yes, love?' I've got the man's attention.

'Hello. My name's Kate.' I put a hand to my chest. 'And we work for a well-known fashion e-tailer and we're just conducting some market research on behalf of the company. Do you mind if we ask you a few questions?'

'Not we. *You*.' Harry leans into me to whisper in my ear. I glare at him again.

'Well, that depends.' The man's expression lights up. 'Will it be you or this scruffy one that will be interviewing me?' He casts his eyes to Harry beside me.

I let out a big belly laugh as Harry forces his hands to his hips. I can't tell if he's seriously annoyed or not, but as he reaches for his phone, he shakes his head in my direction. He begins recording and I secretly hope that my chosen interviewee is so far from on-brand for Poster that they will refuse to post this video on our socials. It's one thing to be captured candidly in a still, quite another to be exposed in motion. And, although a small part of me liked making it onto Poster's Instagram account, I know that any pride I felt was less about the acclaim and more about the fact that I am doing what Amanda told me to the first time she shared about the office merger: be more visible. Not that it really matters now.

'So, if you could begin by telling us your first name and your age?'

'David, thirty-five.'

'Your real age, please, sir.' I grin; I like this guy already.

'Fine.' He rolls his eyes playfully. 'Seventy-five.'

'And what do you think of Poster?'

'Hmmmm.' He spends so long thinking that I break eye contact with him to look at Harry over the top of the phone he's pointing in my direction. He may be shooting our interview, but his eyes are focused entirely on me. My stomach jolts.

'I like them. Really bright, light up a room.'

'So, you buy Poster?'

'Yes, for my wife . . . and my girlfriends.' He winks at me.

'But seriously?'

'Yes, seriously.' David nods and I look towards Harry.

'Why don't you ask about average spend, about what would increase his spending on our site?' he suggests over his suspended phone as my line of questioning runs dry.

'Who made *you* the director?' I quip back to him, echoing his words from earlier, hating that I seem to remember every sentence he says to me so well.

'And how much would you say you spend on Poster per year?' I pose the question to David, annoyed by how much Harry will love that I've taken his suggestion on board.

'I don't know . . . maybe twenty pounds?'

I literally can't think of a product that costs less than that. Not even Harry's socks.

'What would make you spend more?' I ask, as Harry stifles another laugh.

'I don't know, maybe if the edges curl or I go off the picture.'

'You mean the product?' I ask.

Harry's shoulders begin to shake. 'Sir, am I right in saying you're talking about posters, *printed* posters?' he asks from above his phone, which is now trembling in time with his giggles.

'What else would I be talking about?'

Harry's whole body is shaking in an attempt to not laugh in this poor man's face. I purse my lips together, my cheeks flushing red.

'How long did you know he was talking about actual posters for?' I ask, as soon as we've let our unsuspecting first victim disappear into the passing crowds.

'Oh, the second you asked your first question.'

He is trying and failing to hide his grin.

'And you didn't think to *tell* me?'

'I *tried* to tell you to ask whether he knew of our site.'

'Yes, but . . .'

'And do you really think I'm going to miss getting that reaction on camera?'

'You wanker.'

I push my hands into his chest to indicate my annoyance, noticing how solid it is. I'm surprised to feel the warmth of his hands on my skin as he gently pushes my fists away, holding my gaze with his irritatingly gorgeous grey-blue eyes.

'Okay, well, let's see how good *you* are at interviewing the public.' I force the words to break the intense silence that is brimming between us.

'Deal,' he says, squaring his shoulders, challenge accepted.

'Except this time . . .' He takes a small step closer towards me before someone accidentally pushes him from behind, forcing his body so close to mine that I can smell the aftershave on his impeccably white knit. 'Maybe let's choose an interviewee closer to our target *demo*.'

'I hate you.' I look him dead in the eye.

'Oh, Kate.' He holds his heart in feigned affection. 'You say the sweetest things.'

Chapter Ten

Though random interviews with the public weren't my idea – would *never* be my idea – I have to admit some elements of our filming today weren't horrible. Especially the bit where some woman accidentally thought Harry was trying to mug her and proceeded to hit him repeatedly with her handbag. And yet, with every step I take from the tube station to the apartment, I try to reclaim something of the resolve I felt in the office to *finally* follow through on my promise of looking for a new job tonight.

As I turn onto our street, I muster up the memory of being in Gareth Grey's office only hours before. The way he had looked past me and fixated on Cally, maximising her importance and diminishing mine in minutes. Unlocking the front door and walking into the empty living room, I try to recall him mentally pitting us against one another and finding me wanting. And, as I push open the door into my now-bedroom, I try my very best to remember that any advancement at Poster now depends all too heavily on me working with her and—

'*Harry?*'

I immediately stop still upon seeing him standing there in the small box room, a handful of papers in his hands, a look of shock on his face that feels utterly unwarranted when he knows that this is now *my* room.

'What the heck, Harry?' I demand. 'You do *know* what boundaries are, right?'

'Wolf said you weren't in.'

'I wasn't, but *now* I am.'

'I can see that.' For a moment he looks genuinely sheepish. 'Thought you'd be happy to see me?' He smiles and just like that any sheepishness bleats right off.

'If "surprised" and "happy" have somehow become synonyms, then sure.'

Harry is just standing there, all broad shoulders and bewildered smiles.

'You do know what a synonym is?' I ask.

'Do you truly think I'm thick, Kate?' He shakes his head and his smile fades.

'Well, you've just let yourself into a woman's bedroom without permission, so right now, I'm not thinking you're particularly *smart*.'

'Correction.' He takes a small step forward and the room seems to shrink around me as I instantly become aware of how close we are standing. 'I let myself into my friend's bedroom to pick up some important documents he forgot to take on tour and asked for me to mail to him and I technically had permission, from Wolf.'

'You rang?' Wolf appears outside the open bedroom door. I didn't think he was *in*.

I turn to accuse him. 'You could have given me the head's up that Harry is here.'

'Sorry, I fell asleep.'

'With someone else in the apartment?' My head darts between them. 'He could have robbed us for all we were worth.'

'Hey!' Harry objects, documents still clutched in his grasp.

'I know you wouldn't. I'm just trying to make a point, about *boundaries*.'

I swear *both* of them roll their eyes at this.

'I know Pretty Boy is already too wealthy to fall into petty theft,' Wolf jibes.

Harry shakes his head again, making his way out of the bedroom. I still don't know their problem, but from Wolf's side it looks a lot like good, old-fashioned jealousy.

'Don't worry, I was just leaving.'

Harry gives me a sad smile as he heads towards the door, and I suddenly feel quite bad. After our messages and this afternoon, maybe he wants me to ask him to stay.

'Fancy heading out tonight?' Wolf asks before I have time to think further on it. I don't know why but it feels a lot like he's metaphorically trying to mark his territory.

'I was actually going to spend the evening looking for a new jo—' I cut my sentence short; Harry is still lingering by the door. 'Sure you have everything you need?' I soften.

'Yeah, thanks.' He smiles back, softening too. 'Sorry that I scared you.'

'I wasn't scared.'

He smirks again, shaking his head at my feist; normality restored. And, as soon as he has left the building, I feel my heart rate beginning to return to normal too.

126

'Sorry about that,' Wolf says, walking to pick up a long leather belt from the bust-up wooden coat stand that is by the front door, Boner seeming to appear from nowhere now that the coast is clear. 'Fancy a walk?'

'What are you going to do if I say no?' I look from the belt to him, eyes wide. He throws his head back, laughing, and although I *know* that I promised myself I'd spend this evening scouring LinkedIn, after the shock I've just had, I could do with some fresh air.

After a fortnight of being passing ships (or, you know, purposefully-avoiding-one-another ships), heading outside with Wolf feels like a whole new experience. Stealing a glance at his dark hair and open leather jacket, part of me wonders whether he may start melting or twinkling like a *Twilight* vampire in the sunlight.

'I was meant to be looking for a new job tonight,' I say as we stride further and further away from the apartment.

'Meant to be?' Wolf keeps his eyes on the pavement ahead.

'To be honest, I feel like I've meant to be looking for a new job for years.'

'Well, what's stopping you?'

'How much time have you got?' I laugh.

'Enough.' He turns to me, giving me a warm smile that makes me want to open up.

Together, we walk round the back of Maze Hill station and make our way into Greenwich Park, which is teeming with life and colour since the clocks moved forward a couple of weeks ago, the nights drawing out a little longer.

'Wow, this place is gorgeous,' I say, looking from the imposing white museum on my right and up to the tourist-scattered observatory on my left.

'I hardly ever come here.'

'That's because it closes around the time you wake up,' I tease.

'The life of a struggling actor.'

He continues to look forward as he hooks a left to begin walking up the park's steep incline. I try to keep in step with his pace.

'Ever thought of doing something else?' I try to avoid the niggle that is rising from the depths of me, the one that always comes when chatting about careers.

'Never.' He turns to me. 'I was born to act.'

I gaze back at him, trying not to get out of breath as we ascend even higher.

'Must be nice to know what you're born for,' I muse, through increasingly heavy pants. 'I'm thirty in a few weeks and I still have absolutely no idea.'

'That's because you're too chicken to leave Poster.'

'I am *not*.' I stop in my tracks.

'Then what's keeping you there?'

'Honestly?'

Harry's face, cheeks dimpled and flushed with laughter, crosses my mind. I force it out just as fast. He is not the reason. Until two weeks ago I didn't even know he still worked there.

'I took the job because it was on a good starting salary,' I remind myself again. 'I thought it would be a springboard to other things I *care* about, but once you have something to lose, it's hard to justify taking a risk. I'm so close to becoming a director and to start somewhere else now, I'd have to take a massive pay cut—'

'So, it's all about the money for you?'

'Not at all, but—'

'It's a part of it?'

'I don't have the luxury of it not being.'

I stare down his brief look of disdain before we finally reach the top of the vantage point out across Greenwich Park. I look from the Shard in the distance to the high-rises of Canary Wharf, intimidating us from across the water. My family are wonderful, the best even. But we've never had much and ever since my mum and dad decided to take early retirement and go travelling, any safety nets I had are now a thing of the past. I'm somehow too old to rely on my parents but too young to rely on myself. Too old to go home but not secure enough to afford a place of my own. I've found myself in the in-between.

'Money has never been important to me.' Wolf is gazing out across the view too. 'I just know that when I act, I feel alive and like I'm doing something I was made for and—'

My phone buzzes in my pocket. I reach to look at it, at Harry's name on the screen.

> Harry: Are you looking for a new job? Because if you are it would be good to know.

> Harry: For the sake of the microsite development.

'Am I interrupting something?'

'What?' I look up from my phone to see Wolf staring down at it too. 'No, sorry.'

'Who is he?' Wolf asks, arms folded, his deep V t-shirt exposing more of his tattooed chest as he does. He has a knowing smirk on his face. But he doesn't *know* at all.

129

'Just a colleague.'

'One doesn't react like that when "just a colleague" messages them.'

'This one does.' I stash my phone in my back pocket. 'And react like what?'

'Like they stop breathing for a second?'

'I did not,' I argue lamely, feeling caught in the act.

'I wouldn't get involved with someone from work.' He looks genuinely concerned.

'You're not the first person to tell me that. I know it can get complicated.'

'Oh, screw the complications.' Wolf laughs in a way that tells me that he's been romantically involved with colleagues before, possibly even more than once. 'I just meant I wouldn't get involved with someone who works at Poster.'

'I know why *I* dislike the Poster-types so much, but why do you?'

'Well, for starters, I don't like what Poster stands for as a company. And then, well . . .' Wolf stalls for a second, selecting his next words carefully. 'I know I didn't know Sam and his friends that well, but every time they've been round at the flat, they've given off this pretentious, superior vibe and I just don't have a lot of time for people who get everything they go after handed to them on a plate.'

'I get that.' I smile back at him, feeling drawn into his passion. And yet, by the time we get back to the apartment, I can't help but be drawn back into Harry's messages too.

Me: Yeah, I was going to apply for some but got distracted.

Harry: By Wolf?

130

Me: And his Boner.

Me: That's his dog's name if you didn't know.

Harry: Sadly, I did. Poor dog.

Harry: But I thought you loved your job?

Me: I do, but there's only so long you can keep working for a company you don't actually agree with.

Harry: How so?

Me: Well, you heard what people said today. I've always thought Poster was overpriced and overrated, but I thought the public lapped it up. But now it feels like the pandemic has exposed so many inequalities and Poster has been left looking too white, too middle-class, too seedy, too greedy.

Harry: Well, would you look at that.

Me: Look at what?

Harry: We do agree on something.

Me: Well, why are *you* working here if you think that?

Harry: Do you really want to know?

Me: I wouldn't ask if I didn't.

Harry: And you're really going to *listen* to my response?

Harry: Not just jump down my thought like you usually do.

Me: I do NOT jump down your throat!

Harry: Hmmm.

Me: Okay, fine.

Me: Listening . . .

Harry: Well, I used to think Poster was the coolest place to work in the world.

Harry: Ever since I did my internship, I wanted to get a permanent job here.

Me: Even though the company's reputation is on its arse?

Harry: So much for listening . . .

Harry: And yes, I guess I like the idea of restoring something to its former glory.

Me: One set of luxury leggings at a time?

Harry: Hey! I truly believe clothes can change the world.

Me: Now I know you're messing with me.

Harry: The mini-skirt? Originally condemned in the 1960s, now a staple symbolising women's freedom.

Me: And heels make it harder for them to run away.

Harry: 1970s punk? It provided a vehicle for young Brits to voice their discontent with the ruling class.

Me: You're just copy and pasting this from Wikipedia, aren't you?

Harry: The 1980s female power suit? A stark reminder that working women were playing by the rules of a man's world, that we needed to advocate for more rights.

Me: Okay, fine, you've made your point.

Harry: Did I just win an argument against Kate Carter?

Me: No.

Me: But you didn't lose this one, either.

Chapter Eleven

'Kate!'

I hear my name being called above the sound of the 'Coffeehouse Chill' playlist that is currently blasting into my ears: my attempt at keeping my cool this Monday morning. After spending the rest of last week being 'just colleagues' with Harry in the office and most of this weekend messaging him late into the night at home, my mind is scrambling to work out our increasingly unorthodox dynamic. I turn just in time to see Blair standing there, the spring sunlight hitting her face, her chipped-back nails wrapping around her beat-up KeepCup. I look down at the two take-out coffees in my hand and feel a bit sheepish.

'Hey!' I beam back at her, carefully opening my arms to embrace her without spilling any of the overpriced flat whites. True to form, she's wearing all black, her thick, winter trench coat now replaced by a lighter leather jacket. I should really introduce her to Wolf.

'You heading to the office?'

Her eyes narrow at the thought of the tenth floor, nothing

about our being up there making her care anymore for the place and the people who used to occupy it alone.

'Not today, actually.'

'Finally found a way out of working for the Man?' she asks, eyeing my coffees suspiciously. Sure, one of these happens to be for Harry. But she doesn't need to know that. Plus, she's still working for the Man too. Though I can imagine she has sent off more applications to work elsewhere than me. And now I'm here, about to hop through the next hoop Gareth and Georgina have set out for me.

'Sadly not.' I shake my head. 'I'm heading to Sydney's.'

'Sydney?' She looks hopeful, like I might just be able to take her with me.

'*Sydney's*,' I correct. 'The guy who shoots all our product shots and flat lays.'

'Sydney Hollymoor?' Her confusion resolves for a second; everyone who works in fashion – even those tangential to fashion – knows who he is, that he's responsible for some of the most prestigious work in the business, from *Vogue* to Harrods to celebrity campaigns fronted by the most iconic of influencers, from the Kardashians to soft-rock royalty like Rumour Reign. 'Why?'

'We're selecting the products we want to be in our advertising campaign to launch the microsite. We'll shoot them on models, obviously . . .'

'Obviously.' She rolls her eyes, like hearing me talk like this is foreign to her.

'But today, we'll get Sydney to shoot the product flat-lay shots that people will be redirected to when they click on the model's clothes. Should be interesting.'

'If you say so.' She shrugs. 'You're still coming to my birthday drinks on Friday?'

Blair's birthday drinks have completely slipped my mind. It's just that between moving house and juggling my usual responsibilities with the microsite project, I have no idea how we've fallen further and further into April.

'Of course I'm coming to your birthday drinks,' I rally. 'I wouldn't miss it. But if I don't leave for Syd's now, then we're going to miss this deadline.'

'Kate Carter missing a deadline? You've changed.'

'If I wasn't working with Dumb and Dumber, I'd have completed this task in days.'

Blair laughs, but after my messaging Harry all weekend, I can't help but feel mean. Sure, any messages between us start with something work-related, but still, there always seems a reason to keep them going far after the initial question is answered. I hold the coffees in my hand a little tighter, feeling their warmth through the take-out cups and hoping that somehow this white flag of a flat white will make the in-person Harry as warm as the one hidden behind his phone screen.

Blair and I make our way across the small, gated garden in the square outside Poster House, but instead of heading into the lobby with her, I turn in the opposite direction, weaving through the side streets that Harry has specified in the directions he messaged to me just this morning. I detour around tourists swanning down the pavement and businesspeople making a beeline for work, until I'm pretty sure I'm going round in circles. Then, I come to a small alleyway leading me to a row of dodgy-looking buildings, complete with damaged brick-work and boarded-up windows. They are the least Poster-like buildings I've ever seen – so much so, that I have to double-check Harry's directions. But no, I'm on the right street and I'm meant to be looking for a battered green door.

I walk up and down the road, feeling more and more frazzled as I do. And though we've yet to text during work hours, I send Harry a message to confirm whether I'm in the right place. Then, when he doesn't reply, I risk giving him a call. Then another, and another, as my arrival time gets later and my pulse starts to soar.

'You looking for Sydney's studio?' A modelesque woman who I'm sure I've seen lounging around the top floor of Poster House appears from nowhere: my (Victoria's) angel.

She points to the door she's evidently just exited through and disappears as quickly as she arrived. The door is battered, just like Harry said. But it's blue: bloody duck-egg *blue*.

By the time I'm running up the stone steps and reaching the large studio floor, the coffees I'm holding are cold. But it's not like Harry has a free hand to take one, as across the room, his hands are placed carefully on Cally's narrow hips. My stomach somersaults at the sight of it, but I force my sense of shock not to show on my face.

'Kate!' she calls as soon as she spots me standing there. Harry lets go of her immediately, and I see that he's holding a silky-looking garment in his hands. I'm not sure what is more irritating: the idea of him sending me on a wild goose chase for a green door that doesn't exist, him making a move on Cally, or that they've clearly started laying out their chosen outfits together. Without me.

'Nice of you to join us,' he says, as I bridge the gap between us; he begins striding across the space to meet me in the middle.

137

'I would have been here on time if someone had sent me the right directions.'

'Hey! My directions were fine.' He stops walking towards me immediately, literally taken aback.

'I thought you of all people would know the difference between green and blue.'

'What's that supposed to mean?'

'You told me to look for a green door. It's blue.'

'It is green!' He takes a defiant step towards me.

'It's *blue*.' I take one towards him too, until we're standing toe-to-toe, just half a metre and two flat whites between us.

He looks down at the coffees with a smug smile. 'Oh thanks, you shouldn't have.'

I know I should just give one to him, that it might be the very bridge between our messages and in-person moments that we need, but as Cally takes a step forward and puts a territorial hand to his arm, I can't bring myself to do it. No, all I want to do right now is wipe that smug smile off his handsome face.

'It's not for you,' I lie. 'It's for Sydney.'

'Brown-noser.'

'Oh look, you know another colour!'

And then the smug smile is gone. I can tell from his tense jaw that I've hit a nerve. I look from the coffee to Cally and curse myself for messaging him back in the first place. Clearly, whatever digital distraction he needs from me, he doesn't need it here. It's like he's a completely different person to the one who signed off with a simple 'Sleep well x' last night. But I can't think about that right now. No, right now, Sydney Hollymoor, fearful of wasting any of his precious time, has given us full rein of his studio space to 'get ourselves sorted' before

138

we call him in. And I'll be damned if I waste any more of *my* time here too.

'Have the coffee.' I push the take-out cup originally meant for him into his hand before taking a sip of my own. It's completely cold.

Harry takes a sip of his and then holds the cup up in recognition; he knows it's a Kaffeine soy flat white and he's giving me a look that clearly says: *Sure, this was for Sydney*.

I try to move on from it quickly. 'Right. Now that I'm here, we have loads to do before we call in Sydney, so let's set some SMART objectives.'

Harry looks at me like this idea is the dumbest thing he's ever heard.

'Specific, Measurable, Achievable—'

'We know what SMART objectives are, Kate,' he says plainly.

'Well, I didn't,' Cally mumbles under her breath, unsure what the problem is.

'So, we have our data now. I have a wealth of it from our internal database and some that I've managed to purchase from other providers. And we have the qualitative data from the influencer breakfast and interviewing the public, and I emailed out a Q&A to a number of our website users too—'

'You didn't run that by us,' he argues, using his free hand to mess up his hair again before glancing at Cally, whose own hair is piled up high to reveal her pretty face. I know she's probably thinking about how much better it was before I arrived on set.

'I didn't know I had to. It's a pretty standard Q&A.'

'But you didn't mention the microsite, did you? It's meant to be a secret.'

He looks worried and I wonder if our messages are meant to

be secret too. That ignoring me in the workplace is something we wordlessly decided was the done thing.

'Until the launch party, at least,' he adds.

'I didn't even think about a launch party.'

I type frantically into the notes section of my phone, writing myself a reminder to check over the questions I sent out in the Q&A towards the end of last week. I'm sure I didn't mention anything I shouldn't have, but the way he is looking at me now is making me nervous.

'Okay, so first, product selection . . .' I try my best to keep some sort of control, hating how out of it his imposing presence is making me feel. 'Then, we shoot them?'

'Why not shoot them first and then select what photographs best?' Harry asks.

'Shoot over a hundred garments? I'll shoot myself.'

'You do know that Sydney will be the one photographing them?'

'Well, yes, but *we'll* be the ones overseeing it.'

'Yes, *we* will.'

I drain the last of my coffee as Harry sips his leisurely, wandering over to the racks of clothes at the far side of the room. I set up my laptop on a fold-out table and scooch a chair up to read my emails, to see whether any urgent messages have come in from the senior management team. Out of the corner of my eye, I can see him brushing his hand through the garments, like a child running their hand through the wild grass of an overgrown meadow. Every so often, I'll see him pause, picking up a coat or jumper or shirt to feel the fabric in his hands, to gaze closer at the colour combinations: camel and caramel, the pale pinks and blues of a sunset. I force my eyes down to my screen, searching for the document that tells me which trends are generating the most traffic on some of our competitor's sites.

'I think we should go for the caramel tailored trousers,' I say, walking over to meet Cally and Harry by the illuminated white wall.

'For sure, paired with the bright pink pullover.' Harry picks the garment he has in mind out of the huge, messy floordrobe he has just created.

'I was going to say the white knit cardigan. Grandpacore is generating big hits online.'

'This feels cooler,' he objects, scrambling to layer a thick, neon belt that clashes with absolutely everything.

'It may *feel* cooler, but the *Wall Street Journal* recently reported that Gen Z are looking to their grandparents for style inspiration. We should tap into that.'

Harry is already reaching into his pile of items to pull out a pair of black, leather-look leggings, laying them out next to the first outfit he's placed on the studio floor.

'Leather-look leggings are on the way out,' I say.

Harry, who is now on his knees, glares up at me.

'According to the clicks.'

He proceeds to pick out a sheer shirt in a cobalt blue that is so bright that I'm surprised that Poster even stocks it for our usual 'quiet luxury' users.

'The model should wear a Rouge Allure Velvet Luminous Matt,' he says, seemingly ignoring my last sentence completely as Cally nods in encouragement.

'I have *no* idea what you just said.'

'It's a Chanel lipstick,' she informs me, too pleased to be in the know.

'Rouge . . . Do you know that one?' I turn to Harry.

'Man, you never let anything go, do you?'

'You made me *late*.'

'To a job you don't even . . .'

He stops himself from completing this sentence. He's smart enough to know not to say I am looking for new work with Cally in the room. Plus, with all our messaging, I didn't have time to find anything I wanted to apply for. This weekend, I felt like we were getting to know one another, seeing eye to eye, that I was starting to see something in him that I hadn't before. Now, it feels like we're on completely contrasting pages again.

'You do know it's okay to make mistakes?' he goes on. 'You could afford to make some too.'

'More than I can afford some stupid Chanel lipstick.'

'It retails at thirty-five pounds,' he says, my eyes skyrocketing at the price. 'And it lasts for *months*. Sure, you could buy a knock-off for a fiver that breaks each time you use it and replace it every month, but then you're spending the same money and wasting a wealth of resources just to make yourself feel like you're bagging a bargain. But if you need to snub everything you don't understand, Carter, by all means be my guest.'

'Wow.'

I don't have anything better to say, because Harry has just wiped the floor with me. He looks shocked too, like he has no idea where the force of his rant is coming from.

'Sorry, I . . .' he stutters. 'Can you just trust me with this, for a second?' He looks down at the two outfits laid out on the floor, reaching to compose a third: a light blue woollen tank top with distressed denim jeans and an oversized black leather jacket. 'It's my job.'

'And analysing and applying data is *my* job.'

He stands to square up to me, an almost kinetic energy buzzing between us.

'Hey, this looks *good*.' Cally's voice breaks me from his spell as we whip around to see that she's doing *her* job: suspending her phone to take a selfie as she models the outfit that Harry had clearly marked to lay out next.

'Cally, come on,' I begin, hating that after Harry's recent dress-down my voice sounds so weak. 'We've got work to do.'

She begins to peel off the expensive leather jacket, with an expression that informs me that she thinks I'm no fun.

'No, wait.' Harry puts his hand up to stop her undressing. 'That's not a bad idea.'

'What's not a bad idea?' she says. My thoughts exactly.

'Instagramming the styles.'

'What about waiting for the big reveal at the launch party?' I argue.

Cally waits, one hand on her phone, the other on the jacket. Her eyes oscillate between Harry and me, not yet sure whether she's keeping it on or taking it off.

'Yes, but Cally isn't *saying* anything about the new site.'

'I didn't *say* anything either.' Well, I don't *think* I did.

'People will want to know where you've got your clothes from, right?' He turns to Cally, who releases her hand from the jacket: a sign that she thinks he's already won.

'Always. It's the first thing people ask me. Unless I tag the designer.'

'Don't tag the designer,' he says, sure of himself. 'Tag Poster. It'll build intrigue.'

'They already know she's working for Poster now,' I object.

'Yes, but they've not seen her wearing Poster online, and especially not like this.'

The fact Harry knows what she has and hasn't worn publicly is telling. Cally nods, smiling down at the selfie she's just taken, displayed on her screen. She adjusts the brightness and cranks up the contrast until all the colours pop.

'Any more objections, your honour?' Harry asks, eyebrow raised.

'No,' I say, admitting defeat; regardless of the trends, building intrigue is a good idea.

Cally proceeds to upload the photo and she and Harry watch the likes coming in. I, however, am looking at the outfits he has pulled together on the floor. The colours clash, the fabrics too; nothing goes together and yet somehow everything works.

'Right, well, let's get these ones shot by Sydney too,' I begin, remembering our specific brief from Georgina and Gareth. I reach for my phone to call Sydney and let him know that we are ready for him to hotfoot it back from his meeting in Poster House. 'Harry, can you lay out one or two outfits featuring these garments?'

I screenshot the spreadsheet I've opened up on my phone, the one showing which outfits are being bought by our oldest users in the hopes that this may qualify as grandpacore chic. I signal that I've just sent him something and he catches my eye sheepishly, as if he's also remembering how different things felt when he woke up to message me this morning. Then he looks down at his phone, his features hardening, shoulders stiffening.

'I've got to take this.'

'Is it a work call?' I hate that I sound like his mother again.

'Well, no.' He looks down at the name on the screen.

144

'Harry, Sydney is literally just on his way over now.'

'You can hold the fort,' he says, grabbing his denim jacket from the table he left it on, on the far side of the room. I can't believe he's going to boss me around only to bail on us.

'But you're the Creative Manager, remember?'

Is this just because I've asked him to include one or two items that may actually sell?

'Yeah, but you could probably do it in your sleep.'

His sentence lands somewhere between self-deprecating and accusatory, like he's challenging me to find out it's not that easy. But, before I can work out which of the above he's going for, Harry has left the building.

'Ladies!' Sydney walks into the studio almost as soon as Harry has left it. 'Saw Anderson on the way out. What's gotten into him?'

Cally looks to me and I don't know when Harry's erratic moods became my problem. 'He had to take a call.' She smiles her effervescent smile.

'But he's the Creative Manager working on this shoot, is he not?'

'It's just the flat lay of the outfits,' she replies, undermining everything Sydney does here in one fell swoop. Sure, the Gen Z buyer may want to see the garment on models to buy into the look, but that doesn't mean they won't want to swipe through to see the product shots too.

'It's unprofessional,' Sydney says, shaking his head before pushing up the sleeve of his fishnet sweater to look at his chunky watch.

For a moment I feel buoyed that Sydney agrees with me, that anyone as cool as him – with his round, tortoiseshell glasses and rolled-up denim jeans – would agree with anything I have to say. Then, I remember that we're still a team and I'll be damned if Harry makes us look bad. Still, a small part of me dies knowing that I'm going to have to cover for him now.

'I think he said something about a work crisis,' I lie, and Cally's eyes shoot to mine.

'What could be more important than my time?' Sydney puts a hand to his hip.

'It was something to do with the trip coming up,' Cally joins in.

I try to stare her into silence; doesn't she know that when it comes to fibbing, the vaguer the better? Now we have to fabricate a flipping trip.

'To the French investors?'

As far as I'm concerned, Sydney may as well be speaking French himself.

'*Potential* new investors,' she confirms, clearly in the know. So, the trip's real? 'Gareth is busy with . . . well, I'm not sure exactly . . .' Her side-eye to me suggests she knows more than she's letting on. A whole lot more than I do. 'So, he's sending us.'

'Us?' I hate this feeling. Being out of the loop, on the outside.

'Me and Harry. Gareth asked us to go for him. Show them the "future of Poster".'

I will the thin layer of foundation I applied this morning to barricade my blushing, my thoughts morphing into memories of some male middle-manager from the tenth floor telling the basement staff that we would have to work twice as hard to get the same recognition as our counterparts upstairs because *pretty people always go far*. I found the same guy on social media

146

a year later, after he left for a job that he claimed would make him a household name. Turns out he didn't amount to much more, something that might make me feel better if I didn't constantly feel like I am missing the mark.

'When?'

'This weekend.'

'No, I mean, when did Gareth ask?' I say, refusing to let my voice tremble.

'Oh, I don't know . . . first thing this morning?'

So, when I was out buying coffee for Harry, he was busy planning his weekend trip with Cally? No wonder he's been distancing himself from me since the moment I arrived here. I look to Sydney, still standing between us, his closed fists pressing further and further into his hips, waiting to begin. Right now, I'd rather be doing anything else. But unlike Harry, I take my professional responsibilities seriously. Unlike Harry, my promotion to director won't be handed to me on a plate. And yet, as I jump to action, beginning to tell Sydney everything we need to capture for our next presentation back in the office, it is Harry's words that I hold on to to get through the shoot in one piece: 'fake it 'til you make it.'

Chapter Twelve

'So, let me get this straight . . .'

Blair presses her elbows further into the table we're all sitting around in the tenth-floor kitchen, Charlie and Toby leaning closer into the safety of our four-person huddle. Toby is shuffling a deck of cards in his hands; this week, he's learning magic. Blair looks annoyed, really annoyed, and it's precisely the reason I haven't mentioned Harry and Cally's work trip together to her before now. Why I've kept it to myself for the past three days.

'You're working on this interdepartmental project with two colleagues from tenth . . .'

'Well, technically Cally has only ever worked in the newly merged office,' I say weakly.

'Oh *please*, she's the most Poster person I've ever seen.'

Blair crinkles her nose in disdain; I'm pretty sure she's the only person who hates what the tenth floor stands for more than me. I dread to think what she'll say when she discovers I'm messaging Harry. Well, *was* messaging Harry. Before he bailed halfway through the photoshoot to take some mysterious phone call about the trip. Since then, his messages have waned: a half-arsed apology for evaporating from Sydney's studio here, a half-hearted attempt to make small talk when there's an elephant of a work trip between us there. And, with our other work ramping up ahead of fashion's 'festive season', meetings about our microsite have simply been pushed down the priority list. There was once a time when I was blissfully unaware that when it comes to fashion, Christmas begins as soon as summer starts.

'And only *two* members of this so-called three-person team are flying away tomorrow to stay in a shack in Bordeaux to schmooze some potential investors?'

'I believe it's a chateau,' I mumble, too disappointed to feel annoyed about it right now.

'Sounds horrible.' Toby tries to make me feel better.

'And the only member who *isn't* invited on this trip is basement-office Kate?' Blair goes on, angry enough for the both of us.

I would usually fight for any opportunity to show Poster that I'm worthy, but this time, being so blatantly overlooked for Harry and Cally, I feel too embarrassed to bring it up.

'Can we please not make "basement-office Kate" a thing?' I ask lamely.

'I'm just angry for you, babe.' She shakes her head. 'It's discrimination.'

'At least I don't have to miss your birthday drinks.' I try to muster some excitement.

'If you think my drinks will be better than Bordeaux, I'm afraid you're going to be disappointed. It'll just be casual. We'll save the real celebrations for your big three-oh.'

'How many weeks now?' Charlie asks, like I have a terminal illness or something.

'Two weeks tomorrow,' I confirm, stomach churning as I do.

'What are we going to do to celebrate?' Blair asks.

'I don't really want to make it a big deal.'

'But it's a *massive* deal, a huge milestone.'

Yes, and one that I promised myself I'd achieve so much more before meeting.

'If you decide to have a party, I'm happy to perform for free,' Toby says, attempting to flick the fanned cards so that they cascade across the table. Then, the door into the kitchenette flings open, causing cards to fly off in all directions. Each one of us looks up in panic to see Amanda standing there, a look of curious amusement on her face.

'How did I know I'd find you guys here?' She puts her hands to her hips.

'Because it's the only safe place to hide?' Charlie grins up at her.

'Need I remind you that you have jobs to do?'

Her smile falters for a second, her mouth opening up as if to say something more before thinking better of it. I suspect she was going to say something like *for now*. Thanks to the normal flurry of office gossip, we all know the threat of redundancies isn't quite as quelled as she'd like, that this microsite might have more riding on it than I like to think. In my defence, I am trying to bring my best to it. It's not my fault that my best didn't get the invite to Bordeaux, unless . . . *Is it?*

'We should really go back out there,' I say, looking around the coffee-littered table.

'No,' Blair objects. 'Surely it's not time yet.'

'I thought we had minutes, an entire half-hour left,' Charlie adds dramatically.

'Well, you know what they say,' Amanda pipes up, not turning around from pouring a fresh cup of coffee for herself. 'Time flies when you're hiding from your colleagues in the kitchen. Come on, guys, you're heading back to your desks, not out to your deaths.'

The four of us groan, reluctantly standing up and making our way towards the door.

'Kate?' Amanda says my name just as soon as I'm about to walk through it. 'Can I speak to you for a second?' Blair, Toby and Charlie stop walking too, ready to stand or fight for me if they need to. Amanda looks between them shiftily before adding: 'Alone.'

'Sorry I've been MIA these past few days,' she says as soon as the others have dragged their heavy limbs back to their desks for the last hour of the day. She declutters the table with ease, silently clearing up our mess in the way only a good manager can.

'You haven't been the only one.'

I regret the words instantly. Of all the people to talk to about this thing with Harry, I know Amanda isn't the one; she's made Poster's thoughts about office romances quite clear.

'Who else has been MIA?'

'We've just not had much time to talk about the microsite since the shoot.'

'Well, the three of you will have plenty of time to catch up in Bordeaux.'

Amanda beams at me and my stomach somersaults, excitement surging through me, until her next words make me pretty certain that she's simply assumed I've been invited.

'I'm sure the others have briefed you on your mission?

Schmooze the heiresses of the Lavigne estate and get them to buy a big chunk of advertising space on the new microsite?'

I would laugh at the fact that Amanda is pretending to stroke an imaginary cat whilst she relays said 'mission', morphing into the role of a James Bond villain with ease, but I can't. Because right now, I'm too bloody confused to laugh at anything.

'It shouldn't be hard, seeing as Chateau Lavigne is also trying to target a younger demographic with their wines,' she continues, unperturbed by my clearly perplexed expression. 'In many ways, featuring their wines alongside the products on our new microsite feels like a match made in heaven. Do you feel prepared for the meeting?'

'Not one bit—'

'Kate, I would have thought you of all people would know how important a work trip like this is when it comes to proving you have what it takes to— '

'Amanda. I'm not prepared, because I've not been invited.'

'What? Of course you're invited.'

'Well, if I am, I haven't been *told* about it.'

Amanda's confusion is enough to match my own. 'No, that can't be right.' Her nose crinkles; she shakes her head. 'Georgina told me she was handling it. That she'd pass all the information on to one of you to share with the others.'

So, I *have* been overlooked. Just not in the way I thought. Or by the person I thought.

'I should have double-checked everything,' Amanda goes on, hand reaching to her furrowed brow. 'It's been so busy this week, and things are starting to slip through the net.'

Things. *People.* I try to push down the feeling that my missed invite is personal.

'Better late than never,' I say weakly, forcing a smile.

'Is it too late notice now?' She looks concerned. 'You do still want to go, right?'

On a trip that one member of our microsite clearly doesn't *want* me on? Not really, not right now. But I know better than to let Cally or Harry screw up this opportunity for me.

'Yes, of course.' I channel my disappointment into determination, the way I have so often done during my time here. 'But can't you come with us?'

I hate that I sound so needy, but I suddenly feel like I could do with the back-up.

'I would love to drink wine in a vineyard in France, but Gareth has actually approved for you three to go without any directors, because things here . . . They're just . . .'

'Hanging by a thread?' I smile gently and her own face softens too.

'An expensive one,' she nods. 'So, I really need you to get your game face on, Kate.'

As we leave the kitchen and head back across the tenth floor to see Harry sitting there behind his desk, Cally leaning closely in to look at something on his monitor, I have no idea what to think. And yet, when he catches my eye and flashes me his knee-weakening grin, I know Amanda is right: I'm going to need my game face on for this.

Chapter Thirteen

'Have a good trip!' the man behind the checkin desk says in too-cheery tones. I force a smile before making my way through security. I must look so shifty, glancing this way and that for a sight of Harry, that I'm surprised I get through without a strip search.

As I walk past duty-free perfumes on the one side and racks of Ray-Bans on the other, it takes all my strength not to disguise myself under a new pair of overpriced sunglasses or turn back and run the way I just came. As much as I want to go on this trip, *need* to go on this trip, I'm really not looking forward to finding out why Harry didn't pass on the information for me to even *know* about this trip. Because he must have been the one who 'forgot' to send it on; he's been acting so strange ever since that photoshoot, ever since he got that phone call. And I know something has changed between us now. If there was even an 'us' to begin with.

'Kate?'

I look up to see Cally standing before me, her expression caught somewhere between shock and disappointment. It's enough to send my sleepless-night-induced rage into overdrive. Sure, they may not want me here, but I deserve to be on this trip. I deserve to not have a privileged white male like Harry bulldoze his way through my plans.

Her smugness covers over her shock and she still manages to merge herself and Harry into a 'we' with ease. 'We didn't know you could make it . . . to *Bordeaux*?' I can tell this last part of her sentence is trying to confirm whether I'm joining them for the weekend or simply doing my weekly grocery shopping in an airport departure lounge.

I try to save face. 'Yes, I wasn't sure I'd be able to make it either.' It's not technically a lie. Until yesterday, I didn't know I was invited. Not that I'm going to give her the pleasure of knowing this.

'Big weekend plans?' she goads.

'Yeah, I . . .' I begin, searching for my next half-truth, just anything that will make me feel a bit less like the last-minute tag-along I so clearly am to her. Then, I remember Blair's birthday drinks. The birthday drinks that are meant to be happening *tonight*.

Cally doesn't wait for me to answer her question. Or maybe she thinks my apparent lack of plans speaks for itself. Either way, she's peeling off into the open entrance of the Camden Bar and Kitchen, taking a seat at a table squeezed between a banner-wearing hen party on the one side and a loved-up couple staring into each other's eyes on the other. I follow her, my brain too full of Blair's birthday drinks for independent thought right now.

Then I see him.

Harry is turning from the bar, carrying a glass of prosecco and a pint of lager, the shoulder strap of his slouchy duffel bag ruffling his long-sleeved t-shirt just enough that I can see the brown leather belt looped through his distressed denim jeans. He stops to look around the restaurant and Cally thrusts her well-manicured mitts into the air to wave him over. He catches her eye, giving her a nod. Then he notices me, the intensity of his gaze sending shockwaves through my stomach. And I *refuse* to give up and head home now.

'You're here,' he says, with the early glimmers of a grin, as soon as he reaches our table, passing the prosecco to Cally and taking a long, slow draw of his beer.

'No thanks to you,' I bite back, scaring the small smile on his face away.

'What's that supposed to mean?' He pulls up a seat next to Cally and they both take another sip of their drinks; to anyone else it would look like I'm crashing their date.

'It doesn't matter.'

I am not going to give him the pleasure of knowing that he's getting to me. Even so, his eyes are scanning my expression like an X-ray, searing into my soul. I try to hold his gaze, watching his face morph from curiosity to concern.

'Kate, are you sure you're okay?' he asks unsurely. 'Has something happened?'

I want to tell him it's what *didn't* happen that's the issue, that thanks to him I almost missed out on the best opportunity that's come my way since I first started at Poster. But with Cally sitting there, her fingers still lingering on his shoulder, I can't bring myself to say it.

'I'm sure Kate is just anxious for the Lavigne meeting,' she chimes up, her hand stroking back and forth on his shoulder. I'm momentarily speechless at her speaking for me.

Harry makes another attempt to thaw the frost that I'm throwing across the table. 'Let me get you a drink.' But I don't want him to break the ice, to see under my surface.

'Need I remind you this is a *work* trip?' I try to steer us back on track.

'No, your outfit is reminder enough.' He seems affronted by my bluntness.

I look from Cally's cream sweatshirt and Harry's caramel-coloured t-shirt to my black collared shirt and smartest skinny jeans. 'Sorry, I didn't get the fifty shades of beige memo.'

He places his palms into the prayer position before giving me a little nod. 'You're forgiven.' I want to tell him that if anyone should be doing the forgiving right now, it's me.

'Shall we go over the basics for our presentation tomorrow?' I ask, reaching into my backpack for my laptop.

He puts his strong palm to the top of my shoulder. 'Kate, can you just *not*?'

'Harry, this presentation is important.'

'*We* are the presentation.'

'What are you on about?'

'I mean, we're going to visit some high-net-worth individuals who want to learn about our microsite—'

'Yes, and my slides have all the stats that they could ever—'

'Let me finish.' Harry interrupts me right back and though until now I didn't think I had a violent bone in my body, I would love to smack the silly smirk from his frustratingly handsome face. I roll my eyes dramatically so that both of them can see and he promptly shakes away my cynicism. 'These are young investors—'

'Potential investors.'

'Young *potential* investors.' His narrowing eyes dare me to interrupt him again. 'They don't want stiff slideshows and business jargon. They've invited us—'

'The *three* of us.'

'They've invited the three of us,' he corrects himself, still seemingly unsure why he should have to, 'to their chateau for a reason—'

'And that reason is?'

'I'm about to *tell* you.'

Cally sips her prosecco silently, watching every spar of our verbal boxing match.

'Relationship. They want to build a *relationship* with us. To get to know us better, to know what we're about, what our vision for the site and the project is.'

'So, no PowerPoints then?' I sound like a three-year-old who's just been told she can't have jelly with her ice-cream.

His expression softens into a knowing smile. 'Not unless they ask for one.'

'But the microsite isn't *made* yet. What will we even show them?'

'Well . . .' His grin is so gorgeous that for the briefest of moments any anger in me simply melts away. 'I plan to show them a good time.'

'Excuse me, sir. I think you're in my seat.'

Cally looks down at the rather round-looking man sitting in the window seat with confidence as soon as we've got to our row on the plane. His eyes widen as he fixes his gaze on her pretty face, but he makes no attempt to move. I'm standing behind her in the aisle, waiting to take the middle seat. Harry is behind me, getting closer and closer with every new passenger to filter onto the plane, to the point where I can feel the lightness of his breath on the back of my neck. It suddenly occurs to me how *cosy* aeroplanes can be.

'This is my seat.' The man looks around him as if to confirm this to himself.

'21C?'

'This is 21F.' He points up to the seat numbers under the overhead lockers as if he's already way too tired of this. '21C is over there.' He points to the seat across the aisle.

'Oh right, I . . . ' Cally begins, trying to shuffle backwards to rearrange our line-up and accidentally stepping on my toe in the process. I stumble back into Harry, his hands automatically shooting up to my hips to stabilise me. With no room to move, we wait there for a second, the warmth of his hands trickling through my shirt and tingling on my skin.

'Can I just get . . . ' Cally turns around so that she's inches from my face, Harry still holding me from behind, and I suddenly feel so claustrophobic that I step back into him even more, feeling the solidity of his frame lining up along my body.

'You take my seat.' I would raise my hands in surrender if we weren't so wedged in.

'Are you sure?' she asks, already standing beside it.

'I'm sure Cally won't mind the seat across the aisle,' Harry says, looking from the two seats next to the man in 21F and back to the single one on the other side of the plane.

'I really don't mind,' I assure him as Cally sits down and enough space becomes available for him to stop touching me.

I know a big part of me doesn't *want* him to stop and that's precisely why I need to put a whole plane aisle between us.

'You can sit next to Cally,' he offers, turning towards the lone seat across the aisle.

'I thought we were going to talk about model selection for the site?' Cally objects.

'You were?' I raise my eyebrows at him. His body is now mirroring mine only centimetres away as we try to navigate our way around one another. 'Thought we were supposed to be doing this as a team?'

'We *are* a team.'

'Except, you didn't even . . .' I stop my sentence short; Cally has proceeded to sit in the middle seat, next to the large man who is proudly hanging on to his one by the window.

'Didn't what?'

'You didn't even forward my invite on to me.' I lower my voice to a whisper, him leaning even closer to hear, which right now means we're pretty much face to face. 'I know Georgina asked you to, but you didn't want me—'

'Kate.' He says my name so softly that it sounds like a sigh. '*Cally* forwarded on my invite from Georgina; she didn't mention anything about sending it on to you. Maybe I should have thought about it. I've just had a lot on my mind and . . .'

'It's okay.' My cheeks burn with embarrassment. She did *what*? I'm sure I'd be glaring at Cally right now if Harry wasn't holding my attention so intensely. 'And I really don't mind sitting on my own so that you two can discuss models.' I sound as hurt as I feel.

'I know we wind each other up, but I'd never try to mess

160

with your career.' His eyes dart from my eyes to my lips and back again. 'I hope you'd never think that I could—'

A flight attendant cuts through our tension with her forced, cheery tone. 'Excuse me? Sir. Ma'am. Can you please take your seats?'

I tear my eyes from Harry and struggle to put my backpack into the lockers overhead. He reaches to relieve me, stashing my hand luggage with ease.

'Thanks.' I look up to see his body dangerously close to my own again.

'You're welcome.' He breathes deeply, and I watch his strong chest exhale.

As soon as I'm safely seated on the other side of the aisle, I look across to Harry and Cally, who have started chatting animatedly in their adjacent seats. I try to calm myself down, forcing my thoughts away from the tension between me and Harry, the venom that I now know is brimming from Cally. I look down at my phone; I am running out of time to tell Blair about tonight and though I feel terrible about missing her birthday drinks, it's not like I had much of a choice. As I swipe through my messages, I see the last one I sent to Lucy, begging for a reply. I remind myself that she didn't think twice about taking an opportunity that she knew was right for her, even if it meant making me move out of my home. It's all the push I need to finally send Blair my apologies. Her speedy reply makes me laugh and yet feel even more awful at the same time: *Don't worry, Kate, I'll have Toby and Charlie. And as your beloved Meatloaf once said: two out of three ain't bad.*

'Can you please turn that off, madam? The cabin crew are preparing for take-off.'

I look up to see the flight attendant looking down at the phone in my hand accusingly. I do as I'm told and then look forward for the safety demonstration, only then remembering that the overcrowded vehicle we've just wedged ourselves onto is actually supposed to *fly*. I gulp as the air hostess mimes putting on an oxygen mask. The last time I was on a plane was for a school trip to Florence back in Year 8. I swore I'd never go away with school after that, our family holidays remaining firmly on home turf. I feel sick as she puts on her lifejacket and pretends to blow air into it. And, by the time the engine is grumbling, and the plane is wheeling itself into position, I am clinging to the arms of my chair for dear life and wishing my missed invitation had never got to me.

'We're just experiencing some turbulence,' a voice blares from the speakers above us after what can only be described as the bumpiest hour of my life.

I glance towards Harry and Cally, looking for someone to share in my fear. Instead, I find Cally is fast asleep, her head resting lightly on Harry's strong shoulder, her expression angelic. He doesn't look up from his book; I can't see what he's reading but it looks like a full-colour picture book and I'm sure I'd tease him about it if I wasn't so bloody petrified.

Out of nowhere the plane drops downwards and I fling my head between my legs.

'Kate?' I hear him say my name from just across the aisle, but it feels so far away. I try to catch my breath as the plane wobbles up and down, as if trying to navigate the waves.

'Kate, what are you doing?' he asks again and I force myself to look up at him from my braced position. Cally stirs beside him, unknowingly placing her head down to rest on the passenger who refused to give up his seat for her.

'The plane. It just. *Dropped.*'

'Yes, by like an inch,' he says, his voice calm but concerned.

'Really?' I uncoil myself just slightly. 'It felt like a mile.'

'It's just turbulence,' he says, looking amused until I sit up straight enough for him to see the drained-white hue of my usually blushing cheeks. 'Kate, are you *scared* of flying?'

'No,' I say at the precise same moment that another bump causes me to let out an involuntary yelp. 'Okay, well, maybe a little.'

'Why didn't you say anything? In the airport?'

'I didn't want to . . . I didn't even . . .'

The truth is, I wasn't even thinking about it. There's something about my interactions with Harry that keep me firmly rooted in the moment or helplessly harping back to the past. Another bump. Another beep of the seatbelt sign. And I can feel tears starting to make their way down my face. I hate the fact Harry is seeing me like this. But I hate flying even more.

'Just breathe.' He reaches for my hand across the aisle, holding it in his. I concentrate on matching the emphasised breaths he is taking now, each bump seeing me squeeze his hand even more in mine. Every time I've mocked him for 'feeling' his way in work or reducing creativity to crayoning is instantly undermined by the fact he's now having to teach me how to do something as basic as breathing.

'I'm scared.' My eyes swim with tears.

'I know,' he whispers, his entire body leaning into the space between us, his hand grasped firmly in mine for the whole plane to see if they were only to look down the aisle.

'You do know you've got more chance of being hit by a bus than dying in a plane?'

'What part of that is supposed to make me feel better?'

'It's just a stat I know. You love stats, remember?'

'I do.' I breathe in and breathe out. 'I really do.'

Harry laughs and I know he thinks that it's daydreaming about data that's soothing me somehow. The truth is, it's his hand clutched in mine and knowing that he wanted me here after all that's making me feel strong enough to tolerate some turbulence now.

Chapter Fourteen

'Oh my gosh, this place is *incredible*.' Cally strides purposefully into the grand Renaissance Bordeaux and gazes up at the towering industrial tower that acts as an entrance to the hotel. She's clearly full of energy, having slept the entire flight and transfer. Harry looks knackered, having just put in a shift as my in-flight therapist. Though the second the turbulence seemed to subside, he reclaimed his hand.

'May I 'elp you?' the woman on reception asks in a thick French accent.

'We're from Poster,' Cally replies, as if this answers any and all of her questions.

'Ah, I see 'ere, you 'ave the two La Muse City View.'

'Two rooms?' I look to Harry, my panic from the flight still palpable.

'No, no,' he objects. 'It should be *three* rooms.'

'We have three persons written down here.' The receptionist smiles. 'Two rooms.'

'Oh, maybe I forgot to book a third,' Cally says, like butter wouldn't melt.

'Like you "forgot" to forward on my invite?' I'm powerless not to bite.

'No, I didn't,' she says, before throwing a perfectly manicured hand to cover her mouth. 'Oh no. You didn't get it? I must have sent it to the wrong account by accident.'

And the award for best bullshitter goes to @CallyforniaDreamin.

'I'm *so* sorry, Kate. I'm *such* an idiot.'

She looks to Harry with a face that is so sickly sweet that to call her bluff now would make me look like an utter cow. I look between them, my rock and hard place.

The receptionist continues before Cally can interrupt. 'So, ze two rooms—'

'Can we book a third, please?'

'Fully booked, sorry. We 'ave a conference on.'

She looks through the double glass doors and down the spacious corridor leading to a colourfully decadent downstairs bar, which is teaming with suits and business bods.

'You can share, no?'

'No!' all three of us say in unison.

It's then that she signals to the sofas on the other side of the room. Sometimes verbal language isn't needed to say, *This is definitely not my problem.*

'I struggle to sleep in a room with anyone else.' Cally kicks off the debate quickly.

'So do I,' I push back.

'I shouldn't be in a room with Kate,' Harry argues next.

'Nor should you be sharing a room with Cally,' I reply pointedly, offended that he would rather be sharing a room with her, even though I don't want to share with him either.

'I mean, usually, I wouldn't mind . . .' She speaks quickly now, leaning into him in a way that suggests that taking her home isn't out of the question. 'But I really need my beauty sleep before our big day tomorrow.'

'Big day? I thought we were just building a "relationship"?' I say and Harry groans.

'Cally, please, she'll be showing us her PowerPoint in no time.'

'You would be so lucky.' I glare the smug smile off his face, all plane-handholding and back-stroking forgotten; he probably just wanted me to be quiet.

'Look, there's a vacant room in the hotel next door.' He looks at his phone, his expression falling as he scrolls down. 'It's four hundred pounds a night.'

'Small change for Poster,' I say, though I know that the office merger and this microsite wouldn't be happening if the company had money to burn.

'I don't think we can get away with that.' His sorry face confirms that this is true.

'I *can't* share a room,' Cally reiterates. 'I need it pitch black and dead silent.'

'Anything else, Your Highness?' I mutter, just loud enough for them both to hear.

'It's a twin room?' Harry tries to keep us on task for once. 'Well, maybe we . . .'

He looks to me with an expression that tells me this is a last resort. If Cally wanted to come away with just him, why is she being so damn difficult about bunking up together now?

'Look . . .' He pushes through the awkwardness pragmatically.

'We're only here for one night before heading to the chateau tomorrow. All we need to do is *sleep* in the same room.'

'What *else* would we be doing?'

'I just mean, we can take it in turns to hang out in the bar whilst the other gets ready for bed. I could even shower up near the pool.'

'And we'll be getting up at the crack of dawn anyway.' Cally tries to help, but her diva antics have already done enough.

'Fine,' I say, backed into a corner.

'Fine,' he echoes, sounding so far from fine it hurts. I know my reasons for not wanting to share a room with him, but he's looking at me like the thought of it is torture.

'Just sleeping,' I confirm.

'Just sleeping,' Harry nods.

I know no sleeping is going to happen. Well, for me at least.

From the second we arrive in the twin bedroom and push our beds apart as far as is physically possible, my heart begins hammering so hard in my chest that if I didn't know any better, I'd think our eighth-floor twin was at the same altitude as the aeroplane that brought us here. But true to his word, Harry leaves me alone in the room until hours later, when I am already in bed, wearing far more than I usually would and pretending to be asleep.

'Kate?' he whispers, tiptoeing across the room before tripping over the end of my bed. If I wasn't awake already, I would be now. I can tell from the overexaggerated way he is trying to creep around the room that he's likely been sinking drinks in the hotel bar. Part of me wonders whether his liquid looseners

168

could be precisely the tonic that sees our messaging merge into a real-life friendship, maybe even more. Whether perhaps if I were to sit up now, he'd perch on the edge of my bed; whether the next time he laughed, he'd lean in that little bit closer to me and I'd soften into his side and the rest would be history. And yet, the small piece of me that wonders whether he's been killing time with Cally holds me back.

'I'm *asleep*.'

'Evidently,' he grumbles, something like disappointment in his voice.

Through the blurry slits in my all too awake eyes, I can see him pulling off his t-shirt, the definition of his toned torso highlighted by the thin shard of light shining through the gap in the blackout blinds. I see him look back in my direction and I pretend to be asleep, even though the most intimate parts of me are most frustratingly awake. I try to think of anything but how it would feel to press my fingers into his naked chest, to move my hands up to his cheeks and pull his stubbled chin towards me. The stubborn memory of what happened the last time I did forces me to remain perfectly still, except for my shallowing breath.

I risk opening my eyes just a bit more to see the silhouetted shape of his strong body pulling back his covers and lying along the length of his bed. The thought of him lying next to me darts across my mind; it's probably just the heat, the hot and sticky feel of the room. I push the covers away from me at the same moment that he turns on his side to face in my direction, his eyes catching on my own for just a moment. And though everything in me seems drawn to his grey-blue gaze, I feign sleepiness, closing my eyes as I remind myself of all the reasons Amanda warned me away from office romances, all the reasons Harry has given me to know that letting myself like him more than once in a lifetime is a bad idea.

Chapter Fifteen

'Sleep well?' Harry grumbles as soon as he sees that I'm awake.

'I slept okay.' Little does he know I never dozed off in the first place. 'You?'

'Like a baby. I can sleep through anything.'

I believe him. I spent most of the night watching him sleep. And for some reason, knowing that snoozing across the room from me was so easy for him makes me resent whatever it is I'm feeling for him even more.

'We should probably get up,' I say, as he fumbles with his covers, drawing my eye downwards, the combination of this and my words making me blush.

'Ladies first.' He snuggles further into his pillow, looking disgustingly adorable.

'There's no way I'm showering in *there* with you here.'

I look through the panel of glass wall separating the bedroom from the shower, every inch of it visible from where he is lying. He looks from the shower to my rosy cheeks, holding my gaze for longer than is comfortable.

'What is the point of that anyway?' I will my words to dim the tension between us.

'A glass wall between the bedroom and the shower? I can think of some reasons.'

'Yeah, but who can be arsed to put on a show every time they shower?'

'Men don't need a *show*. We're very simple creatures.'

'Could have fooled me.'

The sentence hangs in the vast space between our twin beds.

'Right, well, erm . . .' He struggles for what to say next, any early-morning warmth between us frosted over. 'I'll head to the pool to shower. Message me once you're done.'

As Harry sits to swing his body away from me and pull his jeans on, I know I've said something wrong, that I've shut the conversation down. But then, what is the actual point of trying to really *talk* to him in private, when I know that as soon as he steps out of this room and into our day, we're going to be pulling in different directions all over again?

Cally looks gorgeous by the time I make it down to the reception area bar, the place we decided to meet before picking up our pre-booked taxi to take us to the chateau in Saint-Émilion. Her hair falls in perfect curls down her bare shoulders as she sits sipping her teeny-tiny espresso in a teeny-tiny tube top, which she has tucked into white, tailored trousers. It's a bold choice for a day of sampling the chateau's favourite reds.

'You look handsome,' she says as soon as she sees Harry, pretty much ignoring me completely. I turn around to see him standing there, duffel bag thrown over shoulder. The same outfit he had on for travelling yesterday. I look down at my own ironed pinstriped shirt and best pencil skirt and know that making an effort means different things to each of us.

'Thanks, Cal. You look good too.' He grins. 'You guys ready to go?' he asks, no compliments left for me.

'Physically, yes. But I'd like to go over our game plan in the taxi,' I say, as Cally and I grab our bags and together the three of us head towards the reception desk to check out.

'Why does that not surprise me?' Harry mutters at the exact same moment that I take a massive bite of my recently purchased pain au chocolat; of all of the organisational skills I possess, my beelining for baked goods never fails me.

'Forgive me for wanting to make a good impression.'

'You have chocolate on your chin,' he says, before striding out toward the taxi.

'Right, so what's our strategy for today?' I ask as soon as I've put my seatbelt on. Cally didn't think twice about sandwiching herself in the middle of us.

'To drink champagne and dazzle them with our charms?' Harry replies over her.

What sort of blasé game plan is that?

'We won't be drinking champagne in Saint-Émilion; we'll be drinking crémant,' I point out.

He shakes his head, his lips pursed; he only finds me insufferable because I'm right.

'And I know we want them to take advertising space on the site, but can't we aim a bit higher than that? It would be great to go back with an even bigger investment under our belts.'

I feel a surge of adrenalin rushing through me at the thought of making a mark for the microsite on the trip that I very almost wasn't a part of. I gaze out of the car window as the high limestone buildings along the Garonne river peter out until we're on a busy motorway and flat fields shoot by us instead.

'Maybe so.' For a second, I think he's going to agree with me. 'But Inès and Jade Lavigne have only just started making deals on behalf of the family and are under pressure to make good investments. I worry that if we push them too hard, they'll get cold feet. Trust me, I think concentrating on having fun and building rapport with them first is the way to go.'

'So, we basically need to big them up and make them feel good?' I say.

'It's everything I know about business.'

I see Cally reach for his arm and give it a squeeze. 'You're so right, Harry.'

'Thanks, Cal.' He grins back at her fully as I force my eyes back out of the window.

It doesn't take long for us to turn off the busy road and for the flat fields to start filling with low, spindly vines, planted in neat lines for as far as the eye can see.

'There's so many of them.' I state the obvious.

'They're so short.' Cally does the same.

Only, Cally's sentence seems to prompt some interest from our taxi driver, who until this moment has been completely mute. 'There is a good reason for zis. Our *terroir* produces the best merlot in the world.'

'Your terror?' she asks and the taxi driver laughs flirtatiously.

Must she have this effect on everyone?

'No, no.' The driver is turning around to look at her so frequently that if he didn't seem to know the winding roads so well, I'd fear this could be the end of us. 'The *terroir* is how you say . . .' His sentence peters off. 'There is no word for it in

174

your language. It is the natural environment, perhaps the soil, the topography, ze climate.'

'I see,' Cally says politely; she doesn't sound remotely interested. I am, though.

'That's so interesting.' Harry clearly thinks so too.

'What's your favourite wine, sir?'

'I don't know, maybe a malbec for red? A sauvignon for white?'

So, maybe we have something in common after all?

'How about you, miss?' He looks to Cally.

'I'm a champagne girl,' she beams.

'Well, crémant anywhere in France zat is not from the Champagne region.'

Harry looks to me and gives me a nod. Somehow it feels like one–nil, even though if he and I were keeping score, I'm sure we'd be into the high hundreds by now.

'You see in France, when someone asks you what kind of wine you like,' the taxi driver continues, and I try not to be stung that he hasn't asked *me* what kind of wine I like best, 'We do not say what kind of grape we like; we say what region of wine we like: we like German wines or Spanish wines or wines from Left or Right Bank Bordeaux.'

We all nod in unison, and I make a note to impress the Lavigne sisters with this later.

'*Terroir* is everything.'

I can't help but wonder whether, had Harry and I met in a different *terroir*, the last five years could have played out completely differently.

The roads get narrower and narrower, until we are approaching an imposing set of wrought-iron gates, which

175

open automatically despite looking like a relic from the eight-eenth century. And, as we roll up to the chateau, I can't quite believe what I'm seeing. It's not just one limestone building but an entire village.

'They house all of the workers when they come for the autumn harvest,' our taxi-driver-come-tour-guide explains as we pass an on-site bar.

He pulls up outside a large limestone building and one by one we fold out of the car. Harry stretches his arms high as he spins around to look at the vast vineyard unfolding around us. Cally smooths down her outfit, her heels sinking into the soft, sandy ground beneath her. I force my eyes from Harry to a tan-skinned, bearded man emerging out of the chateau, both arms held open to welcome us.

'*Bonjour, bonjour!*' His smile sends the already deep laughter lines around his eyes even deeper. Now that we're up close, I notice that he's quite the silver fox. He holds out a hand to Harry, who gives it a strong shake. Then, he leans into Cally, giving her a kiss on both cheeks before pulling me into him to do the same. 'One more for good luck,' he adds.

'We're here to see Inès and Jade,' Harry says, stepping so close to where the man has just kissed me *trois* times that it causes the stranger to take a large step back from us.

'Of course, of course.' The man puts his hands in the air. 'My name is Gabriel.' He grins at Harry, before turning back to me. 'But you can call me Gabe.'

'I'm Harry.' He puts a strong hand to his chest. 'And this is Cally and—'

'I'm Kate,' I interrupt him, more than capable of introducing myself.

'Welcome, welcome,' Gabe continues, gesturing so forcefully with his hands that you'd think he was the Greatest Showman welcoming an entire circusful of guests. 'Let me show you to your rooms and then you rest, and then, we *drink*.'

'Of *course* you brought your tote bag.'

Harry leans so far into me to whisper the words that I can smell the shampoo he's just used to freshen up. And, despite making every effort to avoid a naked run-in between us this morning, I can't for the life of me stop thinking about him in the shower.

'Need I remind you again that we're here for *work*?' I hiss back at him.

I need to remind myself of this, because the room that the Lavigne sisters have laid out – or at least, that someone who works for them has – looks more like a wedding. A long wooden trestle table stands, laden with eucalyptus and terracotta and peach roses running down the centre of it, twinkling pillar candles of all different heights threatening to see the whole beautiful thing go up in flames.

Harry and Cally look like they're dressed for a wedding too: him in a white shirt unbuttoned to the centre of his lightly haired chest, her in a sweeping floor-length sundress which matches the colour-scheme of the room so perfectly that I wonder whether she had planned the entire thing herself. I look down at my grey jeans and plain white blouse and wonder how, after days of feeling overdressed on the tenth floor, I somehow feel so underdressed now. Then, Inès and Jade Lavigne enter the room.

177

'Please, please, take a seat.' Inès waves a hand to signal for us to do as she says, the long sleeve of her square-necked gown billowing dangerously close to a candle. Jade pulls out a chair at the head of the table, her satin halterneck slip making her look every bit like Meghan Markle on her actual wedding day. I hide my *Wanna data me* bag under the table.

'I'm Jade,' she smiles.

In fact, thanks to my extensive googling of the sisters over the last three hours, I now know everything I think there is to know about the two of them. Inès, the older sister, is twenty-five and has already graced the pages of *Vogue France* in a piece about the 'Businesswomen of the Future'. Jade, the younger sister, is twenty-three, has walked in fashion shows in Tokyo and Milan and is set to continue to make her own money as well as helping her sister see that Chateau Lavigne remains relevant to the emerging generations.

'Do you know how many calories are in this?' I overhear Cally saying to Harry, leaning to whisper into his ear. I take another swig of my wine.

'So, where do we begin?' Inès says, her French accent evident, though the inflections of her sentences point to countless summers spent in New York and LA.

There is silence around the table, except for the sound of softly played strings that makes me feel like we're in some sort of *Emily in Paris* meets *Bridgerton* mash-up. I look from Inès at one end of the table to Jade at the other, Cally and Harry sitting so very close.

'Well, I've prepared a PowerPoint presentation—'

'Perhaps with the nineteen-ninety?' Jade says. 'Sorry, Kate, what were you about to say?'

Harry speaks up, gently kicking me under the table. 'The nineteen-ninety sounds great.'

'It's an excellent vintage,' Inès nods, as a man dressed in black tie appears from nowhere to fill our large glasses with an inch or so of red wine. I reach for the glass in front of me as Harry does the same, our hands clashing and causing it to topple over in the process. He manages to save it from spilling over the flower arrangement just in time.

'Drink glasses are always on the right,' I hiss at him, as he backs off from my glass.

'I thought it was opposite over here,' he whispers, leaning further across the table.

'That's driving, you idiot.'

'No need to get your knickers in a twist.'

'My knickers are *none* of your concern.'

''Ere on the Right Bank of the Gironde estuary, we produce excellent blended wines,' Inès explains, and Harry and I finally break eye contact to look at her, his long legs still managing to graze against my knees every time he shuffles in his seat. 'This wine is a blend of eighty per cent Merlot grapes and twenty per cent Cabernet Franc.'

'Do the pure wines tend to be more popular?' Harry asks inquisitively.

'No, the blending of the wines is good for structure,' I say, relaying something that I read on the internet just seconds before leaving my room to come down to dinner.

'You and your bloody structure,' he mutters just loud enough for me to hear.

'Harry is right.' Inès beams across the table at him. 'We sell

179

many non-blended wines to local traders and overseas too. Pure Merlot is very popular.'

'Well done, honey,' Cally whispers, leaning into his side as he smiles back at her.

Honey? Since when have Cally and Harry called each other *honey*?

'But Kate is right also,' Inès continues, wiping the grin off his face. 'The blended wines we produce 'ere can often age much better than the non-blended Merlots.'

Told you. I look to Harry, and I can tell from his narrowed eyes that he knows what I'm thinking. He brushes a hand through his hair, holding my eye the entire time.

'The Merlot is the yummy part,' Inès continues, gazing over to Harry as he takes a swig of the wine and proceeds to swirl it around his mouth like he knows what he's doing.

'Mmm, so yummy,' Cally coos, knocking it back and snuggling further into his side.

'But the Cabernet Franc adds strength to the wine and a reliable finish.'

He looks directly at me as Inès continues and I can feel his leg graze my own.

'We call this the "flesh" and the "bones" of the wine,' Jade chips in, drinking her own red wine incredibly carefully so as to not drop a speck on her white dress.

'Does the *reliability* of the blending wine not come at an expense to the primary?'

I don't know why Harry's latest question feels like a challenge.

'Quite the reverse.' Inès looks between him and me. 'In fact, they say blending a good wine is a bit like falling in love.' His eyes burn into mine. 'Ze opposites always attract.'

Chapter Sixteen

'So zis is *your girl*, so to speak?'

Inès gestures across the table to Cally, who, despite being a walking advertisement for Poster when it comes to what she's wearing, is pretty much slumping into Harry's side with the sheer weight of wine we've consumed over the last two and a half hours together. I have to remind myself that 'wine' is synonymous with 'work' tonight.

'Yes,' Harry nods proudly, before clocking that Cally is sliding into the dangerously drunk category sooner than we may have liked. 'She doesn't usually drink.'

'And yet you think our wines will be a good fit for your site?' Jade asks accusingly.

When it comes to consumption, the Lavigne sisters have drunk us under the table.

'Aren't the statistics showing zat more and more of Gen Z are going teetotal?' Inès looks to Cally, like her sloppy demeanour is a good example of why this might be the case. After my 'forgotten' invite and her trying to show me up with each new wine we've tasted, a part of me is sensing the sweetness of

181

schadenfreude at how she's landed up now. Harry must catch my small, sadistic smile as the disappointed expression on his face is impossible to ignore; it sends a stone sinking through my stomach and shame to my cheeks.

'Kate? Did you 'ear me?' Inès repeats again, the increasing frostiness in her tone suggesting that our 'relational' evening is about to take a nosedive if we don't cut it short before we can consume any more booze.

'Didn't you mention you had a presentation to show us?' Jade speaks up.

If we weren't still trying to make a good impression, I suspect Harry would be putting his palm to his face in no time. He looks at me like, *Why did you have to mention that?*

'Yes,' I say slowly; but despite saying everything about how our 'woman' wants to shop and what she wants to wear, it doesn't say anything about how she drinks, which I am realising is completely remiss seeing as we're meeting with the moguls of an alcohol empire.

I look to Harry like a deer caught in headlights. Despite his present disappointment in me, I will him to read my mind: *I need your help.*

He speaks up for both of us. 'It's late and we've had wine; we don't want to bore you with a presentation now.' I know he's coming to my rescue, but it still takes all my strength not to argue that my presentation isn't boring. Woefully untailored to the people we are trying to win over this evening, but definitely not boring.

'Fine, okay,' Inès relents. 'But surely, you must know the basics.'

Every competitive instinct in me wants to scream that I do,

but the only stats that spring to my increasingly messy mind are the bad ones, for us at least: that Berenberg reported that centennials are consuming over twenty per cent less alcohol than millennials drank at their age, that beer companies are now spending over a third of their marketing budget on promoting their zero-alcohol offerings. Essentially, stats that are backed up by the fact that Cally is practically out for the count now, whilst Harry and I are still managing to tread the increasingly treacherous water of this meeting. And only just.

'The basics . . . yes . . . The basics . . .' I begin, but I have no idea what to say next.

'The basics are in flux,' he says confidently as everything in me tightens.

'How so?' Inès raises an eyebrow.

'Well, the stats may suggest that Gen Z aren't drinking as much as their millennial counterparts . . .' He takes a slow, exaggerated sip of his almost-drained glass of red and it's enough to make Jade giggle, going some way to release the tension. He turns to her with a winning smile and I'm almost too worried about how his off-the-cuff non-presentation is going to unfold to recognise the twinge of envy twisting in my gut – well, *almost*.

'But if you truly *listen* to the cultural shift at play, it's an entirely different story,' he continues, three of us hanging on to his words, Cally still hanging on to his shoulder.

'Say more.' Inès leans forward on her elbows, her barely-there cleavage exposed.

'Well, I for one grew up worshipping rock idols like the Gallagher brothers and Kurt Cobain and Courtney Love,' he continues.

I find I'm leaning further across the table too, longing to feel the gentle brush of his knee against mine which has so frustratingly come and gone throughout this entire evening.

'Being a teen in the early noughties was all about heroin chic, Kate Moss's collaboration with Topshop, Marissa Cooper sipping vodka from her hip flask . . .'

I can tell from their expressions that these cultural references are a bit before their time, but that his passion is painting them a compelling picture regardless.

'But as the years have passed, the glamour of drinking has diminished . . .'

Harry looks so poised, so confident, so in his element, that I wonder what watered-down version of him I've been settling for so far.

'We've seen so many of these so-called idols fall: Demi Lovato releasing her confessions of alcohol abuse online, Taylor Hawkins dying in his hotel room, even our very own Marissa Cooper falling apart away from the screen . . .'

He shoots a look to me across the table, and I feel our silent conversation continue; he's asking me to trust him.

'And now centennials are growing up watching Deliciously Ella telling them how to eat green and *Love Island* stars giving them all of the drama with less of the drink and everyday workout plans that no-one wants to water down with cheap wine.'

Jade is leaning so far across the table that she may as well be resting her head on him like Cally. Inès, on the other hand, looks intrigued but impatient, like she wants him to hurry up and get to the point. I'm not sure whether he knows what the point is, but still, I listen on.

'But . . .'

I swear there is an audible sigh around the room.

'But . . . when drinking less and exercising more, your treats need to *count*,' he continues, a glimmer of hope in his eyes that is so damn attractive I'm not sure how to compute it. 'That's why many zoomers are choosing quality over quantity. Gone are the days where many young people want to drink to get drunk; rather, they want to drink to experience it, to savour the taste, the environment they are drinking in, the people they are drinking with.' He flashes another glance to me, and I soften. 'Many of them are beginning to shop in the same way too. Why buy a white t-shirt for a fiver that lasts a month and ends up in landfill when you can buy one for fifty pounds that may well last a lifetime?'

Jade is nodding with so much enthusiasm, I feel her delicate neck might not be able to take it. Inès is reaching for her glass, taking a steady sip but stifling a smile over the rim.

'That's why we think Poster and Lavigne are the perfect fit,' Harry continues, going in for the kicker now. 'Both products are to be savoured not sped through, both products are about quality not quantity, and, if handled in the right way . . .' He pauses to look at each one of us around the room before taking a slow, confident sip that sends a tingle from the top of my neck down to my thighs. 'The clothes, and the memories . . .' He lifts his glass to me, giving me a wink so tiny that if you blinked, you'd miss it. 'They may just last a lifetime.'

'Don't worry, I can take her,' I say, as soon as the Lavigne sisters have retired to their rooms. I don't particularly *like* Cally right now, but she's a young woman and I know better than to return

185

pettiness with pettiness – except maybe when sparring with Harry. I will my legs to keep putting one tipsy foot in front of the other, as I make my way around the table to stand on the other side of Cally, now fully passed out on Harry's shoulder.

'*Can* you, though?'

'I'm not *that* drunk,' I argue, an amalgamation of shame and awe still swimming in my stomach. Shame, because for the first time in my life I wasn't prepared for a presentation. And awe because, well, Harry's speech might just have won us the investment we came all this way for – and he didn't even look like he was trying.

'No, I mean, are you even able to lift her?'

'Just because I'm a girl—'

'*Woman.*' He corrects me before I can correct myself, a cheeky grin on his face.

'Just because I'm a *woman* doesn't mean I can't . . .' I reach to put an arm under Cally, who even in her drunken state still manages to look like Sleeping Beauty, '. . . carry her.'

I heave with all my might to lift her, but her head just flops lightly onto my shoulder. I'm barely giving her a back stretch.

'Don't worry, I'll carry her up to bed,' he says, and I feel a pang of envy in my gut.

'I really think I should do it.'

'I really think you *can't.*' He raises an eyebrow at my pathetic attempts once more.

'But you're a guy and—'

'And what?' He looks offended for a moment. 'You don't trust me with her?'

We both look to Cally, comfortably unconscious and still pretty as a picture.

'No, that's not what I'm saying.'

'I hope you don't think I'm the kind of guy to—'

'I don't know what kind of guy you are.'

As soon as I've said it, the intensity in the room cranks up a notch: our near-kiss, our messages, the way we always manage to wind one another up, all rushing through my mind.

'All I mean,' I continue quickly, 'is that I'm sure Cally will be embarrassed enough about this in the morning without finding out you had to put her to bed.'

'I thought for a second you were happy about this?' He looks down at our lifeless colleague, then back at me, his eyes burning into me in the same way they did when I smiled at her slumping.

'No, no, I—'

'*Kate.*'

'Okay, for a second maybe I let my competitiveness get the better of me.'

'Doesn't sound like you.'

I flash him a look of disdain that is getting harder and harder to fake.

'But honestly? The only person I'm really competitive with is myself,' I say, softly pushing the hair out of Cally's sleeping face, trying to remember that I've always prided myself on being a girl's girl. 'I want to get to the top,' I admit, unashamed, even though I'm no longer sure quite where *the top* is. 'But I'd never want to tear anyone down to get there.'

Harry is smiling at me now, all teasing and taunting paused, if only for a moment. 'Well,' he grins kindly. 'Right now, the only place you need to get to is the top of this staircase.' My heart hammers harder, the tension between us shooting into overdrive. 'And, competitive as you are, we're going to have to work together to get there.'

As soon as he says the words, he's gently ushering Cally's head back onto his shoulder and gesturing for me to help move her legs so that they are crossing his own. I get the impression that he could physically do this himself but thinks it will be more respectful to her if I do it and, when he effortlessly stands whilst holding her in his arms, I know for a fact that's true. As we leave the private room we've just been in, I check the coast is clear. Sure, Cally may have passed out in front of Inès and Jade, but that doesn't mean anyone else needs to know. And now that they actually want to go into business with Poster, I'm hoping that what happens in the private function room stays precisely that: private.

'Are you okay?' I turn around as soon as I've walked up two stairs in the direction of our bedrooms for the evening. He nods, still holding Cally in his arms like a groom about to carry his bladdered bride over the threshold into married life together.

'Are you *sure* you're okay?' I stop halfway up the stairs to whisper again.

'Kate,' he hisses back to me. 'I'll be okay if you keep moving up the stairs.' He strains at the weight of Cally in his arms, which can't be all that much, but still.

'Okay, sorry, sorry,' I whisper back, walking quickly up the staircase.

'I think this is her room.' He nods at the door immediately at the top of the staircase. 'Have you got her key?'

'Why would *I* have her key?'

'I don't know – don't you women share purses and whatnot?'

'No, we're too busy braiding each other's hair.'

'Fine, let's go into my room.'

He gestures for me to walk a couple of paces down the corridor, before stopping outside a large wooden door.

'My key is in my left pocket,' he whispers to me, looking downwards.

'I am not going to go rifling through your pocket.'

'It's either that or you take Cally.' He looks like he's about to drop her.

'Fine,' I say, inhaling deeply as I reach my hand into his pocket. I feel the warmth of his leg under his trousers, trying not to think about how his bare skin would feel on my finger-tips, before feeling the cold hard key and pulling it out of his pocket as quickly as I can. I open the door into Harry's room and he paces across to the largest four-poster bed I've ever seen, perfectly positioned to gaze out of the floor-to-ceiling window, which would boast beautiful views of the vineyard were it not already the dead of night.

I watch as he carefully lays Cally out on the perfectly made bed before scanning around the ornate room – far bigger than my own and also far messier; it's the kind of place you'd go on your honeymoon and I suddenly become aware of how alone we are.

'Right, well, I should erm . . . go to bed,' I begin, forcing myself to turn toward the door.

'No, wait,' he says from behind me and although everything in me is telling me to leave, my heart leaps at the thought that he wants me to stay. 'You can't leave me with her.'

'Oh, I . . . Why not?'

'Well, it's not going to look good, is it, Cally and I sleeping in the same room?'

'But *we* slept in the same room last night?'

'I seem to remember that *you* were conscious. You stay here,' he suggests quickly. 'And I can stay in your room.'

'Okay, but . . .' I begin, as Cally groans from the bed. 'What if she's sick?'

'You can call me,' he assures me as he lets out a massive yawn.

'You said this morning that you can sleep through anything.'

'Okay, well, what if we both stay here for a bit?' he suggests, brushing his hand through his floppy hair. 'Wait until we know she's settled for the night?'

'And do what?' I ask, anxious for his answer.

'Just talk.'

Part of me doesn't want to believe him, but either way, I find myself walking back across the room and perching on the side of the four-poster next to Cally. Harry strides slowly to sit on the eighteenth-century-style armchair on the other side of the room.

'So, this evening seemed to go well?' he says, woodenly, his voice bouncing around the spacious room. Cally stirs and groans beside me.

'Thanks to you,' I reply, a little begrudgingly.

'Pardon?'

For a moment I think he just wants to hear my compliment again but then I see the way he's straining forward in the armchair, that he actually can't hear what I'm saying.

'Thanks to you,' I say louder, and Cally stirs again beside me, resurrection imminent. 'Look, just come over here, otherwise we're going to wake her up.'

'Maybe that's a good thing?' he asks cautiously but he's still too loud. 'She can tell us where the key is and we can all go back to our rooms.'

Cally groans again. 'Trust me,' I say, hating the part of me that feels a bit disappointed that he's looking for a way to avoid us being alone here. 'She's going to want to sleep this off.'

Slowly, he moves across the room, his frame illuminated by the moonlight seeping in through the window, to sit on the floor, his back resting against the side of the bed. I manoeuvre myself gently too, sliding off the mattress to sit on the floor beside him.

'Now, what were you saying?' He smiles across at me, softly, sleepily.

'That tonight, well, it was you who carried the conversation.'

'Only the last bit, when you chickened out from showing your presentation.'

'I didn't chicken out,' I object, as he laughs at how quickly he can wind me up.

'I know,' he softens. 'I don't think I've seen you back down from anything before.'

'I made the presentation so long ago that it wasn't even relevant to this evening.'

'One of the perks of being able to bluff on the spot, I guess.'

'Yeah, but that wasn't bluffing. All the things you said about the culture shift between the early noughties and now, that sounded prepared.'

'Yeah, maybe. Not prepared for tonight, though, it's just stuff I know, things I'm interested in. I may not know the facts and the stats . . .' He breaks off to grin suggestively at me. 'But I guess I'm just curious about what makes our culture tick, sensing the trends.'

'Well, whatever it is you *sense*, consider me a little impressed.'

'Just a little?' He raises his eyebrows; I reach out to punch him on the arm.

'Okay, impressed. Consider me impressed.'

'First time for everything,' he says quietly, and I feel like he's making a dig at me for a moment until I see a glimmer of sadness dart across his eyes.

'What do you mean?' I ask, becoming instinctively curious myself. Curious about him.

'This may not surprise you, Kate. But being interested in Kate Moss for Topshop as a teenage boy didn't make me a hit with the lads.'

'Bet the ladies loved it, though.'

'The ladies thought I was gay.' I clock the sheepish smile on his face.

'You're . . . you're not, though?' I ask, knowing how gutted I'd be if he was.

'No, I'm not,' he says softly. 'Sometimes I wished I was, though. At least then it would make sense of why I was into fashion and pop music and all the things my male peers didn't seem to give a damn about back then. At least then I'd have had a tribe.'

'You must have had a tribe, you're so . . . so . . .' I struggle for the word. '*Cool.*'

He looks at me intently, his profile further highlighted by the odd streetlamp scattered across the horizon outside. He's going to have my life for saying that.

'Trust me, the things I'm into only became "cool" long after I left school.'

'Would you believe me if I told you I was bullied at school too?'

'Yes,' he replies all too quickly.

'Hey!' I reach to punch him in his side again.

'Only because you're so unapologetically *you*. Kids hate that.'

I soften as he smiles, wanting nothing more than to touch him again.

'I don't know, though,' he continues. 'Maybe things are different now?'

'You sense a shift?' I say, putting my fingers to my temples to mock his woo-woo spiritual senses. Now it's his turn to tickle me in the ribs, moving a little closer as he does.

'I don't know,' he goes on slowly. 'Maybe? I feel like it's more acceptable for a guy to be creative nowadays, sensitive even.'

I don't know if it's the drink or the darkness, but I can tell he is opening up to me in a way he was beginning to do via our messages but I've never witnessed in person until now; suddenly, everything in me wants to see him take off another layer.

'Like, when I was choosing what I wanted to do after school, my dad genuinely thought there were two options: be a doctor or be a lawyer.'

'Which one is he?'

'Both.' He looks disappointed, but only in himself. 'He's a law professor.'

'Eeek.'

'Eeek indeed.' Any laughter that he was about to force out is lost somewhere in the heaviness of his sigh. 'At least he was until he got sick.'

The way he says it makes me know he's talking about more than just a cold.

'I'm sorry, is he—'

'It's cancer,' he confirms sadly. 'Late stages. We got some test results on the day of Sydney's photoshoot; that's what the call was about, why I had to leave so suddenly. Probably why I've been dropping the ball on so much of the planning for this trip.'

The realisation of this hits me like a punch to the gut.

'Harry, I'm so sorry. I had no idea.' I reach to place my hand on his.

'It's okay,' he smiles weakly. 'How could you know? So, yeah, he wasn't exactly chuffed that I wanted to "throw away my education" . . . '

Harry brings the conversation back to where we started and although everything in me wants to probe into his dad's illness – what he's going through, what they might expect to go through next – I know that any pushing might see his defences go back up.

'To spend my life crayoning,' he adds with a wink.

I wince, instantly realising how much my words would have wounded him when I managed to reduce his whole career path to something as simple as child's play.

'I'm sorry, I didn't know,' I repeat again, my hand still on his.

'I don't know how you would.' He shrugs. 'He'd like you, though.'

'Yeah?' I don't know whether this is a good or a bad thing.

'You kidding? Data analysis. Now *that's* a proper job.'

'*Your* job is a proper job.'

'Can I get that on the record, Carter?' His grin still can't hide his sadness. 'I think that's probably why you drive me crazy sometimes.'

'I drive you crazy?' My already hammering heart throbs harder in my chest.

'You remind me of him.'

'I remind you of your *dad*?'

This sentence threatens to dissolve any sexual tension between us in an instant.

'Yeah,' he sighs. 'Ever since the day we found out about the office merger; your confidence in your opinions, the way you command a room. Your unwavering belief in *facts*. What if I don't want to believe in facts?'

Facts like a cancer prognosis? I know this is what he's talking about and I guess, I kind of get why my very presence has seemed to get his back up from the off.

'And then there's just the way you look at me, like what I do doesn't matter and then—'

'I never said that.'

'And then the next minute I think I like you more than anyone I've ever met before.'

I struggle to hold his eye, my own desires swinging one way and then another, my understanding of him and our dynamic deepening by the second.

'I guess you keep me on my toes, Carter.'

'Like your *dad*?'

I ask again but the way Harry is looking at me, eyes heavy with wine and want, I'm becoming less and less fearful that the comparison puts us in the friend zone. He laces his fingers through mine, Cally's deepening breath audible through our shared silence.

'I never said what you do doesn't matter,' I whisper after the quiet becomes almost too much to bear. At least, I'm pretty sure I didn't.

'You've made your disdain for the fashion industry quite clear.'

'And the fashion industry has made its disdain for people like me clear too.'

'You do know Poster isn't representative of the whole fashion industry?'

'Well, yes . . . but—'

'I know Poster isn't perfect, but I'd be surprised if the benevolent start-ups you presumably *want* to work for are perfect too. Nothing ever is.'

'Okay, well that's just depressing. I need to believe there's some good in the world.'

'There is. Loads of it. But sometimes it's not about chasing the good *out there* but finding a way to bring the good *in here*.'

'In your *heart*?' I say, crinkling my nose at the cheesiness of it all.

'No, you idiot.' He laughs. 'I mean, where you are, in your job and whatnot.'

'So, what good do you want to bring to Poster?'

'I want to make it more sustainable, to source more ethical fabrics, to reduce our carbon footprint at no cost to creativity.' He answers me cautiously, like I'm about to rip his well-worn wishes apart. 'Now, please tell me all the ways that this is a ridiculous notion.'

'I . . .' His dreams don't sound naïve; they sound a lot like passion, like hope. 'I can't.'

'Wow.' He sighs, reaching to hold my hand in his. 'I never thought when you arrived at the airport yesterday that this would happen.' His voice is a whisper, his breath heavy, his fingers tracing circles on the soft skin on the back of my hand.

'What?' I breathe, willing his words to make sense of everything.

'That I'd finally get to . . .' He inhales deeply. 'Win a fight against you.'

For a moment I think this is all he wants from me, to win. But then he's turning his body to close the small space that's left between us.

'What are you doing?' I sigh, a small, fragile part of me still hating his ability to pull me close and push me away at will.

'Something I should have done properly years ago.'

He lifts his hands to draw my face into his, placing his lips lightly on mine as I feel like I'm losing any last scraps of my control within the sheer power of his kiss.

This time, he doesn't pull away.

Chapter Seventeen

'Morning,' Harry says sleepily from his position on the floor, the sun flooding through the open curtains and into the grand bedroom, highlighting the opulent features of the chateau.

'Morning,' I reply, lying on the bed just above him, still looking at the ornate ceiling. I have no idea when he or I fell asleep last night, but we're waking up close together now.

'What the *hell*?' Cally's shrill cry knocks me from whatever dream-like state I'm in.

'We can explain . . .' Harry says, standing up, not skipping a beat.

'Why am I in a bedroom with you?' she says to him before turning to me. 'And in a *bed* with you?' She sounds far more perturbed by the second half of this sentence.

I remain silent as Harry explains how the previous evening unfolded. Whilst he talks, I grasp at the shards of memory from last night: Harry saying that he wants to change Poster from the inside out; that I drive him crazy; our kiss.

'Oh God, no.' She throws her hands to her sheet-white face. 'Did I screw it up?'

'No,' I begin, looking from her to him. 'Harry managed to save the day.'

She looks a little surprised – I imagine not so much at the thought of Harry coming to our rescue, as at my admission that he did. Even more so at the way he is looking back to me and smiling, our feud finally morphing into something more. Maybe.

'Well . . .' I see the fear on Cally's face for a moment, but then she covers it with a clearly forced smile. 'I'm glad we all got what we came for.'

Her sentence feels pointed, and I'm not sure what she means by it. Did she see us kiss last night? Would it matter if she had? Before I have time to dig into it, Harry is clambering up off the floor and stretching his arms wide as he gazes across the rolling vineyards outside. I study him for a second, a man so full of surprises, and have no idea what today will hold: whether he and I will resort to type or whether our dynamic has changed for good.

'Anyone fancy a walk?' He turns to look at us both. Cally is still stretched out along the length of the bed, whilst I perch nervously on the side of it.

'Absolutely not.' She groans, like even moving onto her side is too much activity for today. Lord knows how she's going to feel on our flight back to London.

'Our taxi comes to pick us up in an hour,' I remind him. 'We need to pack.'

'Let me guess. You're one of those people who rolls their clothes up to perfection?'

'And you just scrunch them all in and hope for the best?'

'Wow, you've really got my number, haven't you, Carter?'

We both know I do, in more ways than one. 'Why pack and roll when you could scrunch and soak up the sun?'

'I . . .' I walk to stand beside him at the window. 'I can't really argue with that.'

'You feeling alright?'

I reach to give him a playful push to the side, but he pre-empts my move, managing to grab my softly clenched fist in the warmth of his hand, holding my eye as he does.

'Sure you don't want to join us, Cal?' he calls over to her lifeless form and I hate that my first thought is that being with me, alone, is simply not enough.

'Just come and get me when the taxi is here,' she groans as Harry nods.

'Okay, Carter, let's take you for a walk.'

'I'm not a dog, I—' I begin, but I'm already talking to the back of his head, following him out into the fresh, French air.

Together, we trace the perimeter of the chateau in something like companionable silence, the crunch of the loose gravel beneath my feet feeling almost therapeutic. As we walk around the back of the stone building, the vineyards we gazed across upstairs unfold before us now, their short stumps and spindly arms managing to be both unique and uniform at once. I steal glances towards the side of his beautiful profile as I follow him further through the vines in the direction of a single wooden bench towards the back of one field, signalling the start of the next.

He falls into step beside me, my racing thoughts of last night stalled in an instant as his hand reaches for mine and he laces his fingers through my own. So, last night *wasn't* a mistake? I feel the cool morning breeze kissing my face, clearing out the last alcohol-induced cobwebs in my mind until I feel my heart slowing, my breath deepening and my limbs uncoiling for what feels like the first time in forever. I never dreamed that the man who can rile me up more than anyone I've ever met could also be the one to finally help me unwind.

'One day, everything the light touches,' Harry says as soon as he's sat down, his open arm scanning across the horizon, his other hand still in mine, 'will be ours.'

'Are you really quoting *The Lion King*?'

'If that's a genuine question, I don't think we can be friends anymore.'

Friends: is that what we are now? I look back at him, daring myself to say this out loud, but then he's looking into my eyes and lifting my chin to kiss me softly, slowly. He pulls away a moment later, his lips lingering so closely to my own, I feel like I'm floating.

'Colin the lion would be proud,' I whisper, refusing to back away.

'Hey! You leave Colin out of this.' He grins back at me, not breaking his stare.

'I'm surprised you didn't smuggle him away on the trip.'

'It's not really his scene.'

'I know how he feels.'

'Me too,' he agrees. If he doesn't feel like he makes the cut at Poster then there's no hope for the rest of us. He relaxes into the back of the bench, reaching his arm around me. I snuggle in closer, wondering whether this – *us* – feels unbelievable or undeniable.

'Did you mean what you said last night?' I begin, not wanting to scare this moment, our new-found dynamic, away. 'About staying put at Poster?' I add quickly. 'If you are as passionate about sustainability as you say you are, why don't you start something new?'

He studies the beautiful vineyard before us; I remain fixated on his profile.

'That's part of the problem though, isn't it?' He turns to me slowly, as my expression morphs into one of confusion. 'As soon as something is broken, we feel like we need to swap it for something *new*. New clothes, new equipment, new furniture, new relationships, new friends. Our culture is becoming more disposable, and I just like the idea of working to change something. Plus, big corporations are responsible for most of the world's global emissions; if we can change the culture from the inside, surely that's a good thing?'

He looks at me, caught between passion and vulnerability, as my stomach jumps.

'It is,' I agree. 'It sounds like a really good thing.'

We sit in silence, staring back at the rustic stone building, the yellow hue of the natural beauty surrounding it telling of scorched summers and hotter than normal springs. *One day, everything the light touches* . . . I smile at his words. I know he was only being silly. But still, something about the silliness itself, the childlike joy of stopping to remember the words of characters buried deep within my past, the audacity of joking that one day the world could be ours, feels like it's stirring something within me. I don't know when my dreams became so orderly – move to London, get a job, get a salary, get a promotion, get a pay rise – or when turning a year older started to feel like a ticking time bomb rather than a cause for celebration. But something about being here, in a foreign land with a man who thinks completely differently from me, just *being* full stop, is making me see things differently; not more clearly, certainly not more logically, but, I guess, a little more curiously.

'We should roll.' Harry breaks me from the thought, getting to his feet, and I wonder whether this is it: the moment when the carriage turns into a pumpkin and I begin to be basement-office Kate again. But then he's reaching a hand out to pull me up to standing.

'Finally coming around to my way of thinking?' I joke, following his lead, my heart still in my throat. How can I love hating this man so much? It doesn't make any sense.

'Hell, no.' He lifts my hand to kiss my knuckles. 'Scrunch-packer for life, baby.'

By the time I get back to my room, there is no time for neatly rolling my clothes. Instead, I force everything into my suitcase and have to sit on top of it in order to see it close – something I will *never* admit to Anderson – before rushing towards our taxi. I can see Gabe waving enthusiastically in the rearview mirror as we pull away. The Lavigne sisters are nowhere to be seen, likely nursing hangovers with treatments in the chateau's not-so-secret spa. It's another world here, but hopefully now they'll want to be a little part of Poster's.

It takes all of two minutes for Cally to fall asleep in the taxi, her pretty head lolling onto Harry's shoulder again. Even so, I can't help but smile as I look out of the window at vineyard after vineyard passing by, until we're finally clambering out of the car and making our way towards our terminal and then onto the packed-out plane.

'I thought Kate could sit next to me this time,' Harry says from his assigned seat, gesturing to the spare one beside him.

I smile back at him, but before I can take him up on the offer, Cally is forcing her way into the same formation we sat in on our way out here.

'I much prefer the middle seat,' she objects with the same kind of conversation-closing defiance she had when informing us that she categorically doesn't share rooms. Perhaps I should thank her for that, given the way that Harry is gazing across at me now?

'But I think Kate and I were going to have a quick chat about the next presentation.'

'Not like you to plan ahead.' She eyes him suspiciously, like she knows something has shifted between us. 'We already know what we want our microsite to look like,' she goes on. Do we? 'Let's just touch base about it when we're back in the office . . . and less hungover.'

'I'm on annual leave next week,' he says, taking the seat next to her as I sit in my seat across the aisle again, my heart rate picking up as my claustrophobia begins to kick in.

'Going away?' I ask, not even trying to sound unbothered by this now.

'Spending time with the family,' he nods with a sad smile.

'Sounds like a good idea.' I mirror his expression before leaning back in my seat and trying to remind myself that if Harry can be this brave about something as serious as cancer, I can face my fear of flying, of being out of control, too.

By the time we're soaring over London, Cally and Harry are both asleep, her head still managing to gravitate towards his shoulder like metal to a magnet. Looking across at the two strangers sitting next to me on my side of the aisle, I try to glimpse the city coming into view through the thick cloud surrounding us, wishing I was still sitting in the vast expanse of the vineyard. When I first moved from Yorkshire to London, I swore I was going to make a difference there, to change the city and not let it change me. I still want to use data for good like I did back then, I know I do. I just thought I needed to leave Poster to do it.

I look back out of the window, stealing a glance at the man sat beside it. His long legs are almost folded up to his chin as he sits with a laptop only inches from his eyes, the bags underneath them telling of late nights in the office, his plain suit screaming of something business-y and nondescript like 'consultant' or 'project manager'. There was once a time where I would have put him in a box instantly, the same way I've always felt the Poster People do with me: safe, secure, wife and two point five kids, a nice house, a bit boring all round. Now, I can't help but wonder what's beneath the surface: perhaps he's less about managing projects and more about encouraging people – the office mentor, always wanting to draw out the best in others? Then, I look to the young woman next to me, her silky, long hair tied up in a messy bun atop her head; she's flicking through a fashion magazine, subconsciously breathing in each time she turns the page to see some slender model advertising clothes she can't possibly hope to purchase since she's travelling in economy like us. She catches my eye and smiles; it's such a gorgeous smile and it pains me that any person out there may feel like they're not enough because of something we put out on Poster. I feel not enough because of Poster. I always have.

I wonder whether I can change that?

Walking out of the plane to be hit by the cool London air, I can't seem to shake the thought. Maybe I don't need to leave

Poster to make a difference? Perhaps I don't even need to be promoted to director to do it? I'm working on a project that is meant to target a new demographic, but what about speaking to that demographic in a whole different way: not speaking down to them, telling them they need to do more and buy more to measure up, but standing alongside them, telling them that they are already enough as they are? It's everything I've wanted to hear myself; I've just been waiting for someone else to say it for me.

'Right, I'm this way,' Cally says as soon as we've made our way through passport control and are standing by the smattering of shops and bars by Arrivals. 'Do you want to share a taxi?' She is looking directly at Harry and I can't help but think about the moments after Harry and I almost kissed for the first time five years ago, when as soon as he remembered he wasn't alone, he jumped at the chance to get into a taxi without me. I wonder whether, now we're on home ground, we'll go back to being rivals again.

'I'm heading straight to the train station,' he replies to her, but he is looking at me. 'Straight down to Devon to see the folks.'

'No worries.' She leans forwards to kiss him on both cheeks. 'See you guys at work.'

Evidently, there is no room in her taxi for me. Though, even if there was, I know I wouldn't want to take it. I want to spend as much time around Harry before he leaves for his parents' as possible. Not that I'm going to be admitting that to him anytime soon. I look to him standing there, knowing that the way he says goodbye now, the next words to fall from his mouth, will set the tone for our relationship now that our game-changer of a trip is over.

'Fancy a drink?' He looks towards the airport bar and my

heart soars in my chest. The only thing better than a good goodbye is no goodbye at all. 'I've got some time to kill.'

'Oh, and I've got nothing better to do?' I bite back; old habits die hard.

'Well, do you?' he asks, cheeky smile in tow.

'Shut up,' I say, already making my way towards the bar.

Moments later, I'm watching Harry return, drinks in hand, to the table for two that I've just managed to swoop into. He places my beer in front of me, and I can't help but think how much has changed since I met him and Cally in the departure lounge only forty-eight hours ago. Turns out a trip away was just what I needed to give me a new perspective, and not just when it comes to what I think about him.

'I've had an idea,' I say, taking a first tentative sip of my drink.

'Don't hurt yourself.'

I breathe deeply, worried about sharing my next thought, the one that began so tentatively as we took off from Bordeaux and seemed to cement as we touched down on the Stansted concrete. It's not based on data, facts; it's based on a belief.

'How about instead of using our usual models for the micro-site, we do something a bit different?'

'Well, our usual models are between thirty-five and forty-five,' he muses. They're designed to target fifty-year-olds, to make them feel just that little bit worse about themselves, on the off-chance that they buy a cashmere jumper to feel better again. 'So, we'll have to get some younger models in to appeal to our Gen Z audience.'

'Radical.' I roll my eyes. 'No, I actually meant maybe we could use *real* women from our demographic in the campaign? Women of all different shapes and sizes and colours.'

'Kate,' he says, a small smile turning up the corners of his mouth. 'I think that's an excellent idea, but . . .'

My smile falters for a second. I knew there would be a 'but'.

'But I'm not sure Gareth will go for it. He likes the "aspirational" quality of Poster.'

'You do know "aspirational" is code for making people feel bad about themselves?'

'I know that, but—'

'And do you not think we should try to change that?'

'I picked my personal battle with Poster a long time ago. Maybe this one is yours?'

He smiles as I remember our chats about sustainability that started this thinking in the first place. Poster has made me and other women feel bad for long enough. If I can't beat them, maybe I can do something to change them, or at least make the 'them' in question broader, more attainable.

'But where do I even begin?' I ask, allowing myself this moment of vulnerability.

'Where you always begin. With research, data, and then a bloody good presentation.'

'Harry Anderson excited about a presentation. What's got into you?'

'More a case of who.'

So, perhaps this influence is a two-way thing after all? Our differences finally beginning to feel like a strength, which is exactly what I want our microsite to show.

'Okay, so I'll get to work on it this week whilst you're away and then maybe we can discuss how plausible it all is when you're back?'

Harry smiles, taking another slow sip of his beer. 'Your place or mine?'

I smile at how suggestive this sounds until I remember a slight snag in the strategy. 'What about Cally?'

'What about her?' Harry grins again.

'Well, we should involve her in this too, shouldn't we?' The thought of her purposefully trying to exclude me from this trip crosses my mind.

'Involve her in what exactly?' He narrows his eyes, a silly smirk on his face; now I *know* he's being suggestive.

'Work. The microsite.' I steer us back onto serious ground.

'Absolutely, and we will.' He nods. 'But maybe it would make sense to work out some of the basic behind-the-scenes stuff together first, just the two of us?' He leans in to place a light kiss on my lips.

'You make a good suggestion, Mr Anderson,' I grin, my hand holding his cheek.

'It's been known to happen.'

'Once in a blue moon,' I tease as he leans in to kiss me once more.

Our trip may have come to an end, but this still feels like the start of something.

Chapter Eighteen

Harry: I'm five minutes away.

Harry: Well, according to Citymapper.

Me: I'll knock off about two mins to account for your ridiculously long legs then.

Harry: These long legs might be the very thing that saves me from Boner the dog.

Me: No Boner tonight, I'm afraid. Wolf's out.

Me: Just me.

Harry: Sounds perfect.

I smile down at the message, before smoothing my hair down in Harry's old friend's floor-length mirror. Thank God for 'vain band boys' or whatever derogatory thing Wolf has called his ex-housemate over the last five weeks we've been living together. Harry and I have awkwardly bumped into one another in this bedroom twice already. Now, he might be invited into it. Unless, this past week that Harry has spent with his family, gathering around his father – hoping for the best but perhaps expecting the worst – has made him come to his senses, change his mind about me? Or perhaps it's been the past three days back at work together where we've barely had a moment to talk? Despite our messaging back and forth outside of the office, he may have decided that when it comes to our in-person relationship our French kiss was exactly that – just a French kiss?

Vera brushes past my leg and I jump out of my skin. In my defence, I didn't even know she was in my room. I stand, pacing the small square of carpet that isn't already occupied by what's left of Sam's things. No, I will not expect the worst from tonight; I always do that. And since everything changed between us in Bordeaux, Harry hasn't given me any reason to doubt him. Tonight, I want to hope for the best. Not just for me and Harry but for my blossoming idea for the microsite too. Our next presentation is only two days away and, glancing down at my phone again, it's now only *two minutes* until he's here.

The past week, while he has been on leave, has been relentless. From analysing the end of one financial year to forecasting for the next, my normal 'back-office' responsibilities have shot through the roof. As for the microsite, I somehow managed to impress Georgina with a report on the click-through rates of alcohol sponsors we have on our main website ahead of the Lavigne advertisement campaign. Planning meetings, however, have perhaps unsurprisingly been on hold whilst *Hazza* has been away, Gareth not entirely sure whether two women can be trusted to steer something so strategic without a man by their side. And the three days that he's been back? Well,

211

Gareth and Cally have been hounding him all day, as if he's going out of style.

Before long, I hear a knock on the door and cross the empty living room to open it.

'Sorry I'm late.' Harry is standing in the doorway looking gorgeous, if not a little flustered. He's wearing a thick lumberjack shirt, pushed up at the sleeves, and looks *hot*.

'You're like three minutes late.' I laugh away his concern, my eyes scanning his strong forearms. I try to breathe deeply, but I'm suddenly feeling a little hot too.

'I know you run a tight ship.'

'I'm not *that* bad.'

I don't need to tell him that his tardiness isn't actually that annoying, now that I know he really cares about some things, that he isn't just blundering his way through life.

'So can I come in?' He looks past me into the empty room behind.

'Oh, you're waiting for permission this time?'

'I *had* permission last time. It's not my fault Wolf fell right back to sleep and . . .'

'Well, he's not here to give you permission today, I'm afraid.'

'Damn.' Harry puts a hand to his chin, pretending to think. 'So, I just have to wait it out here until he comes home to let me in?'

'Unless you know the password?' I put a hand to my hip, my body weighted to one side, my body language as teasing as my tone. I wait for him to answer, but before I know it, his hand is on mine, pulling me closer to him as he presses his lips, his body, into mine.

'Did I get it right?' he whispers, after pulling away, his face lingering by my own.

'I guess you can come in.'

I take a step back to allow him to walk past, still a little stunned by his lips on mine.

'Can I get you a drink?' I ask, as he makes himself at home; his demeanour is completely different now that Wolf isn't here to hound him.

'Got a beer? But just one. I'm only just recovering from Bordeaux.'

'Tell me about it. The last week or so at work has been a killer.'

I hand him the beer, only then realising how inappropriate this sentence is, given how he spent last week with his dying dad. If anything is a killer, it's cancer. And Harry's momentarily stunned face tells me this is exactly where his thoughts have gone too.

'Shit. I'm sorry, I . . .'

'Don't worry 'bout it.' He waves away the insensitivity of my comment like it's nothing.

'How is your dad?'

'Physically? He's been better.'

Of course he has; he's *got cancer*. I berate myself for asking such a silly question.

'Emotionally? He seems in a better place than Mum. My dad has always been good at keeping it together, being the strong one.'

His voice croaks ever so slightly and I wonder how much of his 'faking it 'til he makes it' strategy is inherited from his father.

'And how are you?' I open my can and sit down on the sofa

beside him. Despite the depth of our messages and our late-night chat in the chateau, going beyond banter in real life still feels like breaking new ground.

'Better now.'

He leans over to kiss me on the lips again before I manage to coax myself away.

'You do know you can't just kiss me whenever you—'

My sentence is lost somewhere in our next kiss, as I let myself melt into him, savouring the feel of his tongue lightly encouraging my lips to part, the feel of his strong hands on my side, drawing me ever closer to him. After so many days spent trying to keep him at arm's length, it feels both delicious and dangerous to be so connected to him now.

'So, the microsite?' I whisper through bated breath as soon as he has pulled away.

'Wow, you really know how to kill the mood, don't you, Carter?' His laugh sends the intricate lines around his grey-blue eyes even deeper.

'Wait until you see the data I've pulled together.'

'Stop it, you're turning me on.'

'I may have created a mood board too.' I lower my voice into a sultry whisper.

'Okay, now you're getting *me* in the mood.'

I reach forward to pull my laptop from the coffee table before us and proceed to open it upon my now-crossed legs. I'm not entirely sure whether he expected us to actually be working on my microsite idea tonight or if it was just an excuse to get in my pants, but if he thinks scoring with me is that easy, he's not as smart as I'm now starting to think he is. Firing up my research, I try to quell the fire searing up my legs, the throbbing of my heart, and instead focus on what I've been putting together all week.

'The data all seems to point to the fact that Gen Z want to see themselves represented in their marketing campaigns; the social consciousness of the brands they buy is almost as important to many of them as the items themselves.'

Harry stares back at me, a coy smile on his face.

'What?' I demand.

'I'd just never noticed how sexy you are when you're geeking out.'

'Maybe you were listening, but you weren't really *hearing*.'

I let my comment linger, still scared that at any moment my words could see him retreat behind his usual defences, that any challenges could once again leave me on the outside. And yet, something about the way he's looking at me now is making me feel safe.

'This is the kind of creative brief I had in mind,' I go on, turning around my screen so that he can see the campaigns displayed upon it: stills from Little Mix's *Strip* video, scenes from the first iconic This Girl Can advert, images from Misguided's #LoveThyself campaign, advance shots from Katie Piper's The Unseen. Some images capture the full spirit of the campaigns, the beaming faces of the models, arms wrapped around one another. Others focus in on the intricacies, capturing the delicacy of stretchmarks, the beauty of fabric undulating over fuller body shapes, the uncovered scars that scream, *This is who I really am.*

'Kate, this is amazing.' He literally takes my laptop from me to study it closer.

'I never realised how powerful a mood board could be.'

'Maybe you were looking, but not really *seeing*,' he echoes playfully.

'I hate you,' I quip back.

'I don't believe you.'

He leans in to kiss me now, slowly, gently, like he's relaxing into this too.

'It honestly looks so great, Kate,' he continues. 'There's only one problem.'

'What's that?'

'There's still no wiggle room on the price point.'

'Why's that a problem?'

'Not everyone can *afford* our prices. Of course, the fast-fashion brands selling things for a tenner can convince buyers to "see themselves" reflected in the brand, but if we drop our prices, we'll have to drop our quality and the impact on the environment will be huge.'

'Perhaps it's our job to convince our woman that buying sustainably matters?'

'I've been trying, I swear, but—'

'Harry, this microsite could target a whole new pool of socially conscious women.'

'Okay, so you handle the identity piece. I'll take the sustainability factor.'

'Deal. Hey, look at us working well together!' I laugh.

'Turns out we're a pretty good team, Carter.'

He leans into me again and with every kiss, I feel like we could be.

'I agree, it feels like it's all coming together, just in time for . . .'

'Just in time for what?'

'The launch of the microsite?' I don't mean for my words to sound so unconvincing.

'I don't believe you.' He repeats his words from before, leaning a little closer still.

'Well, just in time for me . . . turning thirty.'

'When do you turn thirty?' A trademark cock of the eyebrow.

'Two days' time.'

'The same day as our presentation?! Okay, now we *have* to pitch your campaign.'

'Just because it's my birthday? Don't patronise me.'

'No, not just because it's your birthday.' He shakes his head at my feist, lacing his fingers through my own. 'Because it's a good idea.'

'Not that Gareth will see it as one.'

'We'll handle Gareth.'

'What about Cally?'

'Let me talk to Cally.' He squeezes my hand a bit tighter before quickly moving on. 'But why didn't you say anything? We could have celebrated in France.'

'I don't want it to be a big deal.'

'But turning thirty is a massive deal.' He grins again. 'What are we doing to celebrate?'

'We?'

'If I'm invited, that is?'

'I was just planning on having a drink with Blair and co. You're welcome to join us.'

Well, welcomed by me at least.

'Sounds . . .' Harry stalls for a moment. 'It sounds perfect.'

He unlaces our fingers so that he can brush them through

my hair, kissing me again and again until I'm not only losing control but losing count. Whatever game was going on between us before, it finally feels like we're both winning, like we're on the same side.

Chapter Nineteen

Me: I've just got to Poster House.

Harry: You've only just got to the office? It's almost 10am.

Me: Finally adjusting to tenth-floor time, I guess.

Me: Plus, I had this guy round to mine last night, and he just wouldn't leave.

Harry: Sounds like a right piece of work.

Me: Meh, he's okay.

Me: When are you getting here?

Harry: I've already been and gone.

Me: Before 10am?

Harry: Finally adjusting to Kate Carter time.

Harry: Plus, Gareth has pulled me into some shoots for the main site this week.

Me: You cheating on our microsite?

Harry: These twenty-pound socks won't sell themselves.

Me: Back in time to grab some lunch?

Harry: It's an all-dayer, I'm afraid.

Harry: Least now you can concentrate on the presentation without some hot guy from across the room distracting you.

Me: Why, is Toby out at the shoot too?

Harry: Ha-ha, very funny.

Me: It's coming together though, just need to update Cally on last night.

Harry: Not *everything* about last night, I hope.

Me: Just the microsite bits.

Harry: She's on this shoot today actually.

Harry: I'll chat to her if you like, bring her up to speed?

Me: You sure?

Harry: Sure.

Me: Thanks. She might be more inclined to go for it if it's coming from you.

Harry: You might be right.

Me: Say it louder for those in the back.

Harry: Once is all you're getting.

Harry: Though, I have to say, this real woman campaign is feeling pretty bang on too.

'What are you grinning at?'

I jump out of my skin, swinging around to see Amanda standing there by my far-flung desk. Today, she's wearing high-waisted jeans and a see-through blouse that would look far too revealing on anyone who wasn't model thin.

'Nothing. Just something Harry said about the microsite.'

She narrows her cat-winged eyes at me in suspicion, entirely unconvinced. 'I'm surprised you're smiling at anything that man says.'

'What do you mean?'

My pulse picks up pace instantly. Has Amanda finally realised that she's seen Harry before, back when he was one of countless interns who circulated through the offices on a monthly cycle? That he was the very person who prompted her warnings against romances in the office, the ones that seemed far too forceful for someone as free-thinking as her?

'Just that you guys seem pretty chalk and cheese.'

'Hmm.' I force something, anything, to come from my mouth. Clearly, Harry is so stereotypically 'Poster' that he's simply blended indistinctly into Amanda's memory. Just a face-less nobody that she made very clear wasn't worth risking my career for. That, or she was so drunk the night of the mixer that there's no memory of him there to begin with.

'I thought you might have come to blows by now.'

'I'm trying to be open-minded, remember?'

'Good,' she nods. 'But don't let your guard down too much, cos I've heard that . . .' She's lowering her voice, even though we both know no-one can hear us from here.

'Heard what?'

'Well, rumour has it that Gareth has just signed off the

additional budget for a promotion for a "member of the micro-site team", promotion-freeze be damned.'

'So, he could be promoting any of us?'

She nods, and yet her excitement is so palpable that I can't help but think it's for me. 'All I know is that *Gina* is really impressed with your data-driven work so far.'

'That's good,' I say, remembering the report I delivered to her just last week.

'And she's a little surprised by how well you understand the Poster demographic.'

'Why is she surprised?'

My mind harps back to some of the outfits I've worn since working up here.

'Don't worry about that.' Amanda laughs, shaking her head and her luscious red hair with it. 'You just keep doing what you're doing, and that promotion is yours.'

Except, I'm about to present something completely out of the box for Poster. I swallow deeply, the familiar feeling of not wanting to make the wrong move washing over me. Then I remember Harry's encouragement, that he thinks I'm on the right track.

'Oh, and I've been pulled into the Christmas campaign shoot this week, so in case I don't see you, good luck with the next presentation . . .'

She breaks off to glance at the latest size-zero model who has just walked out onto the tenth floor to be briefed ahead of their next job and I watch as she subconsciously sucks her belly button to her back. It's all the reminder I need that my idea is a good one.

'And happy early thirtieth for tomorrow, Kate.' She turns

back to me with her winning smile. 'I don't say it enough, but I'm really proud of everything you've achieved. You should be too.'

'Thanks, Amanda.' I grin back at her. 'I think I'm starting to be.'

'Ready?' Blair asks as soon as she's managed to make it to my desk.

'Ready as I'll ever be.'

I close my laptop before me and stash it in my backpack. I thought the day would drag slowly without Harry here, but between the preparation for the presentation tomorrow and the resurrecting hope of my long-awaited promotion, the day has flown by.

'We still on for tomorrow?' she asks, as we walk back across the tenth floor and over towards the lifts. 'Your birthday celebrations?'

'For sure,' I reply. 'I'm looking forward to it.'

'I thought you were dreading it?' She turns to me with an inquisitive expression as she presses the button to call the lift.

'I was, but then . . .' The doors to the lift open immediately. 'Harry.'

'Then *Harry*?'

She gives me her best what-the-heck? look before following my eye into the lift to see Harry standing there before us, a sheepish expression on his face.

'Are you coming out?' she demands with no small amount of disdain.

'No, erm . . .' He looks between us. 'I'm going down.'

We all know that the tenth floor is as high as the lift goes, that Harry has just taken it to the top. His subtle smile lets me know he was coming to find me.

'Idiot,' she mutters under her breath before heading into the lift, standing in between me and Harry as she does. I look across to him, catching his wide-eyed look that seems to say, *What is* her *problem?*

Her problem is that she used to work on the tenth floor and got horrifically bullied when she did. She told HR but they did nothing except transfer her to the basement: out of sight, out of mind. And now, every person upstairs is a not-so-subtle reminder of what she went through back then. I flash him a small smile that I hope says: *I will explain when I get the chance*, but Blair intercepts it, returning my grin through her gritted teeth.

The three of us stand in silence as the lift descends floor by floor and I can't resist checking him out in the mirrored walls surrounding us: he's wearing the same tight green t-shirt he wore on the first day of the office merger, the one that shows every outline of his toned torso beneath it. I find I'm gripping the straps of my backpack just to stop thinking about what it would feel like to kiss the soft skin of his stomach underneath.

'Kate, can I grab you for a sec?' he asks unsurely as the lift doors open.

'Erm . . . sure . . . I . . .' I slow my walking, Blair coming to a standstill beside me.

'It's about the presentation tomorrow.'

'I can catch you up?' I turn to Blair, willing her to leave me alone with him.

'It's okay, I can wait.' She is defiant in her defence of me.

Little does she know that it's not needed anymore, that there are very few boundaries left between me and him now.

'Sure.' His eyes dart between me and Blair as awkwardness consumes us all. I thought he and I were becoming a good team, but I'd forgotten about our respective other players. Even so, all I want to do is find an excuse to talk to him now. 'What time is it meant to be?'

'Typical.' Blair rolls her eyes at him not knowing this most basic of information.

'It's at midday,' I confirm, even though I know he doesn't need me to.

'Great, thanks.'

'Well, as nice as it's been chatting . . .' she says, turning from him to me with a sarcastic smile on her face. My cue to leave. And try as I might, I can't think of a single excuse to stay that won't make the frostiness flowing from Blair absolutely Baltic.

'See you tomorrow?' I smile back to him, wanting nothing more than to hold him.

'Yeah,' he shrugs sadly. 'Tomorrow.'

Together, Blair and I make our way towards the tube station; I have to tell her things between Harry and me have changed, especially as he's meant to be joining us for my birthday drinks tomorrow, but for some reason I can't find the words. I know Harry isn't responsible for her tenth-floor treatment way back when, but ever since we've been working up there, her resolve against the Poster People has only solidified. And after missing her own birthday drinks for Bordeaux, I would hate to do anything to threaten the solidity of our friendship now. But how am I going to find a way to avoid the topic until a better time?

> Harry: I can't wait until tomorrow.

I look from Blair, walking beside me, and down at the messages on my phone. Harry once again seems to have the answer to questions I'm yet to even think about.

> Harry: I'm waiting on the staircase to the basement.

> Harry: Tell Blair you've forgotten something.

'I didn't think you'd know the *way* to the basement.'

Harry looks up from the middle of the stone staircase that I know so well to see me standing at the top of it. I've managed to retrace my steps to the office as quickly as my legs can carry me and yet he still feels too far away. He walks up a few stairs as I walk down a couple, the two of us meeting in the middle. His hands are on my sides instantly, the small step we're standing on forcing us blissfully close together.

'Well, I think it's fair to say Blair isn't my biggest fan.' His face is so near to me now that I can feel his breath on my cheek.

'She'll come around.'

'Like you did?'

'Well, hopefully not exactly as I did.'

'Don't worry, I don't think I'm her type.'

'To be fair, I didn't think you were mine.'

He leans forward to kiss me fully on the mouth, my lips parting at his cues. 'And how about now?' He pulls away slowly.

'Meh, you're growing on me.'

He presses himself a little closer to me and I can feel a part of him that literally is growing.

226

'I wanted to give you an early birthday present . . . ahead of tomorrow,' he whispers.

'If this has *anything* to do with your penis, I'm writing you off as a creep.'

'Head out of the gutter, Carter.'

Harry reaches into his back pocket, pulling out a small, thin box, wrapped neatly in brown paper and tied with a black satin ribbon on the top. He places the parcel carefully in my hands as a kaleidoscope of butterflies flutters through my insides. I will my hands not to shake as I carefully unwrap the paper to reveal a thin, silver box and within it a metallic blue pen, which is engraved with a delicate 'KC' on one side.

'I thought I'd find a use for all those ink cartridges you insist on carrying around.'

'Thank you.' I look to him, too touched by the gesture to say anything more.

'Happy thirtieth, Kate,' he grins, pulling me in for another slow and gentle kiss. 'I think this next decade is going to be a good one for you.'

As I kiss him on the steps to the basement that I have spent so many days of my twenties hiding within, for once, everything within me is inclined to agree.

Vera greets me outside the apartment, weaving through my feet as I walk into the living room, still savouring the taste of Harry's kisses on my lips. Given that it's just gone eight pm, I fully expect Wolf to be out or just waking up in his usual spot on the sofa. Instead, he's up and unexpectedly groomed. Vera must be shocked as well, because as soon as she sees him, she instantly bolts for the open window on the far side of the room, making Boner sit upright.

'You look pleased with yourself.' He looks me up and down as I check my phone screen with a smile.

'And you look, well, *clean*.'

'Why the tone of surprise?' He makes no attempt to hide his smirk, as I make my way to perch on the arm of the sofa beside him. 'I have a meeting with my agent tonight.'

'Sounds important.'

He shrugs. 'Just a catch-up. Want to see why she's not getting me any good parts.'

'Can you not take a bad part and turn it into a good one?'

I know this sentence would have struggled to come out of my mouth a few weeks ago.

'I'd rather retain my artistic integrity.' He yawns. 'Fancy joining for a drink after?'

'With you and your agent?'

'Well, no.' He stands to walk towards the coat stand. 'Just me.'

'I would, but I've got a big day tomorrow.'

'How so?' He's pulling on his oversized leather jacket.

'I have an important presentation in the morning—'

'For a job you don't even like.'

'And it's my birthday.'

'All the more reason to start celebrating now.'

'Thanks, but seriously, I need to be on it tomorrow. It's important and I don't want to let my team down.' I smile at the thought of Harry's present, stashed in my bag.

'Man, one bougee trip to Bordeaux and you think you're

one of them.' He rolls his eyes. 'I thought you were smarter than that, Kate.'

And with that, he's gone, but not even Wolf's broodiness can stem my shine tonight. Harry is right. Some people wait a lifetime for the right opportunity to fall into their laps. Other people make sure to make it happen. And I know tomorrow is mine.

Chapter Twenty

I look up at Poster House, which is coming into view quicker than it ever has before. Because today, for the first time in a long time – perhaps even ever – I am striding towards it.

The tenth floor towers down at me as I approach the iconic entrance. Whoever is gazing down from the floor-to-ceiling windows up there is no doubt judging my simple but smart jeans and shirt combo, but today, I really don't care. Today, I want to focus on what I *have*, not what I don't have, and take a small stride towards making sure other women feel empowered to do the same. And, if it happens to secure me my promotion to director in the process, then I'm not about to argue with that either.

My phone buzzes and I look down at the messages that are threatening to overflow from the screen. *Hola amiga, feliz cumpleaños querida*, the top one reads from Lucy. I've not heard much from her while she's been getting settled in San Francisco, but with my own personal and professional lives ramping up lately as well, I totally understand. Plus, she always comes through in the moments that count. Even Wolf left me a (no doubt drunkenly scrawled) birthday card to find on top of the kitchen counter this morning.

As I push the revolving door into the ground floor lobby of Poster House, I feel welcome bubbles of anticipation filling my stomach, the ones that have been so absent these last few years that I thought I might have just outgrown them. Then, I see the strong frame of Harry standing there in the reception, two coffee cups in his hands, one huge smile on his face.

'It's the birthday girl!' he says loudly, holding his arms wide as I walk across the ornate entrance.

'Careful,' I caution him happily; he's dressed in slim-fit beige chinos, which are turned up at the ankles, and an over-sized white t-shirt that will not look good if stained.

'Oh, sorry – birthday *woman*,' he corrects himself.

'I meant be careful with the coffees, you idiot,' I say, looking his all-light outfit up and down. 'You may like to dress like an off-duty Jesus, but we have a presentation to do.'

'Always so cautious.' He grins back to me, rolling his eyes.

I guess some things will never change.

'Plus,' he continues, 'technically, I don't think Jesus was ever "off duty".'

'Not like you to love a technicality.'

'Only when it means winning against you.'

I smile sarcastically, all lips, no teeth on show.

'This one is for you.' He thrusts my own KeepCup into my hand.

'Where did you find this?'

'The coffee is from Kaffeine,' he confirms proudly. 'Blair helped me find your KeepCup in the upstairs kitchen. Decided that if I'm really going to advocate for sustainability here, I need to start being a bit more consistent about it.'

'Sounds sensible. Wait, *Blair* helped you find this?'

'I didn't say she was happy about it.' He grins back at me.

'Well, thank you. I appreciate it. You all set for today?'

'Got the sustainability points covered,' he nods. 'You?'

'Ready as I'll ever be.'

'Coming from you, I know that means you have it planned to perfection.'

'Maybe. But I would like to run through it all one more time.'

'Classic Carter.'

'Have you got time now?'

'I'm actually off to the second part of this Christmas shoot this morning, but I should be back to run through it one more time before the presentation. You're going to smash it.'

'Thanks,' I grin, feeling the first sip of coffee buzzing through my veins.

'And you know I've got your back in there regardless,' he adds.

'Cally's cool with the direction we're taking?'

'Pretty much.' He nods, leaning in to kiss me before the ding of the lift doors opening into the lobby causes him to pull away.

'Speak of the devil,' I mutter under my breath as I see Cally standing there, dressed head to toe in a tailored white suit, her blonde hair falling poker-straight down her sides.

'Be nice,' he whispers back to me as she approaches.

'I'm always nice,' I hiss back, and he laughs warmly.

'You ready to go?' she asks Harry, pretty much ignoring me completely, one hand on her hip and the other clutching some sort of portfolio, I assume for the shoot.

'Just about, yeah.'

'Good, because Georgina has our work cut out for us.' She giggles.

'But we'll be back in time to run through the microsite presentation before twelve,' he says, half confirmation, half question.

'Oh, that?' she says nonchalantly, like this is no big deal to busy old her. 'Sure. I've actually been brainstorming some ideas with Gareth that I want to run past you both.'

'I think we're pretty set on our idea.' I try my best to hold on to my good mood, but you try being bossed around by someone who has been working here all of two seconds.

'Good.' She says this to me, but she's beaming at Harry. 'Rumour has it that if you play your cards right, you may be in for a promotion.'

Well, *one of us*, I correct, remembering Amanda's assurance from yesterday. That said, provided I'm finally using data for something that matters, I can make my peace with Harry getting the pre-freeze promotion, so long as he's buying all of the coffees from now on.

'Have a good morning, birthday woman.' He beams at me. 'We'll see you soon.'

'Oh, it's your birthday?' Cally pretends she's bothered. 'Happy birthday! How old are you?'

'Thirty.' I smile, because now that I'm here it doesn't feel so scary.

'That's big.' Her eyes widen before she makes her way towards the exit, beckoning for Harry to follow her. I'm not sure whether she means the number or the occasion, but as he looks back over his shoulder to wink in my direction, I'm not sure I even care.

I try and fail not to watch the clock all morning. So much so, that the mountain of reports waiting for me in my inbox like some sadistic birthday present with no receipt feels like a welcome surprise. I complete them all too fast, tearing myself away from my usual desk to walk across the tenth floor to deliver them one by one. Half of the upstairs staff are seemingly out at 'the shoot' – my favourite one of them included – but a smattering of those who remain look up at me as I pass them, some nodding, some smiling, one even wishing me a happy birthday shortly after Blair, Toby and Charlie have cornered me to do the same. I guess birthdays can bring out the best in even the moodiest of models. Still, I can't help but see it as some sort of good omen for my presentation today, the one that I have read over no less than twenty times before it even turns ten thirty. All there is to do now is wait for Harry and Cally to return for our final run-through. And wait. And wait some more. Eleven thirty passes without sight nor sound of them. Then eleven forty-five. And, when it hits eleven fifty-five, I know I have to head over to Gareth Grey's office without them. Harry may have rubbed off on me in some ways, but my punctuality and professionalism remain intact. Especially on a day like today.

With shaking legs, I head across the open-plan floor, the smiling faces of the staff who look up at me reminding me that today will be different to the other times I have sat in Gareth's grandiose office, only to leave feeling as small as a mouse. At least Harry and Cally have an excuse to be late. I, on the other hand, need to make a good impression on what may prove to be the most important meeting of my working life so far. I knock confidently on the slightly ajar door to his office, though I know he can already see me through the glass.

'Cath! Come in, come in.'

Okay, so not off to the *best* start.

'I actually prefer Kate,' I say as politely as I can through gritted teeth.

Gareth leans back in his imposing leather office chair; today, he's wearing a razor-sharp navy suit and open-collared shirt. I hate that I've worked here so long that I recognise it as Burberry. What I don't recognise is the kind smile on Gareth's face.

'Sorry, Kate. Please take a seat.' He gestures to the chair across from me. 'I've just heard from Georgina that their taxi is literally pulling up outside now.'

'I can come back in five minutes if you like?'

'No, no, no bother. I've wanted the opportunity to say how well you're all doing on this new initiative.'

The way he says 'new initiative' makes me sure he knows what we're up to about as well as he knows my actual name. Still, I can't help but feel encouraged by his words.

'You, Cally and Harry make a good team.'

I mentally edit out the 'C' word. Though, I guess in the spirit of embracing our differences, with which I hope to dazzle Gareth and Georgina over the next half-hour or so, she does add a certain something to our group. I proceed to fire up my laptop.

'Oh look, here they are now.'

I follow his gaze out of the glass walls of his office. My

heart leaps in my chest as I see Harry striding – I swear, as if in slow motion – towards us, Georgina and Cally walking a few steps behind him on either side, creating the perfect triangular formation. I'm not sure if he catches my eye or not, as he looks as beautifully brooding as the first time that I saw him advancing across the office. Except this time, it couldn't feel more different. This time I won't be fighting him, we'll be fighting for change together.

He walks into the office, smiling at Gareth and then pulling out a chair next to me. I turn towards him, giving him a huge grin, but he simply nods his head back at me. In the past, I would have thought this gesture cold. Now I know that underneath the frosty exterior, he's thawed and fragile and warm. Georgina and Cally do the same, Cally still with the large portfolio from the shoot tucked under her arm. Gareth smiles at her too, the full and unreserved smile of a family friend, before looking her all-white outfit up and down. She looks stunning, and maybe even fitter than ever. I know that convincing a man like Gareth that we should break the Poster mould, use models who don't have the so-called 'perfect' dimensions, will be an uphill battle. I bat away the thought that this world isn't designed for people like me and prepare to advocate for those who feel unwelcome here too.

As I listen to Gareth quiz the three of them about the shoot and Georgina provide him with a quick round-up on our microsite so far (and, I imagine, reminding him about why he's even in this meeting in the process), I try to catch Harry's eye. For once, he's not leaning on the back two legs of his chair or looking at his phone or glancing around the room; he's poised and present and ready. I know this matters to him too.

'And now these guys are going to present their big ideas for the branding of the site,' Georgina goes on. I know they say that behind every great man there's an even greater woman, but when it comes to Gareth and Georgina, it's really taking the mick.

'Let's hear them then.' He leans back in his chair, folding his arms before him. I take a deep breath, remembering all the reasons why it's Poster that needs to change, not us.

'From our research we feel that perhaps—'

'Well, as I was explaining to you yesterday—'

Cally's words cut across mine as she reaches to place her portfolio on the desk.

'Kate, if you start first, then we'll hear what Cally has to say,' Gareth orders.

'But—' Cally begins, and Gareth gives her a reassuring smile, as if to say *This will only take a second*. I swear I glimpse her wink in return. I glance at Harry, who seems to be getting more and more nervous by the second.

'From our research,' I begin again, trying to not let his anxiousness rub off on me. This is a good idea, a worthwhile idea, I know it is. 'We feel that perhaps the "exclusivity" of Poster feels a bit dated. While it once looked aspirational to have a certain standard of beauty, certain skin tones and dimensions to Poster's "woman", now it reads as a lack of inclusivity. Most shoppers are looking to brands where they can really *see* themselves represented in the clothing. We propose that we launch the microsite with our most inclusive campaign yet, one that looks like a snapshot of life in the city, make it a real celebration of diversity.'

I swing around my laptop to show the mood board Harry

and I have purred over: all different shapes, sizes, races and cultures captured in motion, their strength and attitude clear to see in their open smiles and fluid dance moves.

'Okay,' Gareth says slowly, his smile unwavering. I hope this is a good sign. 'I get it.'

He does? I can't help but turn to Harry and smile, but he's still looking forward.

'But . . .'

I knew there would be a 'but' and I'm prepared to fight it.

'The very essence of Poster is that not everyone can get it, not everyone can wear it.'

'I understand.' I nod, hoping my bared teeth look more like a grin. 'But if you look to brands like Abercrombie & Fitch, brands who had a very defined "person", who wanted to create an in-crowd, they've come under so much scrutiny in the media that they've had to move with the times too. It makes a lot of business sense to do so.'

Georgina is nodding and I feel like I've got her onside, that I may be impressing her like Amanda said I was. The thought of the pre-freeze promotion darts across my mind before I push it back out again. For once, this isn't about the promotion.

'I'm not suggesting we ban burqas. I'm not a monster,' Gareth says, putting a hand to his chest in defence; he doesn't look all that sincere about it.

'I believe they banned a *hijab*,' I interject.

'I just think our woman still needs to be aspirational.' Gareth ignores my correction completely. 'No-one is going to be spending the big bucks when just anyone can wear it.'

'That's why we're going to make sustainability a big part of our campaign,' I go on, teeing up Harry to interject with the points we discussed late into the evening. I look to him but he remains mute, clearly not wanting to interrupt me whilst I'm on a roll. I take another deep breath and continue. 'In addition to welcoming more women to really see themselves in our campaign, we want to invite them "behind the scenes", to show how our clothes are made, be fully transparent about our supply chain, so they can see what their hard-earned money is being spent on.'

As I speak, I'm reminded of Harry's heartfelt pitch to the Lavigne sisters in France, right before everything changed between us. And though he's inspired me in a thousand different ways, this time, I know the passion is all mine.

'Hazza, what do you think about this?' Gareth turns to my trusted male counterpart.

I turn to him too, studying the gorgeous contours of his face.

'I think . . . I think it could work,' he nods back at his boss.

Okay, so not quite the heartfelt spiel of Bordeaux-days gone by. What has happened to the data and statistics he had to back up his facts? Harry continues looking forward, his tanned skin seeming lighter than usual. I know better than to think he's hungover this time. He's either really flipping nervous of stepping out of line in front of Poster's CEO or something else has happened, something on the shoot? As I try to measure the pace of my breathing, my mind darts to our day at Sydney's studio, back when Harry received that first mysterious call: has something happened with his dad? I feel my insides fall at the thought.

'Okay.' Gareth nods at Harry's subdued response. 'Cally?'

The stone in my tummy tumbles even further.

'Well, as I was explaining to you yesterday,' she says, a

beaming smile almost breaking her face in two as she opens her portfolio on a page that is mostly filled with filtered images of herself. She looks from Gareth to Harry in such quick succession that I'm not entirely sure which one she is talking to. Harry glances down at his clenched hands. 'I think this microsite should reclaim the It-girl. In a time where many companies are scrambling to be as politically correct as possible . . .' She doesn't need to look in my direction for me to know this dig is meant for me. '. . . influencer culture remains dominant amongst our target demo; people buy what they are wearing not only because of the product but because they want to *be* like the person they are following. We need to put this influence at the heart of the site, to have one girl wearing the looks that we launch with. One girl everyone wants to be.'

'But it'll deter so many people who would otherwise buy clothes from our site,' I argue; I know because I'm one of them. I look towards Harry for back-up.

'We don't need to attract everyone, Kate. Just the *right* people,' Cally says.

'But that's discrimination.'

'It's target marketing.'

'I honestly believe that with a more empowering campaign we'll be able to attract a much wider pool of people,' I go on, my voice becoming shakier by the second. 'That doing something *unexpected* for Poster would make the right sort of noise. We could put a competition out on social media for people to *become* the models on our site themselves.'

'That would take a lot of time,' Gareth muses, leaning back in his chair in a way that I find infuriating, but if it means

240

he's still sitting on the fence, that he hasn't already decided in favour of Cally's idea, then I'll take it.

'The best things often do.'

I look to Harry as I say the words, remembering everything we've been through these last weeks that has led us here. He holds my eye and for a moment, everything in me stills.

'But we don't *have* time.' Gareth's voice breaks our contact in two. 'The Lavigne sisters called late last night to confirm that they want to take advertising space – and they're paying a good chunk of cash for it too. They loved every yarn you were spinning about this cultural moment, Hazza. About the centennial approach to alcohol.'

He wasn't *spinning yarns*. He believed every word he was saying. Didn't he?

'But they are worried that if we don't launch soon, someone else will be taking the same messaging and running with it.'

'But the cultural moment won't shift in weeks, will it?' I fight back lamely, feeling more and more maimed as I do. 'It'll take months, right? Years.'

Harry is simply staring back at me, mute. Say something, Harry. Anything will do.

Cally speaks up now. 'Apart from that people are already talking about what we're up to.'

Georgina manages to get a word in edgeways. 'How so?'

'Because of the questionnaire *Kate* sent out to our users,' Cally continues smugly as my stomach somersaults again. 'Fashion journalists and influencers are already speculating that we're going to launch a site for Gen Z, so if we want to surprise them, or be the first among our competitors to launch a new digital shop front, we need to do it soon.'

'Let them speculate,' Gareth says, and for a moment I think that he's defending me. 'It won't matter – we've agreed with the Lavignes to launch the site two weeks tomorrow.'

'That's too soon,' I say, feeling like I'm the only one making any sense. Harry isn't speaking at all, and it makes me want to hold him and hit him in equal measure.

'Not if Cally models the clothes herself,' Gareth says. 'She's already an It-girl.'

'I still think our real woman campaign is the way to go,' I say, hating how close to tears I sound. It's just for the first time in a long time, I really care about this. Really care about other women never having to feel the way I do now. Overlooked, isolated, alone.

'What do you think, Hazza?'

Everyone turns to him, and I will him to look at me, to have my back like he said he would. Silence hangs between us for seconds that feel like hours. Then he fixes his eyes on mine and for just a moment, everything slows down, everything stops.

'I think,' he begins, turning back to *Gazza*. 'I think we should go with Cally.'

Chapter Twenty-One

'Harry, you coordinate with Sydney to shoot the products on Cally . . .'

As Gareth continues to put the next steps of Cally's plan in motion, I don't know where to look or what to think. Or what the point of thinking here is at all. This place is never going to change. I can feel Harry shifting beside me and I want nothing more than to ask him what is going on, why, after encouraging me in this direction in the first place, he seems to be distancing himself from my plan now. Distancing himself from me?

The four of them continue to bounce around ideas, honing a plan that sounds like it was already underway long before today as my mind swells with confusion. Sure, it was unlikely that Gareth would go for my real woman campaign without a fight. I thought we might have to make a tweak here, a compromise there. But I didn't think it would be railroaded completely, that after finally feeling like I could make a difference here, I would find myself once again on the wrong side of the brick wall I've been hitting for over five years now.

My heart feels heavy with disappointment as the conversation draws to a close and Gareth stands to usher us out of his office. And though my head is filling with thoughts of all the women this campaign could have helped, another one threatens to be heard among them: Harry could have helped me too. But he just sat there. He did nothing. But I know him well enough now to know that there has to be a good explanation.

'Hazza? Can you hang back for a second?'

I also know, as Gareth beckons him over, that I'm going to have to wait for it.

Walking past colleague after colleague in the direction of my deserted desk, any friendliness I had felt before seems to have ended abruptly now that the rest of the tenth-floor staff have returned from this morning's shoot. I feel my ears burning and my cheeks blushing as I see one woman lean into her friend to whisper something, looking bang in my direction. And though it's unlikely that they care enough to be gossiping about me, I feel floored by a familiar insecurity that I do not belong here, that I probably never will.

By the time I get back to my desk, I half expect Harry to have followed me, to have realised that he's screwed up, to have his apology raring to go: a call from his mum during the shoot, impending bereavement causing a breakdown, stealing his headspace completely. Or even a call from the hospital with the worst news of all. But as I turn around to look back across the office, I see that Cally has joined him in Gareth's office, that they are chatting animatedly, that it looks as if they are laughing, that she's reaching a hand to his arm.

I force my stinging eyes away, willing myself not to cry. Opening up my laptop, I try to bury myself in the analysis work that once brought me so much joy, provided I was psychologically able to keep myself miles away from Poster, so long as I was able to stay in my lane and convince myself that my turn towards better things was only a short ride away.

cb@poster: Hey K. See below for my It-girl pitch.

I see Cally's message force its way onto my screen and look up to see that she's now sitting behind a hot desk only a stone's throw from Gareth's office, Harry pitching up beside her too. Why he isn't making the effort to bridge the gap between us now is beyond me. I read her message, my mood feeling lower with every scroll downwards. The pitch is everything I thought it would be, everything I hate about this place, about this industry. And she's not even bothered herself to flesh out the wider ethos of her influencer-based campaign for me first-hand; she's simply forwarded on an email she previously sent to Harry. I scroll to the bottom of her message and am just about to exit it, but then I see them: the three little dots that indicate that there's a longer thread below. I stall for a moment, not knowing whether to read on. I've read what she asked me to. And yet, something encourages me to scroll down.

The emails between Harry and Cally go back and forth, back and forth: about their ideas, their projects, their weekends. I try not to read them all, not wanting to know whether their relationship is anything like ours, but the thread between them just keeps going and going and going. Until it doesn't. Eventually, I hit the end: the first message, sent from Harry to Cally on her very first day, displayed on the screen in front of me. I brush a hand over my already tear-damp cheek and reread the words again, heart hammering in my chest.

245

ha@poster: Do you want to send over your initial thoughts on the microsite?

ha@poster: P.S. You look really nice today. What are you up to tonight?

ha@poster: P.P.S. It's Harry, btw.

I double-take, rereading the messages again, the words feeling impossibly familiar. In quick succession, I recheck the sender, the recipient, the date, the time. They were sent just moments after Harry sent the exact same messages to me. My pulse races as I remember again how random his messages felt, how at odds with how he'd treated me in person. Of course it felt random. He'd meant to message Cally instead.

I slam my laptop shut, not needing to read anymore. Especially not today. On my thirtieth birthday. On a day when I was finally starting to think things could be different. Forcing my laptop into my tote bag, I begin to make my way back across the tenth floor as quickly as my shaking legs can carry me. I need to leave this place, now.

'Kate? Kate, are you okay?' Blair is half-walking, half-running as she follows me towards the lifts. I am swallowing my tears, refusing to cry here more than once in a lifetime.

'I'm . . . I'm . . .'

Behind her, I can see Harry rising from his seat next to Cally and walking in our direction. And I really don't want to deal with this now, not today.

'I'm not feeling very well.' I press hard on the lift button.

'How did the presentation go?'

She narrows her eyes suspiciously, seamlessly drawing a line between my sorry expression and my even sorrier performance in today's meeting. She knows me well enough to know that falling flat on my face at work can knock me for six. And what she doesn't know, she's bound to find out in ten seconds when Harry arrives by our side.

'Not so well,' I say quickly.

'And you're surprised by that?'

'My idea was really good.'

'I thought you of all people would know not to put your hope in the Poster People.'

Something about the way she says this makes me sure she's not just talking about the presentation. She looks combative and I've got no more fight in me today. And, out of the corner of my eye, I can see that Harry is now just a few more steps away.

'Look, Blair, I need to go. I need to rest. I'll . . . I'll . . .'

'What about your birthday drinks later?'

'I'll . . . message you.'

The lift doors open and I immediately jump in, jamming my finger into the basement button with urgency. As the doors close, I can see him standing square on to the lift, looking directly at me, his expression heavy and concerned. Then, all I see is me. My own reflection staring back from the mirrored lift, sorry and ashamed and not belonging here once again. *One trip to Bordeaux and you think you're one of them. I thought you were smarter than that, Kate.* Wolf's words circle my mind as I watch the floor numbers descend. I don't know why, at thirty, I'm having to learn the same lessons over and over again.

As soon as the lift doors open, I see Harry standing there in the empty ground-floor lobby; his chest rises and falls visibly from having run down the stairs.

'Where are you going?' he asks quickly, worry etched in his brow. 'What's wrong?'

'I'm not feeling good.' I use the same lame excuse, trying my best to brush past him. He reaches for my hand, the gentleness of his touch making me flinch.

'Kate, please.' I shrug my arm so that his hand slips off it, his face suddenly stung.

'Oh, so you're acknowledging me now?' I sound pathetic, but then, I feel it too.

'Look, I know the presentation didn't go to plan today—'

'Didn't go to plan? You didn't do anything. Other than side with Cally.' I bite back the tears at the mention of her name, his messages to her still reeling in my mind. But this isn't about her; it's about us. If there was even an 'us' to begin with.

'I can explain.'

'Please do.' I fold my arms before me, my brain struggling to make sense of the last six weeks and how to square that with the fact that the flirtation between Harry and Cally has always been undeniable. I guess I've just chosen not to see it.

Harry looks genuinely scared. 'I was going to tell Cally about your idea, but then she told me about hers, and the deadline, and the fact Gareth was on board, and I thought—'

'You thought it was better?'

You thought she was better.

'No. I kept trying to find the right time to convince her—'

'You said you would handle it. It's been two days now.'

'I've been trying, but each time I tried to speak to her the timing didn't feel right—'

'I don't care how it *felt*.' I don't mean the volume in my voice

248

to rise. 'I never should have trusted you to speak to her in the first place. I should have handled it myself.'

Harry looks stunned now, struggling to hold my eye as he looks around the room. 'Trusted me? This is *our* microsite, Kate. You don't get to control everything.'

'Maybe not, but I thought you might at least have tried to warn me before the meeting.'

'I did, I sent a message. Did you not get it?'

'Nope.'

I look down at my phone, the birthday messages filling the screen that made me feel so loved this morning now just feeling like salt in the wound.

Harry reaches for his phone too, his face falling as he does.

'The signal . . . it didn't send . . . I . . .'

'Are you sure you meant to send it to me?'

'Yes. Who else would I—'

'Cally? I know that you meant to message her when you first messaged me.'

If he looked taken aback before, now he looks downright petrified. 'That was . . . I can explain . . . I . . .'

'You wanted Cally and I was just the next best thing?'

'It wasn't like that.'

'What was it like?'

I take a step forward and he retreats back. It might be a coincidence that he does this at the exact same time that the lift releases a smattering of people into the room, but all it does is highlight to me that so much of what's happened between us has been when we're alone, when no-one is around to judge him for being with me in the first place.

'Yes, I meant to message Cally, but then you messaged back

249

and we started chatting and I just couldn't seem to stop myself from replying. I really liked talking to you.'

'So, I was a good stand-in until Cally finally got back to you?'

'Not at all . . .' He takes a step towards me now. 'Kate, I really like you.'

The room is filling with more and more people, and I hate that Harry is looking to the lifts every time one opens to see who is streaming out. Is he waiting for her even now?

'Okay,' I say, as the lobby gets even busier. 'Prove it.'

He glances around the room; it feels like a thousand pairs of eyes are on us. And he's hesitating. He's just the same as he was five years ago, more interested in what other people think than in me.

'I shouldn't have to prove it, Kate. You should just know.'

'I know that all the facts are pointing in the same direction.'

'And what about how you feel?' He asks this latest question with eyes still darting to the latest colleague to walk in.

'That's irrelevant now.' I feel my defences shoot right up.

'Is that what you really think?' He looks gutted, but I know better than to believe him. His eyes look to the lifts again.

'I think that you care more about what people think of you than what you actually think yourself. That you always have, ever since the first time you tried to kiss me.'

'At that mixer? Years ago?' And now his eyes are back on me. '*You* tried to kiss me.'

'That's not true and you know it,' I snap back. 'You only want me when no-one else is around, because you think people expect you to be with someone like Cally.'

'I don't care what people think—'

'You bailed on our microsite idea because Gareth thought it was better.'

'No, I got *conflicted* because he started talking about the promotion and—'

'Conflicted?' I crinkle my nose at the word.

'It's what people feel when they don't see the world in black and white.'

'No, it's what people tell themselves when they don't have the balls to say what they really want. When every decision is made out of fear that they're a . . .'

'Fear that they're a what?' Harry demands as my sentence trails off.

'Nothing.'

'A *what*, Kate?'

'It doesn't matter.'

'Fear that they're a . . .'

He's holding my eye so intently that I know he's not going to relent until I admit what I was about to say. And I know it'll break him. But this thing between us is breaking me too.

'Disappointment.'

I don't need to say who to; we both know I'm talking about his dad. That I'm throwing things back in his face that he told me in confidence. But how am I supposed to know what parts of him were real and what parts he was just faking to get ahead?

'Nice,' Harry says, biting his lip and looking towards the door. 'Really nice.'

As soon as I've said the word, I regret it. I really, really regret it. But I also regret trusting him, letting down my guard, caring about the presentation, caring about him.

I can feel my eyes filling with hot, angry tears. But no, I won't let him make me feel like the bad guy for hurting him now when he's delivered a thousand cuts by omission. He begins to leave, but stalls as soon as he sees Cally striding confidently into the lobby.

'It's okay.' I force a sad, sarcastic smile. 'I'll leave you two to it.'

With every step I take away from Poster, from Harry, the anger subsides, leaving only sadness. This was meant to be my turning point, my fresh page. A new, confident decade, where I finally feel like I'm doing what I was born to do and spending time with the people who make me feel more and more myself. Not wasting time with people who didn't even want to talk to me in the first place.

I try to stop my tears from falling, to hold it together, to be strong, but as I see the shabby door into the flat in the distance, the tears come thick and they come fast, until I find that I'm sobbing like a small child, all snot and shoulder-shaking, on the doorstep. Vera appears from nowhere to witness my wallowing. I miss living with Lucy; I miss believing that my next big break is just around the corner. And I know that even though what me and Harry had might not have been real, I'm going to miss the technicoloured feeling of messaging and making out with him. Even getting mad at him.

Blair: How are you feeling? Still on for drinks?

I look down at the message, my heart dropping on seeing someone other than Harry's name on the screen. Whether or not he meant what he said about joining us for birthday drinks tonight, I know better than to think he's going to show up now.

Especially after what I said to him earlier. Now, all I want to do is hide in my room and wait until this terrible day is over.

Me: I'm still not feeling well.

Me: Think I caught a bug or something.

Me: Rain check?

Blair: You're hanging out with Harry, aren't you?

The tears fall onto my screen as I read the words. I can't believe she's accusing me of lying.

Me: No. I'm really ill.

Except that I totally am.

Blair: Okay then.

Blair: Rest up, friend.

Blair: And happy birthday x

Even though her text-tone softens, her words still leave a sting. I wipe away my tears and force my heavy limbs to open the apartment door and head inside. I'm not sure whether I'm surprised or not to see Wolf stretched out on the sofa, but his face falls when he sees me.

'Is something up?' he asks, pushing himself to sit up straight.

'What gave it away?'

I don't need a mirror to know this morning's mascara is now halfway down my face.

'It's your thirtieth birthday and you're here in this shithole?'
Despite my misery, I laugh.

'Come on,' he says, slapping the sofa cushion beside him, gesturing for me to sit down. I don't have the strength to object.

Soon he's getting to his feet, heading to the fridge and returning with two cold beers. I know by now that this is his answer to everything, but if it'll drown out the questions and regrets currently swimming in my mind, I'll take it.

'Misery loves company.' He lifts his can to 'cheers' mine.

'What do you have to be miserable about?'

'My agency dropped me,' he says, taking a swig.

'I'm so sorry,' I say, detecting the pain in his voice. 'That sucks.'

'Their loss. Your turn.'

'It's nothing.'

'Tell your face that.'

'Fine.' I take a massive sip of my beer before launching into the shitshow that is today. 'My presentation went terribly, I had a massive fight with my . . . colleague.' I break away and he raises an eyebrow; he must know I'm talking about Harry. 'Things with my friend Blair are as frosty as they've ever been, my parents are on the other side of the globe so they're sleeping through my thirtieth, oh, which I'm spending alone, and I'm turning another year older without getting any wiser and I'm still working for bloody Poster.'

'Wow,' Wolf says, his eyes scanning my sorry-looking expression. 'You win.'

We sit there in silence for a moment, both sipping our drinks, until my phone chimes, my push-notifications telling me that Poster has just posted an image on social media at the least opportune time. I swipe my screen to see a photo of Cally beaming out from the frame.

'But you're wrong about one thing,' he says, turning towards me now.

'What's that?'

'You're not spending your thirtieth alone. We're going out. Anywhere you want.'

'Really?' I look up from my phone.

'My treat.'

'But why?'

'Like I said, misery loves company. And people like us have to stick together.'

'People like us?'

'You know . . .' Wolf gazes down to Poster's account. 'People not like *them*.'

Chapter Twenty-Two

The lift doors open onto the tenth floor of Poster, and it takes all my strength to force my legs across the lobby and further into the office. Not only am I about to come face to face with Harry for the first time since our fight, but after a weekend of drowning my sorrows with Wolf, it's not just my heart but my entire body that feels bruised.

My eyes clock the back of his head and, as much as I try to tell myself that he doesn't matter, that he never did, the rapidly increasing beat of my heart begs to differ. I will myself to keep moving forward, to remind myself of all the things that felt so flipping clear before Harry went and made everything blurry. I'm using Poster in the way it uses us. I'm getting promoted to director and side-stepping into something better, something more. Something I was made for. And I'm not going to let him distract me again.

I hear his laugh boom out across the open-plan space as I make my way towards my own social Siberia. Where the sound of it once felt like winning, it now feels like chalk on a black-board. And I hate that out of the corner of my eye I can see that it is Cally who is responsible for it. Poster might be going with her It-girl campaign, might be making Harry think the pre-freeze promotion has his name on it, but I know as I pass them, head held as high as it's possible to hold it when you're five foot three, that I'm not going down without a fight.

Slamming my laptop down on my desk, I try to drown out the sound of the two of them flirting and get on with my work. I try to remember the countless reasons Wolf gave me this weekend to not trust this place or these people. And yet, I can still feel a small knot in my stomach squeezing tightly, making the disappointment deep within me impossible to ignore. I'm disappointed that they couldn't see my real woman campaign was worth fighting for. I'm disappointed that Harry isn't trying to fight for me either. But then, I did suggest he was a disappointment himself. And not just to me but to his dad. Or at least, that's how I know he has taken it. I guess we've always known where to hit each other where it hurts. I force my tired eyes towards my screen.

bhp@poster: Amanda wants to see us in the kitchen.

I read the email as soon as I receive it, cursing the small part of me that had thought it could be from Harry.

As I approach the small kitchen tucked away on the tenth floor ten minutes later, I try to shrug away my sadness. I suspect from Blair's email and the location that this meeting is just going to be for the basement staff, the very people I used to love working with before the office merger made everything so complicated. And yet, as I push the door open, to find Blair, Toby and Charlie perching on the edge of the kitchen counter, the devs team gathered around the table, and countless others standing, huddled into the small space, I feel a pang of disappointment that Harry isn't here.

'Can't believe you've graced us with your presence,' Charlie whispers as soon as I've wedged my way into an inch of standing space between them. His voice is cheeky but cutting. Evidently, they think I've been fraternising with the enemy. Little do they know that any fraternising is well and truly over.

'Thought you'd be too busy with your fancy new microsite,' he continues.

'Shut up, Charlie,' Blair hisses back at him, shooting a quick glance my way. I try to catch her eye, but as I do, she forces hers towards Amanda, leaving a sting as she does.

'Right, guys, quieten down, *Be quiet*,' Amanda shouts over the low hum of chatter. The room falls silent. 'It's been a couple months since we moved up here from the basement and I think it's fair to say we've all acclimatised to the dizzying heights of the tenth floor.'

A collective groan echoes around the small space. The fact we're hiding out in the only place where the upstairs staff fear to tread tells you just how unacclimatised we really are.

'The celebrity-led campaigns for the central site have been seeing good returns, and our new microsite aimed at zoomers will be launched a week on Saturday . . .'

Toby nudges me in the side. I feel like I might be sick: partly because Cally's It-girl campaign will only perpetuate everything we hate about this place, but also because the photoshoot for the site will take place towards the end of the week, which means the three of us will have to work together and Harry and I will have no place left to hide.

'And yet, sadly, our KPIs are still not recovering as we'd like, post-pandemic . . .'

As Amanda continues, my mind races faster. The one thing worse than still being here would be not having a job at all; if I once dreaded the thought of moving back to Yorkshire with my tail between my legs, now I don't even have that option; when my parents decided to live out of a suitcase, they thought I was settled here, sorted.

'So, the Senior Leadership Team has decided we should go through a consultation process to see where more cost-cutting can be done. They've decided to start with us.'

She brushes a piece of red hair out of her face – a tell-tale sign that she's nervous – as a silence falls across the room. Then, the objections come.

'Of course they bloody have!'

'This place would crumble without us.'

'Why not start with the deadweight upstairs?'

'They hardly have any *weight* between them.'

I listen on, trying to make sense of this. If I lose my job, I lose everything I've built here. And yet the upstairs staff are immune, their beauty protecting them from the fall?

'Now, I'm not saying anyone is going to lose their jobs,' Amanda goes on, clearly disgruntled about this too. 'Not if I can help it, but let's just say, the pressure's on.'

If there were any more pressure in this place, we'd all explode. Maybe then the Poster People would be happy. But no, I refuse to let them overlook and belittle us anymore. As we fold out of the kitchen and back to our battle stations, I know that this means war.

'Kate? Can we talk?' The steadiness of Blair's tone is almost scary. 'In private?'

Cally's giggle dances across the open-plan office and I can't help but look across at her, sitting way too close to Harry. She catches me looking and flashes me a smug smile.

'Sure,' I say, my heart in my throat. 'Where?'

'Where do you think?'

She doesn't wait for me to answer before she's leading us away from the chatter of the tenth-floor staff who are all 'too blessed to be stressed' and down towards the basement.

'You weren't unwell on Friday, were you?' she says accusingly, as soon as we're perched on the top of the stone steps to the old downstairs office.

I might not have been then, but I feel sick now. Someone passes us on the stairs, forcing us to sit a little closer, even though right now, we feel miles apart. The basement has been taken over by some sort of recipe delivery service. This place was our stomping ground, our safe space, for years. Now it feels like we're simply in the way.

'I didn't feel good,' I reply, choosing my words carefully.

'We all know you cancelled on us to hang out with him.'

'That's not true.'

'Isn't it?' She looks angrier still. 'Look, I know we're just colleagues, but—'

'Just colleagues?' My voice begins to tremble. 'How can you say that?'

'Well, for starters, you forgot about my birthday, and then

you bailed on us on yours. We had a surprise planned for you, you know? Toby had practised his magic and—'

'Blair,' I say, risking reaching for her hand.

'I thought that guy being up on tenth would make you hate it even more.'

'Me too.'

'You know how they've treated us, for years.'

'I thought he was different.'

'And?'

My eyes fill with tears. 'I promise I didn't bail on you for Harry. It's not even . . . he doesn't even . . .'

I bite back the words, hating that he hasn't even attempted to talk to me today.

'Whatever *thing* was going on between Harry and me . . . it's over. I found out last week that he's been messaging Cally.'

'They do seem pretty cosy.'

'And he only messaged me by accident.'

'Ouch.'

'And the presentation on Friday . . . it didn't go well. I don't think I'm getting promoted.'

'That sucks.' Blair states the obvious. 'And now we might be losing our jobs.'

'The one thing that sucks even more.' I nod as she softens before me, realising we're still on the same side. I don't need to ask her how her job hunt is going. The market is still reeling from the pandemic, and she's still killing time on the stone steps with me.

'But it's more than the presentation,' I go on. 'I genuinely started to care about what we were doing; felt I could make a difference here for once.'

261

'I learnt a long time ago that people don't make a difference at Poster. It's Poster that makes people think they need to be different.'

'Unless you're Cally.'

Blair bites her lip, like she's trying to stop herself from saying something.

'What?' I ask, wondering why my sentence isn't met with her wholehearted agreement. 'You think Cally hasn't benefitted from pretty-privilege her whole damn life?'

'I *know* she hasn't.'

'How can you possibly know that?'

She looks shifty suddenly, and not just because someone else is squeezing past her. She pulls her long black hair to hang over one side of her shoulders, studying her shoes.

'I'm not supposed to say . . .' She looks from her black toe-nails, peeking out of her sandals, up to my weary expression. 'But . . .' It's like after the last few days she knows I need something to remind me that our friendship is back on track, and nothing does this quite so well as our shared hatred for our employer. 'You know I used to work upstairs?'

'I still can't imagine it.'

'Well, I didn't dress like this back then,' she says, her face falling. Blair hardly ever talks about what went down up there.

'What did you wear?' I narrow my eyes, trying to imagine Blair in Barbie pink.

'That's not the point,' she deflects. 'I used to help Mark with the internship scheme, filter through the work experience applications and help email out the responses.'

Mark was one of the old managing directors here, the one Blair used to PA for. Apparently, he was a real piece of work.

Then again, I know that helping a man do the jobs he doesn't want to would be enough to get Blair's back up on a good day.

'Cally applied to do her secondary school work experience here but got rejected. And though every application was meant to be confidential . . .' Blair bites her lip, still not wanting to put a foot wrong after all this time. '. . . honestly, Kate, you wouldn't recognise her. I barely did when she started working here for real, but I swore her full name rang a bell.'

'How do you know what she looked like if she didn't get a placement?' I ask. 'And please don't tell me Poster used to make people attach a photograph of themselves to work here?'

'Wouldn't put it past them. But no, they asked for social media handles, websites, blogs that the candidate runs, just to make sure they were serious about working in fashion.'

'And Cally's two million followers didn't cut it?'

'Before CallyforniaDreamin . . .' Blair says slowly as she pulls her phone out of her back pocket and starts to type something into her search engine. 'There was Caroline Brown.'

It's then that she hands me her phone and I look down at the face of a teenager who looks nothing like the Cally who is currently sitting upstairs, laughing and joking with Harry. This girl is smiling at the camera, her teeth so crowded that it looks like she was born with too many for her mouth. Her hair is short and thin, her bare cheeks rosy and red, her skin pimpled and shiny and problematic in the same way mine was at that age. Her eyebrows are bushy – before fashion decided to celebrate this – and her nose is hooked. She's unfiltered and flawed but beautiful in her own way.

'This isn't Cally.' I hand the phone back to Blair.

'Look at the eyes.' She zooms in closer.

They are the same sparkly hue that captures so many people's attention today.

'I could have sworn I'd seen them somewhere before when she started here,' Blair goes on. 'They're so unique and then I recognised her name and put two and two together.'

I swipe down to another of the three photos uploaded on the old WordPress site, which was last updated more than six years ago. Although the angle from which the photo is taken makes it impossible to see the girl's whole body, her chest is so flat that it makes me sure that Cally's perky C-cups must be fake.

'Wow, she must have had—'

'Veneers, nose job, boob job, hair extensions . . .'

'So, she could pay to fit in? If that's not privilege, I don't know what is.'

'If that's not the *patriarchy*, I don't know what is.'

'Why hasn't she deleted this?' I ask, looking down at the dormant website.

'I don't know,' Blair says slowly, reclaiming her phone. 'Maybe she gradually stopped posting and then just forgot the website existed.'

'Or that Caroline Brown existed, full stop?' I say, stunned by the transformation.

'I have no idea. All I know is she was this girl before she became an It-girl.'

I watch as Blair flicks from the website to Cally's current account. Our It-girl that everyone will want to be. Our It-girl that it might just cost people everything to look like.

Chapter Twenty-Three

The feel of cool kisses on the tip of my nose stirs me awake and I open my eyes to see Vera's whiskers tickling my face. It takes me a moment to realise the date, then the time. It's the day of our shoot. And I'm going to be really late.

'I hate you,' I hiss to Wolf as I rush through the living room; the fact even he's up and making himself a big breakfast to soak up last night's alcohol tells you just how late I am.

'The wine didn't pour itself.'

'I never used to drink on a school night before I met you.'

'You're welcome,' he grins as I throw a sofa cushion across the room at him. 'Meh,' he shrugs. 'Softer than the pen refills.'

Though it would be easy to blame Wolf for our blow-outs of late, I know that hanging out with him has been a welcome release from the heightened tensions in the office as we've finalised the details for today's shoot. From the moment Blair told me about Caroline Brown, Cally has been everywhere. In every meeting room I enter, every café I try to escape to, she's there, looking more and more confident in her own skin. Except, now that I know what she used to look like, it doesn't feel like her skin at all. Harry has been alongside her too. And he hasn't said a word to me, his silence almost as infuriating as his words once were. Today marks a week and a day since the presentation, my discovery, our epic fall-out.

'Make good choices!' Wolf shouts as I rush out of the front door and I hate that this semi-ironic utterance taunts me all the way to Covent Garden, our location for today's shoot. Even more so that it's the first thing I think of as I enter Neal's Yard to see Harry standing there beside Cally as he styles her next look.

Cally narrows her eyes in my direction as soon as she sees me turn into the courtyard. 'I told you she would be here,' she says to Harry.

My forehead prickles with sweat and not just at the thought of the two of them talking about me. Despite the fact we've only just slipped into the month of May, the sun has decided to shine on today's shoot. The bright brick buildings, with their colour-pop painted windows, jar against my heavy mood, but I need to shrug off the hangover. The consultation period for the review of the basement jobs has been cemented and this may be my last chance to convince Gareth and Georgina that any promotion should be mine.

'I'm here.' I pin on my best fake smile as I walk across to join them.

'Wonderful,' Cally says, her voice dripping with sarcasm.

If Cally looked gorgeous from a distance, up close she is devastatingly beautiful; she's wearing the pair of tightly tailored caramel trousers and the oversized pink jumper that Harry paired with them, back when we were about to capture the items with Sydney. I know from the frosty meetings we've shared over the past week that the brief for today is natural, pared back: the girl anyone can relate to and want to be. I don't know whether to laugh or cry at the dream we're trying to sell.

'Not like you to be late,' he grunts, barely meeting my eye.

He speaks. He looks gorgeous, too, in camel chinos and an oversized white tee. I try to remind myself that he sold me a dream too, that none of what he was spinning was real.

'Learnt from the best,' I bite back.

'Didn't know I'd had such an impact on you?' He gives me a cocky smile and I clench my fists by my side.

'Only when it comes to timekeeping.'

'And style?'

'Style?'

'When I first met you, you wouldn't turn up in anything other than a suit, but now . . .'

He looks down at my Boner-chewed blue jeans and slightly discoloured white t-shirt, thrown on moments before rushing out of the door. The door he once kissed me against, a week after kissing me for the first time in Bordeaux. Back when I was naïve enough to think that the only barriers Cally's presence was putting between us were physical.

'Things change.' I look into his eyes as I will myself not to mistake his bullshit for banter.

He breaks away to look at Cally, who flashes her perfect veneers back at him.

'So, we were discussing your role today,' she goes on.

'Oh, were you?' I look between the two of them, feeling more and more left out.

'Can you get some behind-the-scenes shots for social?'

There's an inflection to the end of her sentence but I can tell this has already been decided.

'You can upload them directly to my account.'

Which one? I can't help but think of her old blog.

'It'll be great to get some BTS footage before Gaz arrives.'

She grins at the thought of him; it must be nice to know you're the favourite. Harry smiles across at her too; strike that, it must be nice to know that you're *everyone's* favourite.

'So, you're cool with that, yeah?'

Before I can object, she's thrusting her phone into my hand, the perfume wafting from her wrist enough to turn my tummy.

'Are you hungover?' Harry eyes me suspiciously. I hate how he can read me.

'No.' I swallow a yawn.

'I don't believe you.'

I want to tell him that I wish my lie-detector was as good as his.

'It was a networking event.'

'Who with?'

'What's it to you?'

He stares back at me and for a moment, it feels like it's just the two of us again, like the fashion circus around us and the cliques of colleagues just fade into the background. He squares his broad shoulders, the way he so often does, and I try to stand a little taller too.

'Make sure you capture the clothes . . .' He looks down to Cally's phone in my hands, refusing to answer my question; a power play to put me back in my place?

'No shit, Sherlock.'

'. . . from the right angles.'

'Meaning the angles that make Cally look even tinier than she already is?'

'Aw, thanks, babe.'

Somehow any shots fired at him seem to translate into compliments for Cally.

'Do you want to take some photos of the setting whilst we get the next look ready? Gareth wanted us to include our followers so that they feel a part of it all.'

Cally keeps saying *our* followers, but we all know she means hers. And, as she and Harry head off to style the next look and I make my way to the far side of the courtyard, I've never felt less a part of it all. I'm the spare piece the tenth floor have always made me feel.

After an excruciatingly long time, Harry and Cally emerge from one of the two local stores that we have been able to commandeer to use as a makeshift dressing room and break-room on either side of the courtyard. I watch as they make their way to the centre of it, sick to my stomach at the sight of him brushing a loose strand of hair out of her perfectly made-up face. I study Cally's sculptured figure, made even more enviable in the leather-look leggings I once told Harry were going out of fashion. But they *were*. Now that I'm posting them to her two million followers, perhaps the data will begin to tell a different story. My blood simmers. I've spent my life making decisions based on cold, hard facts because, in reality, I never truly believed I had the power to change anything, until Harry fooled me into believing I can. Fooled me into believing in him.

I look over Cally's phone at him, standing just outside of the real photographer's frame. He's looking her up and down as she twists and poses in time to the music that is being blasted over the courtyard. Then, he looks over at me. He smiles softly and for just a second, he looks like the man I thought I was starting to like, maybe even starting to love. Then he snaps his gaze away. I guess there's a thin line between love and hate.

'Yes, yes, yes. This is *precisely* what we need.'

I hear the unmistakable voice of Gareth Grey before I see him striding across Neal's Yard, his sharp dark suit acting like a shadow against the vibrancy of our selected location. Cally, now wearing a pair of blue denim boyfriend jeans with an off-the-shoulder cream blouse, stops her posing for what feels like the first time in three hours and I lower her phone. Recording social media stories of Cally isn't exactly what I'd hoped I'd be doing today, but I have to admit that the engagement our posting has received is out of this world and I really hope Gareth will credit me with the timing and the captions and the comments.

'Thought I'd check in to see how my favourite triple threat is doing,' he continues. Harry steps forward to join them, completing what I assume is the trifecta he's referring to, seeing as he keeps calling me Cath. Gareth reaches a hand to rest on Cally's shoulder for a moment, and she seems to soften into him comfortably: the tender actions that scream *not just my boss but firm family friend*. 'How many looks have we done?'

'All but two,' Harry says with a smug look at his watch. I know he has an agenda too.

'Excellent stuff.'

'Happy with the styling?'

I get the sense Harry is fishing for compliments just to make me angry now; I roll my eyes and he clearly notices, shaking his head at me in return.

'Cally looks stunning, as per usual,' Gareth coos and she beams back at him.

'Agreed,' Harry says, looking me dead in the eye. If he felt in any way remorseful for having led me on in private only to reject me in public – again – he clearly doesn't now. Now, I'm just an obstacle in the way of him getting the kind of promotion that can convince his dad that he's made good choices before it's too late. My heart lurches at the thought of what his family is going through, but I silently try to talk the feeling into place. People go through trauma every day. It's not an excuse to be a dick.

'Guys, you say the cutest things,' Cally coos, her feigned embarrassment not fooling me. 'You look pretty sharp today too,' she grins up at Gareth. Is she *flirting* with him? Like having Harry wrapped around her little finger isn't enough for her?

'I'm glad you suggested I get this one.' He pulls at the lapels of his jacket. And she's choosing his outfits for him now? Before I can linger on the thought, Gareth is turning to me.

'And how's the social media going?'

'Well, it's not my area of expertise,' I begin as our CEO looks back at me like he has absolutely zero idea what that is. 'That's data analytics,' I remind him, strongly. Well, as strongly as anyone with my hungover disposition can. 'But we're getting good traction.'

I flip the screen of Cally's phone around to show them the boomerangs and filtered minutes I've captured and posted from her account.

'*Cath*, wow, these images are amazing.'

If he calls me Cath one more time . . . My fists bunch up by my side and I swear it looks like Harry is about to crack a small, sadistic smile. What is wrong with him?

'Turns out it's not that hard to be creative when photo editing is involved.'

Harry bristles beside me, his lips pursing as I say the words. 'Or when your model is this naturally beautiful.'

He wipes the smile off my face. Naturally beautiful? I struggle not to say the words out loud.

'Yes, we certainly have our It-girl,' Gareth beams. 'The one that every young woman will aspire to dress like and be like.'

And become broke to look like? And diet to look like? And get surgery to look like? I hand the mobile back to her, but I know the comments of girls that appear as young as thirteen will stay with me: *Omg body goals. I need Botox asap. I'd die to look like this.*

'And I like the way you've shot her, Cath. Can you take some more stills like this? This behind-the-scenes unfiltered vibe.'

'The stories have a filter on.'

'Yes, but not a *real* one.' I think this means not one that people will notice. 'And can you upload them to the office's shared file by the end of play tonight? I'll get Georgina to send an office-wide alert out early next week. We want everyone to get excited about this. We need to let them know that *this* is the future of Poster.'

'You think my job is easy again?' Harry says frostily as soon as Cally and Gareth have headed inside to prepare the penultimate shoot. 'You've changed your tune.'

Says the man who has essentially ignored me all week.

'Stand and take photos of pretty women? Yeah, *news flash*, it's not that hard.'

His face looks furious, his hands automatically shooting to

272

his hips, and I'm not sure which is worse, his silence or his rage. Any playfulness to our back and forth before seems to be well and truly dead now.

'News flash . . .' He mocks my words back to me. 'That's not what I do.'

'After all this time, I don't think I understand what you do.'

'Kate Carter not understanding something – now, *that's* newsworthy.'

'What's that supposed to mean?'

'It means you're a know-it-all. Always have been.'

'Better than someone who bumbles through life not knowing what he's doing.'

He looks at me for the longest time, his cheeks pinkening in frustration. I hate how handsome he is, how he still has the power to make me go weak at the knees. 'If that's what you really think, why did you message me back in the first place?'

'You messaged me!'

'I know,' he replies. 'But you still messaged back.'

'It was a mistake.'

I'm not sure whether I mean his first, semi-flirtatious message to me or that I bothered to reply to it. Either way, I can tell I've finally hit his last nerve.

'I can't deal with this right now,' he says, slowly, quietly, like he's giving up, even though I didn't think he was holding on to this in the first place. Whatever this is.

'Deal with what?'

'With you, Kate.' He searches for his next words. 'You're impossible.'

I stare back at him: the man who once made me feel like anything was possible.

'I'm going to go and get Cally. We need to finish this.' He looks beyond me.

Yes, we do, I think silently, though I know he means the campaign shoot. I need to stop pretending that if Harry hadn't accidentally messaged me instead of Cally that the whirlwind of whatever I'm feeling now would never have happened.

As soon as he turns away from me to walk in the direction of the pop-up dressing room, it's like he takes my feist with him, leaving only the fragility of my true feelings in its place. A lump in my throat forms almost immediately, rising within me until I feel dangerously close to tears. I make a dash in the opposite direction, towards the breakout room bathroom, before anyone can see. The usual shop front is blissfully empty as I make my way past the central counter and to the corridor towards the back of the building, in search of the loos. Then, I stop still, silent, stunned by what I'm seeing before me.

Towards the end of the corridor, cast into shadow by the lack of windows bleeding light into the room, I can see the slight figure of Cally standing against the wall and a much taller, broader male figure pressed up against her, his hand on her thigh and his head in her neck. I watch, unable to look away, as she giggles coquettishly each time he goes in for another kiss, whispering his name over and over again. My insides squirm as he pulls away and she tenderly pulls him back into her.

Without thinking, I turn to rush out of the building and across the courtyard, which is still scattered with staff members and freelancers. And I keep walking. Walking out of Neal's Yard, out through the tourist-scattered scenes of Covent Garden. I keep walking and rushing and panting and pacing until I find myself on Waterloo Bridge, gazing out across the

Thames and trying to catch my breath. I look to the murky river, hiding whatever is below the surface, and try to slow my throbbing heart, my racing mind, because I really need to make sense of what I've just seen: Cally's svelte figure pushed against the powerful frame of Gareth Grey.

Chapter Twenty-Four

Harry: Surprised you left the shoot without saying anything.

Me: Surprised you've still got my number.

Harry: So, I guess you found out about Cally and bounced?

I stare down at my phone screen, the messages coming through sporadically as I make my way home, trying to lose myself in the depths of the Underground. I know I've left any semblance of my sanity at the shoot; around the time I saw Poster's CEO entwined with a woman more than two times younger than him, around the time I heard her giggling back at him, enjoying every compliment, kiss, and graze. I study Harry's latest message. So he knows too? Is that why he's decided to pick up his phone to me for the first time in days?

Me: About Gareth and Cally?

Harry: That he gave her the pre-freeze promotion, yeah?

Me: No, I . . .

Harry's next message appears before I can work out what I want to say next.

Harry: Turns out neither one of us were in the running after all.

Harry: I guess that makes us both losers, Carter.

There was once a time when Cally getting promoted over Harry would have surprised me, but now it all makes sense. Not even *Hazza* can compete with her when it comes to what I've just seen. As I look down at his latest message, the desire to write him one back, to apologise for what I insinuated about him being a disappointment to his dad, is almost overwhelming, to the point where I find I'm typing out the messages I really want to send:

Me: So, are we just going to pretend the last few weeks haven't happened?

But they did. And he's only messaging me because we've both been overlooked, because he needs someone to stroke his ego now. I delete the characters one by one and begin to write anew, this time sending a message to someone else completely.

Me: What are you up to tonight?

I click send and wait for his reply, unsure as to whether it'll even come.

★　　★　　★

As I wait behind a wooden table in Rosa's, scanning the passers-by for any sign of Wolf, I realise how long it's been since I've had a date. Not that that's what this is. All the same, I may have kissed Harry in France almost three weeks ago, made out with him all night at our apartment, kissed him again on the stairs to the basement the next day, but I've not sat down for dinner with someone of the opposite sex for ages. I've been too obsessed with climbing the ladder at work to care. Turns out my rung was broken.

Wolf walks into the restaurant and I notice a table of two girlfriends looking up from their noodles as he does, one of them leaning over the table to whisper something to the other that makes both giggle. I study his figure as it walks towards me, from his chunky Doc Martens and grey, ripped jeans, past his narrow hips and his tight black t-shirt and up to his long hair, which is tied up into a neat bun on the crown of his head. I guess when you take him away from the clutter of the apartment and his position sprawled across the sofa for so long that the cushions have moulded to hold his shape, he does look pretty hot.

'Sorry I'm late,' he mutters, wasting no time in reaching for one of the prawn crackers I've ordered to eat while I wait for him.

'Expected nothing less.' I grin sarcastically. We live ten minutes down the road.

'We'll take a bottle of white,' he demands of a passing waitress.

'I can't drink much,' I object quickly. 'I've still got some work to do this evening.'

I can't believe that after today, I now have to relive it all while selecting the most natural but filtered images of Cally to upload into Poster's shared files.

'So you can get a promotion at a workplace you don't even care about?'

'Unlikely. They've already chosen Cally over me.'

The story of my life of late.

'And so, remind me, why are we not drinking much tonight?'

'Well, when you put it like that . . .'

I know in my gut that this is a bad idea, that I should still try to keep my job, but all I need to do is upload some photos and right now I really want to forget what I've seen today.

Wolf tops up my glass and starts to tell me all about the latest conversation with his ex-agent and although I have a thousand things that I need to get off my chest today, listening to his problems is soothing me somehow, as is my wine. And the second glass too.

'And then she said, *It's not me, it's you.*'

He laughs fully, pouring himself a third glass of wine before flagging down a waitress to order us a second bottle.

'She actually said that?' I hold my hand over my glass, but he simply pushes it away.

'Like she was a lover breaking up with me.'

'How long has she been your agent?'

'About two years. So, I guess that makes her the longest relationship I've ever had.'

'I'm sorry for your loss.'

'I can promise you the loss was all *hers.*'

'How are you so *sure* of yourself?'

I marvel at the size of his ego, surrendering to another sip.

'I just know my worth,' he grins. 'You should know yours too.'

He leans in closer across the table, the young women who

have been checking him out eyeing him up again as they make their way out of the restaurant.

'If the vapid airheads of Poster can't see what's right in front of their eyes, then screw them.' He takes another defiant glug of his wine. 'You're perfect as you are.'

You're perfect as you are. Five words that every woman wants to hear. And, after today, they feel like balm to the bruises that Harry and Cally and Poster have left on my skin.

Somewhere between leaving Rosa's and staggering down Trafalgar Road on our way back to the apartment, Wolf reaches for my hand. My first instinct is to pull away, but the feel of his fingers lacing into mine steadies me somehow, reminding me that someone sees me and likes me precisely as I am. And so I let him hold on, trying my best to let my thoughts of Harry go.

'Are you really doing your work right now?' Wolf says, kicking off his shoes, as I slump down on our sofa to open my laptop before me. It takes me a moment to realise it's my vision that's blurry rather than the images of Cally from the shoot on my screen.

'I'm a woman of my word.'

Slurry words at that.

'So, this is Cally?' His eyes widen at her beauty, and I feel a bit jealous. Not that he finds her attractive, but that everybody does. 'With that following and that face, I can see why Poster would want to keep hold of her, promote her—'

'Oh, and she's sleeping with the CEO.' The words spill out of me before I can stop them.

'So, that's why she's getting promoted over you?'

'No, I'm not saying that; they might really like each other and—'

'You're too good, Kate.' He grins at me. 'And a little naïve.'

'I'm not naïve, I'm nice – or at least, I am to most people.'

Harry's furious face from earlier darts through my mind.

'From where I'm sitting,' Wolf continues. 'She sounds like a savvy young woman who will stop at nothing to get where she wants in life.'

There isn't an ounce of disdain in his voice; if anything, he sounds impressed.

'I'm not sure that's true,' I object slowly. In a world post-#MeToo it seems absurd to jump to conclusions about their dynamic, but I can't for the life of me get the sight of her smile, the sound of her infectious, flirtatious giggle, out of my mind. Maybe Wolf is right?

'I'm ambitious too,' I argue back, the thoughts in my head feeling so dense that they are becoming impossible to wade through. 'In a work-hard, don't-cut-corners kind of way.'

'And how's that working out for you?'

We both know the answer to this question.

'So, what? You're suggesting I make a move on Gareth Grey?'

'I'm not saying you should make a move on anyone.' He shakes his head quickly. 'But I am saying you should make moves in the direction you want to go. Don't wait for someone to give you permission if you want to make a change. It might never come.'

'You been ordering the fortune cookies again?' I joke, but he isn't laughing.

'I'm just saying you could be more of a go-getter.'

'That's easy for you to say. You work for yourself; you can't get fired.'

'Hello. No agent, over here. Plus, this Cally has a job to lose too. She still takes risks.'

'*This Cally* has an uncle who is friends with the CEO and enough money to revamp her entire identity – oh and *face* – to become the poster girl for Poster.'

'A revamped face? Like surgery?'

'Lots of it.'

'Show me.'

'No, I . . .' I regret mentioning the photos instantly, some sort of siren going off in the dark corners of my all too blurry brain. I promised Blair I wouldn't show anyone. Wolf is looking at me like a dog with a bone. But no, I can't. 'I promised I wouldn't.'

'There's that "too good" I was talking about.'

'I can't,' I object again.

'Chicken,' Wolf teases, not knowing that he's hitting a nerve as he does; isn't that what he said about my leaving Poster? That I was too chicken to do it? I know deep down that he's right. That among all my reasons to leave or stay at my job, there is one reason that trumps them all: what if I try to leave and I'm not good enough? What if I'm only good at my job amid the so-called 'vapid airheads of Poster', if I can't really make it in the 'real world'? What if I'm not enough? Or too much? Or bad at it? Or too good? As Wolf's eyes search me, the weight of these questions becomes too great and something snaps within me.

I don't want to be scared anymore; I want to take chances, just *do something*.

'Fine.' It might be his goading, or the fact my mind feels like it's swimming with wine, my laptop right in front of me, the photos of Caroline Brown just a quick click away. 'I'll show you, but you can't tell anyone else. You have to *swear*.'

'Housemate's honour.'

Wolf holds up three fingers in the scout salute as my own fingers type to reveal Caroline Brown's old blog, which stands in stark contrast to the photos from the shoot.

'Wow, that's erm . . . quite the transformation. I bet she'd hate for anyone to see it.' There's mischief in his eyes.

'Yes, she would and I'm not showing anyone.'

'I thought you wanted to make your real woman campaign happen?'

'These photos are *not* for the campaign,' I object.

'Bet they'd fit the brief though,' Wolf encourages me on.

I study the photos, hovering over them to momentarily add them into the relevant folder on the company's cloud so that I can study them side by side, knowing that I'll remove the Caroline Brown ones again in a minute. But for just a moment I allow my mind to dwell on the real woman campaign that briefly made sense of my time working for the Man. I know the images from today's shoot will be edited soon, photoshopped to within an inch of their sanity, bits of Cally that up until now she didn't think needed to change deleted and tweaked. The photos I took on my phone are real in comparison to what the final product will be. But they'll still make everyone who doesn't look like her feel lacking in comparison. I study the photos, suspended side by side, my vision getting blurrier by the second. This is the kind of campaign I would love to see. One that truly says, you are beautiful as you are, but if you want to change, we're going to be honest about it, transparent about it, to tell you of the cost.

Wolf makes his way back over to me, two beers in his hands, and I know I should stop drinking now, that I've consumed more than enough alcohol to help me forget all about today – enough to wipe out this evening too. I shake my head and he places the beers down on the coffee table before he gently lifts my laptop from me and onto the table too. I gaze back at him, struggling to focus on his strong frame before me as he reaches for my hand, pulling me to my feet.

The next thing I know, his hands are on my stomach, gently pushing me against the cold living-room wall behind me. His fingers reach their way up my top until I can feel the heat of his skin burning into my own. I breathe heavily, his face hovering inches from mine, my blurry brain struggling to make sense of the scene unfolding before me; it's like I'm barely in my body at all, my mind harping to a parallel world where it is Harry standing in front of me whispering that I'm *perfect as I am*. But he's not. Wolf inhales, his focused eyes darting from my distracted gaze to my slightly parted lips. It's like he's hunting to have me. And then I let him. I feel the hard pressure of his lips on mine, the rough touch of his searching hands, as I will him to erase these last few weeks.

Chapter Twenty-Five

I wake up and instantly wish I haven't. My head isn't banging, it's *screeching*. I take in my surroundings, the unfamiliar dark blue walls lulling me into a false sense of security that it's still the middle of the night. I almost believe the lie, everything in me wanting to go back to sleep and force my fragile frame into a reset, waking up in a world where I didn't drink all the Grigio in Greenwich last night. But then, I realise where I am, who I'm with. Wolf's bedroom. With Wolf's tattooed bare chest breathing heavily beside me.

'Shit!' I don't have the strength to think the word without saying it out loud.

He jolts awake at the sound of my voice.

'*Fuck*,' he mutters, and I really hope we *didn't*.

'Why are we . . .' I look to his naked torso lying next to me in his bed, down at my own body, bare but encased in his scratchy sheets. 'Did we . . . We didn't . . .'

'Have sex?' If he registers the horror on my face, it doesn't bother him in the slightest. 'No, we didn't. But I deserve a medal for saying no to you; you wanted it.'

He laughs, my mind trying and failing to register this fact. I can't imagine I did.

'I was so drunk I can't even remember walking home,' I say flatly, everything in me wanting to ask him why he feels he deserves to be rewarded for not taking advantage of someone who by that point probably couldn't remember their own name, never mind consent.

'Fun night, though.'

My stomach swims with wine and remorse. We may not have had sex, but in the blurry recesses of my mind, I am beginning to remember a kiss. For some reason, it feels like cheating. Which is ridiculous, given that Harry hasn't said a single nice word to me all week.

Wolf stretches his arms in the air before resting back down on his pillow, his heavy head now cradled in his own hands. I try to recall the events leading up to our drunken dinner: the It-girl photoshoot, Harry's harshness, Cally's promotion, her kiss with Gareth Grey. A groan escapes from my lips, lips that have so recently snogged my housemate, as I remember that despite it all, I know I'll be dragging my sorry body into the office today. That as bad as things are, I am not brave enough to be a bad girl, the one that bails.

'What time is it?' It takes all my strength to sit up.

'Ten twenty.'

'Twenty past *ten*?'

'The very same.' He yawns nonchalantly, nowhere better to be than here, as adrenalin pumps through my veins. Harry may have rubbed off on my stringent timekeeping of late, but that was before Amanda told us about the basement consultation, the fear of redundancy sweeping through the downstairs staff like wildfire. Now is not the time to be screwing up.

'Crap. I need to leave.'

I jolt out of bed and instantly wretch, a wave of sickness cascading through me.

'No, stay in bed with me.' He pushes back the covers where I've just been lying, stroking the space in the sheets that I've left vacant. 'Please?'

'I need to go to work.'

'Do you, though?' He snuggles further into the sheets.

'It's my job.'

'That you're terrified of losing.'

'Yes, because without it I'd be homeless.'

'You'll always have a space in my bed.'

It's tempting. Tempting to stop striving, to just be looked after by someone, even if it's someone who can barely look after themselves. But no, that's not how I was raised, not what I wanted for my life. I wanted to make something of myself. And though Poster may not see my value, and though Harry might not see it either, I am hardwired to try my best, to keep trying, full stop.

'I need to go.' I force the words, pushing down another urge to vomit.

'I don't get why you still care about a place that clearly doesn't care about you.'

'Because . . . because . . .' I don't know why I need to defend myself. 'I just *do*.'

I care about my basement colleagues; I care about my career. I still care about *him*.

'Well, in that case . . .' Wolf closes his eyes, not even bothering to finish his sentence.

As I drag myself towards Poster House, I find myself slowing as I pass the stairs to the basement office, longing for the days when I would walk through the heavy-duty door to welcoming smiles and the sound of Charlie's singsong chorus of 'Morning, Angels'. Yet I can barely look down the stone stairs, knowing the memory of Harry beckoning me back to meet him there, kissing me tenderly, giving me the most thoughtful of gifts, is still so very close to my surface. Then, a flash of red catches my eye.

'Amanda?' I ask, as her petite figure, perched on one of the steps, comes into focus.

She turns around, a deer caught in the headlights, a lit cigarette in her hands. 'My dirty little secret.'

'It's safe with me.'

I sit down on the step beside her, inhaling the second-hand smoke.

'I didn't know you still came down here,' I muse.

'Only for my elevenses.' She takes another long draw of her cigarette. 'I used to have croissants in the morning before I started working on tenth.'

'And here I was, thinking you were immune from their influence.'

'Toxicity is like burnt toast,' she says quietly. 'The stench will get everywhere.'

'Woah,' I say. 'What happened to perky, positive Amanda?'

I search her face for signs that she knows what I know. That our almost-sixty CEO is with our early-twenties Innovation Executive. That this may be the only reason he overlooked a campaign that could actually change things around here for one that thrust his young lover even further into the spotlight.

'She's still there.' Amanda pins a smile to her face. 'But when they start making cuts and purposefully come after my team first, there's no more Ms Nice Guy. Anyway, you should head in,' she says, taking another drag of her cigarette.

'You coming with?'

'Postponing my return as long as possible.'

'Great, I'll wait with you and—'

'Kate,' she says sternly, moving from mate to manager seamlessly. 'I might be avoiding my inbox today, but last time I checked, you have a microsite to launch.'

Walking reluctantly up the steps to the iconic entrance into the building, I know that the pre-merger days aren't the only ones I am pining for. More than that, I miss the brief moments when I'd felt foolish enough to believe that I could change this place from the inside out, that this microsite could matter. The fleeting moments where it felt like I could be valued for my ideas, for who I am. That a man like Harry could value me too. But, by the time I ascend to the tenth floor, the pit in my stomach reminds me that Amanda is right: this place is toxic from the inside out, packed with so many lies that I'm not sure what's true anymore. The lift doors open out onto the tenth-floor lobby, and I force my shaking legs to make their way out into the open-plan office. Any hopes of passing Harry and Cally as quickly as I can are dashed as soon as I turn the corner to see the two of them embracing in the corridor.

I stop still, studying the shape of them entwined together, the same way I had with Cally and Gareth only yesterday, my stomach sinking even further. But I double-take as Harry pulls away and I see that Cally's shoulders are shaking, her usually pristine makeup making ugly dark tracks down her cheeks. She's crying. She's crying really hard and somewhere within the mix of jealousy and anger inside of me, I feel a hint of empathy trying to lurch its way to the fore. He keeps one arm slung around her as she cries into the palms of her hands, pulled high to cover up her pretty face. Then he leans to whisper something into her ear and before I have time to move or hide or turn to look in the opposite direction, she's rushing past me so fast towards the exit that I have to jump out of her way. Harry remains in the corridor between me and the office.

With no other choice, I walk towards him, desperately trying to work out what I've just witnessed. Has she just told him the truth about her and Gareth? That their own message-crossed love affair has to come to an end? Harry makes no attempt to move. I'm not even sure he registers me approaching. He simply looks into the middle-distance in the direction where Cally has just disappeared. He looks gutted. And it makes me mad that he would care about her hurting heart more than my own.

'Excuse me, you're kind of in my way.'

My words come out sassier than I intend them to. They always do around him.

'And you hate that, don't you?'

He folds his arms before him. The arms that were just holding her.

'What do you mean?'

'Whenever anyone gets in your way.'

'I really don't understand you.'

'And I don't get you either.'

'No, like seriously, Harry.' Our bodies are so close, facing up to one another in the tiny space, that I can feel his breath on my skin. 'I don't understand what you're on about. Where is Cally going? Why is she crying?'

She got her promotion, her man; my pulse is racing, my mind blurrier still.

'As if you don't already know.'

'I can assure you, Harry, I really, *really* don't.'

He looks down at me like he doesn't even recognise me.

'Caroline Brown?'

The whole world feels like it's plummeting as Harry says the two words I never expected to fall from his mouth. The room spins, the heat of my hangover hitting new heights as the penny finally drops. I forgot to take her photos out of the shared folder last night.

'Everyone's seen them.'

'No, no, no, no.' I say the word over again, trying to put a lid back on what he's telling me. 'I didn't mean to . . . I . . . I was just messing around with the campaign and then . . .'

Then Wolf kissed me. And I'm not even sure I wanted him to. I don't know why, after his failure to reach out to me since our fight, I still really don't want to tell Harry about kissing Wolf.

'You forgot?' Harry fills the silence before I can. 'Doesn't sound like you.'

'If you think I'd share those photos on purpose then you don't know me at all.'

'I don't,' he confirms sadly. 'I don't know you at all. I thought you were different. That you weren't like the mean girls who work here, willing to screw others over to get their own way. It's why I liked you, or at least thought I did.'

'You thought you were messaging Cally.'

'For like a *second*. Bloody hell, Kate. You never let things go, do you?'

'Unlike you, who lets things go all too quickly.'

His expression softens for a second and I feel like he's about to say something about why he's not tried to get in touch, but then he hardens again; clearly thinking better of it.

'Well, I don't think I'll be letting this one go quickly. You've really hurt Cally.'

'What? Because I've accidentally shared something that's real?' I say weakly, furious that he's still on her side, more so that I'm still here in a place where people can't be themselves, furious at myself for getting wrapped up in a world that was never meant for me.

'It wasn't yours to share,' he argues back, voice rising a couple of notches.

'And I didn't mean to, but some people would kill to look like she does in her "before" photos. Is it not a bit vain to care so much about showing them to the world?'

'It's not vain to care about appearances,' he argues lamely, and I think of all the times he's looked past me to see whether anyone else is watching us.

'I almost forgot that you work on the tenth floor.' I shake my head; he's cared about how things *appear* with the best of them.

'I love how you basement people think you're so different from us.'

'We *are* different from you; we're kinder than you guys up here for a start.'

'You've just uploaded photos that you know Cally didn't want anyone to see.'

'I've told you, I didn't mean to. I—'

'Really? You've been furious ever since your real woman campaign got shot down.'

'Yes, because I was finally going to do something that matters here.'

'No, Kate. You thought you were finally going to *be someone* who matters here. You're so obsessed with "the mean girls" that you've not even realised that you've become one. You've just screwed over a young woman to get your way.'

'She's not as young as you think she is, Harry. She knows what she's doing.'

'What are you getting at, Kate?'

'Well, I know Cally is sleeping with Gareth, for a start. You may think she's young, in need of protection, but she seemed totally in control of herself yesterday. I saw the two of them together at the shoot. That's why they left early.'

'That's not what happened.'

The way he's looking down at me now, face set like he'd fight for Cally any day, when he doesn't seem to care that I'm hurting too – it's enough to crack my heart for good.

'I know it's hard to believe that your precious Cally would do something like that.' I know I sound sassy again, that Wolf's theories about Cally may be way off, but I can't seem to stop. 'I know what I saw. I've been grafting for my promotion for years and she just—'

'For someone who loves facts so much, you could do with checking some of yours.'

He looks unrecognisable, the dark circles around his usually flawless face only further highlighting how tired he is, how tired of this he is, how tired of me. His square jaw is tensed, his usually dark skin seemingly drained of all its colour.

'I know it must be hard to hear—'

'That the CEO of the company I work for molested a young woman? Yes, yes, it is.'

His words steal my breath and then give it back at double the rate.

'What?' The whisper bleeds out of me.

'You heard what I said.' He lowers his voice even further as someone passes me in the corridor, forcing me to take a step even closer to Harry; there are only inches between our heaving chests now. 'Backstage on the shoot, Gareth made a move on Cally. That's why she left.'

'But that's not . . .' I breathe, the corridor walls seeming to close in from both sides. 'That's not what I saw. Cally looked like she was reciprocating, enjoying it.'

'What would you have done differently?'

'Pushed him off? Screamed? Told everyone in the courtyard?'

'She was *terrified*. And what if she told everyone? Would they believe her?'

'Of course,' I say, my words losing force. 'Everyone knows he's a slimeball.'

'Yes, but he's a slimeball who runs this place. A slimeball who is paying them.'

I clutch both hands to my stomach now, sure I'm going to be sick. He looks at me, and I swear there are tears in his eyes. A stray tear escapes from my own.

'For a smart woman, you sometimes miss what's in front of your eyes.'

'I'm . . . I'm . . .'

I'm speechless. Of course, the power discrepancy between them crossed my mind for a second, but Cally has always *seemed* so powerful . . . even more so in that moment, giggling and laughing with him. Then Wolf got in my mind, and Harry got in my heart, and I just . . .

'I liked you, Kate. I really did like you, but now, after this . . .'

'If you liked me, how come you dropped things so suddenly after our fight? I know I said some things, but after the presentation, and the messages to Cally, and . . .'

Tears are falling down my cheeks freely now. I quickly wipe them away.

'Believe it or not, I've had other things on my mind. A big part of me want—' Harry is speaking in shards, landing on the most jagged note of all. 'My dad . . . My dad . . .'

He doesn't need to complete his sentence; the beaten expression on his face says it all.

'He got taken into hospital last weekend.'

'You never told me,' I whisper, this latest piece of information breaking me in two.

'You never thought to ask.'

Harry doesn't speak to me for the rest of the day, and I don't blame him. Cally doesn't return to the office, and I don't blame her either. Even as I rush back to my desk to delete Caroline Brown's photos from the company's shared files, I know the damage is already done, that there's no repairing this. I watch as clusters of colleagues gather around computer screens, analysing the before and after photos I've unknowingly shared with them, their hands thrust up to their mouths to hide sniggers and smiles and shock. Each squeal or giggle makes the broken pieces of my heart clang together even more. All this time I've been obsessed with not being 'Poster material' and yet I've acted precisely like the people I have been trying to distance myself from: selfish, underhanded, stereotyping too soon, refusing to accept that people can evolve and grow. Because deep down, buried in the basement, I know that I've always wanted to be upstairs. Still wanted to fit in with them, even if I didn't exactly *like* them. Turns out I'm a fraud too. No wonder I flipped the second I thought Harry's feelings weren't genuine. When you know you're faking it, you feel like everyone else is too.

As I make my way back to Greenwich, back towards the apartment I've never once felt at home in, I long for the days when I knew who I was. When I wasn't so obsessed with making something of myself before I hit thirty. I never should have shown Wolf Caroline Brown's photos. I promised Blair I wouldn't show anyone. A pang of panic surges through me as I realise that I haven't seen her all day. That she's probably seen the photos too. That she'll know I'm the one to blame.

Me: I didn't see you in the office today?

Blair: I went home early.

Me: Feeling okay?

Blair: I got my letter today. I'm at risk of redundancy.

I hate that for a second, I feel relieved, like maybe she hasn't seen that the photos were leaked. Then I register her words. They can't get rid of Blair.

Me: There's no way they'd want to lose you.

Blair: What? The one person that Cally can point to as the source of the photos?

Me: I'm so sorry. I never meant for anyone to see them.

Blair: I trusted you.

Me: I know, and I'm sorry. I'll make all this right, I swear.

Blair: And how do you plan to do that?

Me: I'll think of something.

Blair: No offence, Kate, but there's not enough data in the world to reverse this damage.

Chapter Twenty-Six

The tears are already streaming down my cheeks by the time I get home. And I don't know whether I'm disappointed or relieved to find the apartment empty and a note from Wolf on the kitchen counter: *Gone away for a few nights, W.* Either way, I'm not surprised. I don't know him all that well, but from what I've witnessed these past weeks, he isn't above leaving just when things start to get tough. Boner has naturally gone too, Vera also getting the memo. Somehow, Vera heading home to be with her real family – whoever they might be – makes me feel very far away from my own. I know from the brief interactions with my parents since my birthday that they're now camping in the outback of Australia, in a totally signal-free zone. Even so, I call them, just to hear their voices on the answerphone. It does nothing to quell the tears. If anything, it just makes me sob even harder.

I cry for Blair, at risk of redundancy and already too mixed up in the mess I've made. I cry for Harry, for the loss of whatever was blooming between us, but more so for the loss his family are facing now, holding on to hope that things might by some miracle get better again. And I cry for Cally, for the parts of her that thought she needed to change and the parts of her that men like Gareth Grey feel like they are entitled to own, to violate for their own gratification. As I sit on the sofa that I once kissed Harry on, before kissing goodbye to any chance of us seeing eye to eye again, I allow every tear I've held back to fall.

I've screwed up. I've really, really screwed up. And not just today, not just with Cally's photos. Choosing Poster over Do Good Data caused my whole life to unfold in jagged lines as I tried and failed to get back to where I'd meant to be by now. And yet, here I am, newly thirty and still in the same job. Still promotion-less, still directionless. Still single, unmarried, childless and hopeless. Even bloody cat-less. But if I thought rock-bottom was turning thirty whilst working for Poster, I was wrong. Turns out rock-bottom is caring so much about what you're not that you forget who you really are.

I reach for my phone, looking for a lifeline. Someone to call who'll tell me that everything will be okay. I flick through my contacts; they tell of bridges burnt or bridges too remote to rescue me. Instead, I find myself turning to social media and scrolling through images of married bliss and career highs until my eyes are growing as heavy as my heart, and before long, I slip into the blissfulness of feeling nothing at all.

The sound of my phone vibrating on the coffee table wakes me from my nap – though, thanks to the sunlight streaming through the open curtains, I soon realise that it wasn't a nap at all but an impossibly long sleep. The events of yesterday fill my mind like an unwelcome montage, the pit in my stomach reminding me the nightmare was real. Still, my phone demands attention. I reach for it, dreading what might await me next.

'Lucy?' I answer the call as soon as I see her name on the screen.

'*Hola, niña.*'

Just hearing the warmth in her voice makes my eyes well up. At least there's one person who is far enough away that I've not been able to royally mess up our relationship.

'Thanks for calling back.' I sigh so heavily I'm sure she can hear it in America.

'I'm calling you, you donut.'

She laughs fully as I realise that though I hovered my finger over her number countless times last night, I couldn't bring myself to actually dial her number.

'Oh, I just . . . Is everything okay?'

'Yeah, just got the urge to call you.'

'Well, that's good, because I really need to talk to you.'

'Must be fate.' She laughs again, and I can't help but think of Harry.

'Hmmm,' I reply, entirely unconvinced.

'I know you don't believe in anything that you can't back up with cold hard facts,' she goes on. 'But sometimes God or the universe or something just comes through for you.'

'Maybe,' I say with a sigh. 'Either way, I'm glad you're here.'

We both know that in reality she's eleven hours and over five thousand miles away. 'I'm glad I'm here too.'

'So, you did kiss the hairy-backed housemate?'

'That's what you got from everything I've just said?'

300

I laugh properly for the first time in ages. I've lost count of how long Lucy and I have been on our transatlantic call, but it's been long enough to fill her in on everything that's happened, from the microsite and the message mix-up to managing to mess everything up.

'No, that's where I'm *starting*.'

I settle into the sofa, soothed by the fact that she isn't going anywhere fast.

'It was a mistake,' I confirm. 'Not the biggest mistake I've made lately, but a mistake, nonetheless. But he doesn't have a hairy back and he's disappeared since things screwed up.'

'This is going to sound weird, but I think I know where he's gone.'

'How on *earth* would you know where he's gone?'

'How do you think?'

'Your parents?'

'It's tight-knit in the biz, *niña*.' She dons her usual fancy-pants voice to mock them.

'Tight-knit as it is, *darling* . . .' I'm surprised I even have the energy to mimic her tone. 'I'd be shocked if they know Wolf. He's not really in anything; his agent just dropped him.'

'They don't know his work, *doll face*. They know Wolfgang's parents.'

'Who the hell is Wolfgang?'

'Wolfgang is the son of the minted mutual friends of my parents and your landlord, they're all in Cannes together ahead of the festival, and I believe he's your hairy housemate.'

'No. That can't be right,' I begin. 'That's not my housemate. My housemate is a poor, out-of-work, anti-establishment actor with a chip on his shoulder.'

'From what my parents have said, he has a chip on his shoulder alright. Thought his privilege would buy him opportunities or something, but the world doesn't work like that.'

I struggle to get my head around what she's saying, around how I could have got Wolf so wrong. I'm struggling a bit with Lucy's sentence too; privilege does buy *some* opportunities.

'But if he's from such a wealthy family, why does he live here, with me?'

'The wealthy background thing can make you pretty unpopular with your peers.'

'Is this where I'm supposed to get my tiny violin out?' I ask, before I feel something shift between us, even at a five-thousand-mile distance.

'Sometimes being from a wealthy background also makes people think you had things handed to you on a plate, that you don't really deserve what you've worked for.'

I know we're not talking about Wolf anymore. I cannot afford to lose another friend, another relationship that matters to me, this week.

'I promise you that's not what I think. I know you got your job at Do Good because you're *good* at what you do. I'm just jealous I couldn't do the internship too.'

'It's okay.' Lucy softens, and I sigh. 'I'm a bit jealous of you too.'

'Jealous? Of me?' I get my second big laugh of the day.

'Yes, of you,' she confirms without skipping a beat. 'You may not have grown up rich in money, Kate, but you were rich in other ways.'

'What do you mean?'

'Well, your parents were always *there*. They may be travelling

302

now that you've left home, but they made damn sure they were there to scoop you up after school every day and give you the confidence you needed to even move to a city like London. The fact this Cally felt the need to change herself so dramatically at such an early age and had no-one there to stop her? That's so sad to me. Everyone needs to know they're enough as they are.'

'That's what I wanted to show people through my real woman campaign,' I agree softly, my heart still so heavy that I betrayed Blair's trust, that I hurt Cally too.

'And that's great,' she says slowly. 'But you have to start believing it yourself.'

'I know you're right . . . but I've been so scared of trying and failing and I've been saying I'm going to move on from Poster for so long that I barely even believe it myself. I'm the boy who cried wolf.'

'I think you mean the boy who cried *Wolfgang*.'

'I absolutely do not.'

'But seriously.' Her tone softens. 'I don't see you as the boy who cried wolf. I see you as a person who is fearsomely loyal to her friends, even if it means staying somewhere longer than you mean to.'

'But what if I'm just scared of moving on?'

'Then you wouldn't be the only one,' Lucy laughs. 'We could all be a bit less scared.'

'But I'm always talking about moving on and I never do.'

'I think it's great that you've always got one eye on the future, that despite everything, you never give up dreaming, but . . .' Her sentence softens, stalls, until only silence remains.

'Go on,' I urge her.

'I think you have to let go of your past.' She forces herself to say what she's thinking, what she may have been thinking for some time. 'There is no parallel you out there who was able to take the internship at Do Good, who is working there as a director now; there is only the you that you are now, who has made choices and needs to own them, to live them.'

'You're . . . You're right,' I say, streams of realisation washing over me. 'I've been telling myself that I screwed up back then so often that I've been scared of putting a foot wrong now and . . . well, I've ended up putting a thousand feet wrong in the process.'

'People make mistakes.'

'I know. I've made many.'

'You're not the only one though, Kate. Sounds like Blair and Cally have made mistakes too – not to mention Harry.'

'What mistakes has Harry made?' I swear I can almost hear Lucy smiling on the other end of the line before she replies.

'For starters, he never should have let you go.'

Even so, I know I need to find a way to own my mistakes and move on, move forwards, even if it means making more mistakes along the way. After years of holding on to 'should have's and 'would have's and 'ought to's, I know I need to accept that life is messy sometimes. That it can't be controlled and predicted and calculated. That sometimes you need to let yourself simply feel your way and see where the mess might take you. I'm not there yet. How could I be, after a lifetime of trying to do everything as logically as I know how? But I know I want to try. Even if I fail a thousand times.

'I know,' I whisper, and even though I don't feel like I deserve forgiveness, that I might not be able to make things right, I know I need to at least try to find a way forward, to continue to believe better things are ahead than the things we leave behind.

Chapter Twenty-Seven

I'm barely able to see the doorway over the towering bouquet of black lilies that I am holding in my hand. I know lilies are often used when people die, but I hope that's not what this is: the funeral of a friendship. Of all the things Lucy was right about yesterday, one rings particularly true: I've always been rich in relationships.

It had taken another hour or so to finally say goodbye to Lucy, each one of us promising to speak more often. Perhaps we will. Or maybe our lives will go on, busy and bursting at the seams, and it will never quite feel like the right time to ring. Even so, I know we will always be there for one another when it matters most. The best kinds of friendship are brimming with forgiveness. I take another deep breath and go to knock on the door.

'What are you *doing*?'

Suddenly Blair is in the open doorway looking back at me, one hand raised into a fist. I must look menacing. She, on the other hand, looks cute, her face fresh, her dressing-gown fluffy. I don't know who is more surprised.

'I, erm . . . I came to give you these.'

I thrust the flowers into her face; she looks embarrassed. For all the hours we've clocked up together in the office and at the pub after work, I've very rarely been to her house. And never this early in the morning.

'Great, well, erm . . . thanks?' She may be dressed like a cloud, but she's clearly still frosty. And understandably so.

'Can I come in?' My now flower-free hands clasp together to show her I'm not above pleading.

'My housemate is asleep.'

'Can I come in?' I repeat my question in a stage whisper. She doesn't crack a smile. 'Look, Blair. I'm really sorry. And I don't have any answers or solutions or game plans to make it better.' She stares me down and I inhale sharply. 'But I would rather sit with you and have you tell me everything I've done wrong than not be speaking to you at all.'

She studies me silently for the longest time and then lets out a deep exhale.

'Fine,' she says, throwing her free hand in the air. 'You have five minutes.'

Five minutes. I have five minutes to say sorry for screwing up in a thousand different ways. I follow Blair into her living room, surprised afresh that it isn't a dungeon of darkness but a really very tasteful-looking sage and cream number. I guess when you are only seeing one side of someone you can forget the depths underneath.

'Cute dressing-gown,' I grin as she pulls it further around herself before sitting down.

'Is this really how you want to spend your five minutes?'

'Oh, course not, no,' I go on quickly, perched on the edge

of the sofa to show I know I'm not really staying. 'Look, I'm so sorry that I showed those photos of Caroline Brown to anyone, that I was so careless with them.'

She listens on, her expression neutral, waiting to hear more of my explanation.

'The truth is, ever since the merger my head's been all over the place. I'd thought my identity was solid, but I think it had just stopped being challenged, never brushing up against something different, people who think differently to me too.'

I can't help but think of Harry. I wonder if Blair notices it too.

'I guess there's still a little girl inside me who's always wanted to be in the in-crowd, who thought it was finally happening, and it gave me the confidence to dream big again and then . . . Then as soon as those dreams were dashed, I was angry at myself for even letting myself dream about something other than leaving Poster in the first place.'

Blair doesn't say anything; she just glances at the clock behind her. Okay, three minutes. I have three minutes left.

'Then I found out that Harry meant to message Cally first, that she got the only promotion going this side of Christmas, and then . . . then I saw her kissing Gareth Grey and—'

'She was kissing Gareth Grey?' Blair's naturally beautiful face twists with emotion: disbelief, confusion, disgust.

'Yes, and I got it all wrong. I had my new housemate in my ear – not that it's his fault,' I backtrack quickly. I know I need to own this, to move on from this. 'But I just thought, why does she get everything, and I get nothing? And I was wrong. About everything. I was seeing in black and white and not really looking at what was truly going on.'

She bites her lip, like she's holding something back. Okay, one minute left.

'I'm sorry, Blair. I'm sorry for everything. For getting so distracted with Harry and being the kind of woman someone like him might want to be with, that I momentarily forgot what was more important than any of that. It's you, my friends, my family: the me I am when I'm not trying to be anything I'm not.'

She looks back at me, arms folded. Time's up. I smile sadly, getting to my feet.

'Wait,' she says, stopping me in my tracks, beckoning for me to sit back beside her. 'I'm . . . I . . .' She stutters, and I wait. 'I'm sorry too,' she softens. 'I never should have shown you those photos in the first place; it's part of the reason I reacted so strongly. I was angry at myself for breaking my word.'

'It's OK, I . . .'

'I guess I know a thing or two about losing yourself as well.'

'But you're so unapologetically you.' As I say the words, I realise they're not mine; they're what Harry once said to me.

'If by that you mean I won't be forced to wear this season's Poster then—'

'No, it's more than that,' I go on. 'You just own who you are. I'm over here trying to fit in with whatever crowd I'm surrounded by and hiding my Meatloaf fetish and—'

'I didn't know it was a *fetish*.' She cracks a coy smile for the first time since I arrived here.

'You know what I mean,' I grin back.

'I'm more than just one thing though,' she says. 'The Poster People just see me as a goth so I kind of play up to it just to make them angry, but I'm so much more than that.'

'I know you are,' I say softly. 'But maybe the Poster People are more than just that too. Ever since I've known you, you've seemed to hate them and—'

'Sometimes it's easier to hate than it is to love,' she says quietly.

'What do you mean?'

'You know that Amanda warned you against relationships in the office?' Blair goes on, and I watch as her knees start to chatter against one another under her gown.

'Yeah, she said something about having seen people held back in their careers by having relationships in the office . . .'

Blair looks at me, tears welling in her eyes. 'You know how I worked on tenth before getting moved to the basement?' She continues cautiously, like her words are treading a path she's not taken for a while.

'For Mark,' I nod. 'Before the tenth-floor staff were awful to you and HR shifted you to the basement?'

I'm attempting to bond over how awful they are again, but it doesn't feel right anymore. They may have stereotyped us, but we've put them in boxes too.

'That's . . . that's part of it.' She stalls for a second, silently contemplating whether she can trust me with whatever she has to say next. 'Mark and I . . . We . . . we had a relationship,' she goes on. 'It started slowly, just flirting and stuff, and I thought it was harmless because he was married so nothing was ever going to actually happen and then . . . well, things did happen and I tried to stop it, but there was this one time where he just wouldn't take no for an answer and . . .' Tears are falling from her eyes now, my own starting to swim with tears too. 'Obviously, I thought of reporting it, but then he warned me not to or he'd tell everyone it was me who came on to him and before I knew it there were rumours going around the office that I was easy or something ridiculous like that and so, yeah ... The bullying happened ... It just ... it just wasn't the whole story. Amanda knows I had a relationship on tenth, that it didn't end well. I think she was trying to protect us from the he-said-she-said in the workplace and—'

'Blair, I am so sorry.' I feel so awful for never looking for the real reason behind her hate for them. So awful for jumping to conclusions with Cally too.

'It was a long time ago,' she says, brushing a stray tear from her cheek.

'It still matters.' I risk reaching for her hand. 'The truth always matters.'

It's then that she pulls me into a massive bear hug; I hold on to her tightly.

'It was kind of my fault anyway. I was seeing a married man and—'

'No, it was not.' I pull away to look her in the eye. 'At least, not all of it. But I think I'm learning that regardless of who is to blame, you must find a way to forgive yourself.'

'Well, I forgive you.' She looks back at me, her hands still clutching my arms.

'Thank you,' I whisper. 'No more mistakes, I promise.'

'You can't promise that.' She shakes her head. 'No-one can.'

'I can promise that I'll try.'

'And I'll try to dial down the hate for the tenth floor too. After all, for a moment you and this Harry guy looked quite good together, so you never know.'

'Oh, I think I do.'

'What happened to not jumping to conclusions, looking under the surface of things?'

'Hmmm,' I reply, void of better arguments. 'But first I need to apologise to Cally.'

'No, *we* do. And when we do, we've got to be *nice*, Kate.'

'I never thought you'd be telling me to be nice to people from the tenth floor.'

'Turns out we have a lot more in common than I thought.'

Things are still far from sorted; if anything, Blair's latest revelation is making me think that they're even messier than I'd thought, but at least we're here now, holding on to one another in the midst of it all.

'So, you know you can hack into pretty much anything?'

'Yes,' Blair says, oh-so slowly.

'Can you find out Cally's home address?'

'There is no way I am giving you that.'

'Because of what happened with the photos?'

'Because it's *illegal*.'

'I know,' I groan; it was worth a shot. 'I just want to apologise and she's not replying to my emails and—'

'It's also unnecessary.'

'Unnecessary?'

'Everyone knows she spends her Sunday mornings in the Lazy Lounge.'

'Do they?' I ask, confused, until it dawns on me. 'Wait. *You* follow @CallyforniaDreamin?'

'What?' Blair pulls her gown around herself. 'She has some good interiors ideas!'

★   ★   ★

We walk to the nearest tube station as quickly as we can, slowing at the small florist that is set up outside it. Surely taking a bunch of blooms to say I've bloody screwed up can't hurt?

As we disappear underground in silence, Blair's words about me and Harry looking good together, about jumping to conclusions too soon, circle my mind. I didn't really give him a chance to explain his side of things before I was already going for the jugular. Maybe his dad is a bit disappointed in him – perhaps that's why it hit such a nerve – but I know now that so many of my own actions have been because I was more than a bit disappointed in myself. But I'm moving on now and Cally is still the next step on my redemption tour. That Blair is by my side encourages me that I'm not the only one who has ever made a mistake.

We take the Northern Line all the way down to Tooting Bec and run out onto the busy streets. There is absolutely zero guarantee that Cally will be in her usual haunt, especially after everything she's been through in the last forty-eight hours. And yet, for some reason, despite everything, I fancy our chances. I recognise this as a tiny bit of hope. But that doesn't stop my whole heart lurching as I see her there through the window, nursing her coffee.

'What are you doing here?' She looks stunned to see us approaching her.

Unlike Blair and me, she looks entirely made-up, her cheeks contoured to perfection. Her hair falls in loose curls down her back, and I recognise everything she's wearing from our site. And even though I'm the one standing, she's looking down at me and I feel that familiar sense of rivalry threatening to rise to my surface. I silently tell it to simmer the hell down.

'I came to apologise,' I say.

'I don't really want to talk to you.' She lowers her voice, looking around the hipster coffee shop setting we're in. I wonder how many people in this room follow her. How many people know who she is? I know I've not scratched the surface myself. I've not even tried.

'I know. I wouldn't want to talk to me either,' I say, Blair still close by my side. 'I just wanted to let you know that I'm genuinely really sorry. I never meant to hurt you. And these are for you.'

I gently place the sunflowers on the table, not giving her a chance to refuse them.

'I know they don't even begin to make up for what I've done, but for what it's worth, I think your photos are really beautiful – the ones from the shoot and the ones you didn't want anyone to see. Oh, and I think Gareth Grey is a complete and utter knob.'

Cally looks from us to the flowers and back again, biting her plump bottom lip.

She breaks our silence quietly. 'Sunflowers are my favourite.'

'I honestly didn't mean to share those photos; I shouldn't have even seen them.'

'That's my fault,' Blair chips in. 'And I'm really, truly sorry.'

'I've kind of been waiting for someone to find them.' She doesn't ask us to sit down across from her, but she does look at the empty seats at the table.

'I wondered why you didn't delete the blog?' She looks down at her coffee so sheepishly that I feel the need to add: 'You don't have to explain yourself to me, though.'

'I don't.' She holds my gaze forcefully, tears brimming in her eyes. 'But I want to.'

I smile softly, simply holding space and willing her to fill it.

'When I was younger, I desperately wanted to change what I looked like,' she continues. 'I wanted to fit in and stand out at the same time; it doesn't make sense.'

'It does,' I urge. 'It really does.'

'But I never wanted to *erase* myself,' she continues. 'After I had my surgeries, that blog was the last record of my old self, and it didn't feel right to delete it. Perhaps I wanted to hear, one day, that someone could love both versions of me, that I could love them both too.'

I don't know why out of the three of us, it's me who's started to cry. Cally remains entirely composed, as if she knows that she has nothing to hide anymore.

'I reckon if I'd had the permission and the money, I would have been tempted to change some things; I wanted to look like the people filling Poster's website too,' I admit.

'It was a massive boost to my confidence,' she nods. 'But I still struggle with my self-image sometimes; I hated the idea of taking my makeup off in front of you guys in France, that's the real reason I didn't want to share a room with either of you guys.'

I bite back my tears, remembering how she had acted then, how she had unknowingly pushed Harry and me closer together.

'No amount of surgery will make up for not loving yourself,' she adds.

'You should post about that,' I smile, wiping a runaway tear from my cheek.

'Maybe one day I will.'

'I'm so sorry for sharing them before you were ready.'

'And I'm sorry for shooting down your real woman

campaign. I've worked so hard to be an It-girl and I thought if just anyone could be a model, then there would be no space for me.' A nervousness darts across her features. 'And I'm sorry for not forwarding on your information for Bordeaux.' I *knew* she hadn't. 'I know it was wrong, but you were coming up with all of these ideas and impressing everyone and I wanted a chance to . . .'

'Why do women always feel like there's not enough space for us all?' I ask, breaking off her explanation gently. I meant what I'd said: she doesn't need to explain herself to me.

'Because men like Gareth Grey make sure there's not?' Blair adds somberly.

'It's funny really,' Cally continues. 'I spent so long wanting to be the kind of woman people would see, notice. And now, I'm beautiful in all the ways the world tells us we should be, and people still don't really *see* me. Now they just see hair and boobs and nice teeth.'

'They really are nice teeth,' I agree lamely.

'Thank you.' She lets out a sad little laugh.

'I'm sorry I didn't take the time to get to see you properly.'

'I'm sorry I didn't really give you an opportunity to.'

'Maybe when we get back to work, we can start again?' I ask.

'I'm going to be taking a bit of time off, not because of the photos, but because . . .'

She looks down at her coffee, tears escaping from her eyes now. Blair reaches out a hand towards her.

'I know,' I say softly. 'I saw what he did to you.'

'You saw?' Her head shoots up, her eyes widen.

'At the shoot.' I nod.

'Would you be willing to put that on the record? I know it

315

might have looked consensual, can be awkward to get involved career-wise and I know Poster hasn't got the best reputation for taking these kinds of allegations seriously and it's our word against his, but—'

I reach for her hand across the table too and holding it firm, look her dead in the eye, knowing that believing her, supporting her, is what I should have chosen to do from the start.

'Abso-bloody-lutely.'

She smiles back and for some reason, I find I'm standing up to drag my chair from its position opposite hers until we're sitting side by side, the way we always ought to have been.

'I know you're taking some time off, but you're still coming to the launch, right?'

'No, I don't think I can.' She shakes her head sadly.

'What if Harry and I create a kind of forcefield around you all night?' I stammer on the words; it feels like there's a forcefield between me and him.

'People will still be talking about the photos.'

'Let them talk,' I say, trying to install some fight into us both.

'Would you?' She raises an eyebrow. Blair does too.

She's right. I probably wouldn't have made it out of my bed by this point.

'What if I can promise you that people won't be talking about Caroline Brown at all?'

As soon as I've said the sentence, I feel Blair's own words rattling around my mind: *You can't promise that.* But I can also feel a plan beginning to formulate in my mind.

'Then maybe,' she says. 'But how on earth are you going to do that?'

'I think I have an idea.' An idea that may well just get me

316

fired before the company can make me redundant, but an idea nonetheless. 'But you're going to have to trust me.'

I have no right to ask her this. I'm not sure I trust myself. But then she smiles.

'Okay, Carter. You're on.'

Chapter Twenty-Eight

I look down at Harry's number on my phone for the thousandth time, willing myself to message him. Maybe after things with his dad get better, one way or another – my heart aches at the thought – I can explain that I never meant to hurt him, that my quick reactions were simply self-preservation on speed. Any hate I felt for him has frustratingly vanished. All I feel now is sadness that we ended what we had before it could even get going. Sadness, and a strange sense of peace. And I know that peace is partly to do with the fact that the apartment is still completely empty.

As I walk across the vacant living room, I gaze out of the window to the small ground-floor patio space outside. Thanks to Lucy, I know that the 'few nights' Wolf said he'd gone away for might in fact be another two or three *weeks*. I breathe deeply, looking up to the empty space around me. I really don't mind living alone; I think I might actually like it. Not that London cares about that. But perhaps I could live somewhere else, somewhere further north, somewhere cheaper. The only thing tying me here is my job. And, if I really go through with the idea I had when speaking to Cally, the one that has since turned from a spark into a full-blown strategy over the rest of the weekend, then holding on to my job seems as impossible as living alone in a city like London.

I stash my phone; if I tell Harry what I am about to do he will try to talk me out of it. Walking towards the door to begin another Monday-morning commute, I expect to be startled by the soft fur of Vera brushing through my legs. But that cat has been so noticeably absent since Wolf left that I wouldn't put it past him to have packed her a little pussy suitcase and taken her to Cannes with him. I'm not sure anything about that man would surprise me now. I guess I never really knew him. I'm not even sure I gave him the chance to know the real me either. But he's about to. Everybody is.

By the time I see Poster House coming into view, I'm anticipating the familiar feeling of fear, about to bubble up inside me. But it doesn't come. Instead, the strange sense of peace I felt in our all too quiet apartment seems to stick to me like a second skin. The microsite is set to launch at the end of this week, and I know it's going to make an impact on a younger demographic, like Poster always hoped it would. Whether a good or a bad impact remains to be seen. The nerves only slightly set in as I approach Georgina's office for the first meeting of the day. I know Cally is taking some time away this week, but I fully expect to come face to face with Harry for the first time since Friday. As I get closer to the side-office, though, I see only two figures through the glass: the svelte figure of Georgina sitting across from a flash of red hair that I know belongs to Amanda. I tense up, remembering that our team is at risk of redundancy; I can't imagine what this place would be like without Amanda. Then, as I get closer, I hear laughter and the warm hum of two women talking about everything and nothing all at the same time.

'Kate.' Georgina smiles up at me as soon as I appear in the doorway. I smile back before grinning at Amanda, a silent *Hey, she got the name right* passing between us. 'Take a seat.' Her slender arm indicates for me to pull out a chair beside my boss. 'I'm afraid Cally isn't very well at the moment and so won't be joining us.'

'I know.' I say the words with as much emphasis as I can. I want to tell them that I know the truth, about Blair too, about the toxicity of this whole place, but I know this is not my news to share. Still, I'm there when they need me, an ally to add my voice to theirs.

'And Harry . . .'

I inhale sharply, not wanting the emotion to show on my face.

'Harry is spending some time with his family over the next few days.'

I still don't know whether this means they are holding on or healing from the hit.

'Okay,' I say slowly. 'Does this mean we're pushing the launch back?'

I'm scared that if we do, I'll not have the fight to go through with my idea: the one that might just make Cally – and everyone else – feel like they can be themselves here.

'Nope.' Georgina smacks her lips together in an expression that I swear says, *I think this place is ridiculous too.* 'Gareth says it's now or never.'

Amanda makes no attempt to hide her disdain. I look

through the glass windows to the open-plan office behind. Where even is he?

'He's gone to confirm things with the Lavigne sisters himself.'

I must bristle visibly at the thought of Gareth hurting another young woman as Amanda reaches for my hand, giving it a squeeze and saying, 'We're on it.'

For a moment, I don't know whether she's read me properly, whether she knows what I now know about Gareth and Cally, about Blair and the many other toxic incidents which have scarred this place. Then she gives Georgina a sad little smile and though no-one has said anything, I just know we're all thinking the same thing.

'We're building a case with HR.' Georgina finally fills our silence.

'But HR are rubbish and just do whatever Gareth wants and—'

'An external HR company,' she confirms. 'And the police.'

'We don't want him to just get a slap on the wrist for this,' Amanda adds. 'So, we're making sure to build the case, the story, properly.'

'The story?'

'The media will be all over it,' she nods sadly.

'We want to share the news in a way that doesn't take the whole of Poster down with him. Believe it or not, there's still a lot of good, a lot of talent, in this place.'

I think of Blair, of Toby and Charlie, of Cally and Harry.

'And the bad?' Amanda raises her brows. 'We're going to smoke it the hell out.'

'But I'm afraid for now it has to be business as usual: we

can't raise suspicion, so the microsite launch has to go ahead, but please know, there's a new era of Poster coming.'

I nod. If I had a penny for every time that I'd heard that, I wouldn't need to worry about losing my job here at all. And yet, coming from these two powerhouses, I believe it.

'I'm going to help you with the launch,' Amanda says. 'Anything you need.'

'Well, I did have an idea to shake it up a bit.'

'Now's not the time for us to rock the boat,' Georgina says, and Amanda nods.

'Yes, but what if it's not us who rocks it? What if it's just *me*.'

'I love it,' Amanda says, as soon as I've finished telling her about my idea for the launch. She leans against the counter of the upstairs kitchen, as always looking entirely at ease wherever she is. 'But—'

'Why is there always a but?' I groan.

'Because until we are ready, Gareth Grey is still in charge around here.'

'I bet he won't even bother himself to come to the event.'

'He's gone all the way to France to bring the Lavigne sisters back on his private jet.'

'He has a private jet?'

'That's not the point—'

'And we flew to Bordeaux in coach?'

'Kate . . .' She says my name more seriously now. 'If you do this, he will fire you.'

'I know.'

'But if you do decide to go through with it,' she goes on, the beginnings of a smile turning up the corners of her perfectly painted lips. 'I'll be so proud of you.'

'What's this? Lovers' corner?' Charlie's voice breaks us from the moment and we look up to see him, Toby and Blair all standing there.

'Don't tell us you're at risk of redundancy too?' Toby looks genuinely concerned.

Gareth Grey won't even get a chance to make me redundant.

'Just dreaming.' Amanda shrugs.

'Nothing more dangerous than women who dream,' Charlie mutters, mocking the toxic masculinity that hums through this place from the top down.

'What would you say if I asked you to show me an embarrassingly real photo of yourself?' I ask. 'You know, something from your past you hoped no-one would see, a secret hobby or artist or something you're into that you worry people would mock you for?'

I wait for one of them to mention the Caroline Brown photos that they now know I'm responsible for leaking. They don't, though – because they all know how sorry I am about it.

'Are you working for MI6 now?' Charlie asks suspiciously.

'Are you trying to bribe me with my tea-towel collection?' Blair narrows her eyes.

'I'd say.' Toby beams back at me. 'How long have you got?'

It doesn't take long after chatting to the guys in the kitchen to get the entire basement staff on board, but that was always going to be the easy part. Not because they're more at ease with their warts and whimsies than the tenth-floor staff. Far

323

from it: most of them have been trying to keep the little titbits of knowledge they've just shared with me quiet for years. But because they trust me. The staff from the tenth floor, however, have been groomed to despise those from downstairs for as long as we've been taught to begrudge them. Perhaps some of the higher-ups here have always known that provided we're focused on fighting with each other, we aren't going to join forces and start fighting for change.

As I walk towards a collection of women I've spent the past few months actively trying to avoid, I can feel my heart picking up pace. And then, as one of them fixes their blazing green eyes on me, my breath catches in my throat too. I can't believe I didn't recognise her from my first mixer all those years ago. She's dyed her blonde hair jet black, but her face hasn't aged a bit; it's the one who wore that plunging red dress and urged Harry to some after-party, somewhere better than me.

I feel any confidence evaporating out of me as I morph once again into how they've always made me feel: insignificant, a nobody. But as they turn around to see me approaching, I remind myself that this is exactly why I am doing this. To make Caroline Brown and every girl who looks like her know they can be somebody, exactly as they are.

'Hey?' I don't mean my first word to sound like a question.

'Hey,' the one who was in the red dress says. Today, she's wearing a pair of oversized boyfriend jeans that make her look even smaller, with a black racer-back sleeveless sweater.

'Can I talk to you for a second?'

'I think that's what we're doing.' Another one of them eyes me suspiciously, this time a model-tall, model-thin woman who can't be older than nineteen.

'It's about the microsite that launches on Saturday.'

'The one that Harry Anderson is heading up?'

'He's not heading it—' I have to stop myself from fighting with him by proxy. 'Yes, that one. I wanted to run an idea past you.'

'Past us?' A third woman looks startled that I'm speaking to them; I push down the voices telling me that I shouldn't even be looking them in the eye. They're just people. Flawed and scarred and vulnerable too. And this new microsite idea will help show that.

'And you're sure we won't get fired?' the woman who was in the red dress, who has since introduced herself as Amber, asks.

'If there's even a hint that anyone is getting in trouble, blame it on me.'

'But won't Gareth and the management team know where you got the photos?'

'People get hacked every day.' I shrug, hoping I'm not coming across like a creep.

'Anyway, if everyone gets involved, it's safety in numbers, innit?' The extremely tall teenager, Josie-Anne, is beaming back at me.

'Why would you take the blame though?' The third woman, Teegan, looks unsure.

'Because this campaign matters to me. It always has.' Okay, well, that's not technically true. 'Well, as soon as I saw the potential in what this campaign could do.'

I can't help but smile at the impact Harry has had on me.

Even if we never exchange messages or share another real conversation, I know I'm glad that our paths collided again.

'I can see why Anderson likes you.' Amber eyes me from toe to top.

'Really?' I look surprised. 'You never gave off that impression.' I want to reclaim the words as soon as they've escaped from me.

'What do you mean?' Her smile wavers slightly.

'You won't remember this,' I begin slowly, hating myself for even going there. Of course she won't remember that stupid summer party. 'But back at my first summer mixer at the company, Harry and I kind of, I don't know . . .'

'Hit it off?' Eyebrow raised again. *Pissed each other off*, more like.

'Something like that.' I shrug. 'And you and your friends laughed about it and then one of you said something like "Told you he wouldn't do it". It doesn't matter now; it was a long time ago and everything, but . . .'

'I remember,' she says softly, slowly. 'I'm sorry I wasn't very nice to you. It's no excuse but I was only just feeling like I was finding my feet at Poster and sort of felt like any new girls were a bit of a threat. It was just insecurity, you know, and, well, I'm sorry.'

It never crossed my mind back then that a woman like her could feel insecure at all.

'And the "Told you he wouldn't" thing . . . was kissing me, like a bet or something?'

'No, not at all,' she says. 'My friend knew someone who knew him and said he was a nice guy but had zero game. We saw him making a move on you and thought he'd bottled it.'

I stand there with my mouth hanging open. Zero game? When for so long I'd thought he was just messing with me then, had been playing games with me ever since.

'Well, erm, thanks. I'm kind of glad you brought it up,' I say sheepishly.

'Technically, *you* brought it up. To be honest, I'd almost forgotten Anderson used to intern here. Anyway, count me in for the launch. Oh, and have you invited any celebrities?'

'To the event? I think some influencers are coming and—'

'No, I mean, to be a part of *your* idea for the launch?'

'Oh, no. I haven't. Should I?'

'I think if you got a celebrity on board, you might just get away with keeping your job. Hell, Gareth might even take credit for the whole damn thing himself.'

Time misbehaves in the final days before the microsite launch, moving at a snail's pace and a rate of knots at precisely the same time. The minutes draw into hours as I watch my personal email address for the photos I've been promised. And yet, despite people from the basement and the tenth floor vowing to send me their most unfiltered shots, for the first twenty-four hours my inbox is as empty as the apartment I return to. And when I reach out to every celebrity and influencer I can think of to join in with the launch plans, none of them wants to know, most of them wondering why I'm not emailing them from my work account.

At the same time, the hours speed by. Amanda and I check the technicalities and add the final touches to the event as Tuesday seamlessly blends into Wednesday and Wednesday fades away. When Cally messages me on the Thursday morning to ask whether she should still come to the launch, I send her a whole-hearted 'Yes!' that in that moment feels like a lie. But then Toby's photograph comes in. Then Blair's. And Charlie's. And before long, my inbox is flooding with unfiltered images of Amber and Teegan and Josie-Anne and countless other people from both offices. Well, from *our* office, seeing as we're now one and the same. To the point where I almost feel excited when I wake up on Friday. Getting ready and locking the apartment door behind me, I still don't know when or even whether to expect Wolf to be coming home (or when the landlord will start chasing me for his part of the rent). I stride onto our side street leading to the main road into Greenwich, only to stumble on something underfoot.

'Vera!'

I don't hesitate to scoop her up and she snuggles into my arms like a long-lost friend.

'Mira!' someone shouts in the distance, the repeated sound moving ever closer.

I look up to see a familiar face, one that I recognise from somewhere, before I realise it's not from real life but from screens and magazines. I never expected her to be here, in joggers and a sports bra, a famous singer-songwriter down some random side street.

'*You're* Rumour Reign.'

I wish I'd chosen something more insightful to say.

'And *you're* holding my cat.' She looks fuming about it.

'Vera is *your* cat?'

I'm not sure what's more surprising, that I'm standing in the street chatting to a celebrity, or that Vera has been leaving her famous owners to come and slum it with us.

'No, *Mira* is my cat.' The cat that still happens to be held in

328

my arms. 'Who the hell calls their cat Vera?' Rumour shakes her head.

'When I first moved here my housemate told me Vera likes to let herself in through my bedroom window and I sort of just got used to it.'

I nod towards the door I've just come out of, Vera – or Mira – still held in my hands. I gently put her down on the pavement, but she simply weaves through my legs, staying close.

'He must have heard us calling her name and got it wrong,' she muses, looking to the unassuming terrace two doors down. 'Hey, she clearly likes you.'

'You live there?' I look surprised. Sure, we only rent the ground floor and she probably owns the entire property out-right, but I never dreamed she'd be living close by.

'Yes, but please don't tell anyone. I can't be dealing with any of that celebrity crap.'

'But you're Rumour Reign.'

'Yes, so you've said.' She looks at me like I'm a crazy person who has been intentionally stealing her cat. 'I like to sing,' she shrugs. 'I want to do something significant with my life, but I can't stand all the fakeness that comes with it.'

'I want to do something that matters too,' I say as Vera meows beneath me.

'What is it you do?'

As I tell Rumour Reign about my job, the one I'm likely about to lose, I hate the small part of me that is wondering how the hell I'm going to explain this fateful bump-into to Harry. I know that if he speaks to me again, I'm going to have to admit that no number of statistics can make sense of the mundane moments that somehow start to shimmer with magic.

Chapter Twenty-Nine

Amanda: All set for later?

Amanda: You do know we can just go with Plan A.

Me: But Plan B is so much more fun.

★

Blair: How you feeling about the launch?

Me: Shit scared if I'm honest.

Blair: Stepping out of line is never easy.

Me: Nope.

Blair: Want me to say something cheesy about you being born to stand out?

Me: Not really.

Blair: In that case, I'll just see you there.

Me: See you there, friend.

Lucy: You live next to Rumour Reign?

Lucy: RUMOUR REIGN?!

Me: Well, next door but one.

Lucy: One rock star next to another.

Me: Thought Wolf was an actor?

Lucy: I was talking about you, you donut.

★

Me: You definitely coming tonight?

Cally: I don't know. I'm still embarrassed.

Me: I promise by the end of the night you won't be the only one.

It's surprising that I've been able to get ready between all the messages that have been lighting up my phone screen. I feel like it's my birthday again. Except, this time, I am not waiting for the higher-ups of Poster to give me permission to make a difference. This time, for the sake of Cally and Blair and every young woman out there who is feeling on the outside or clinging on to their place on the inside, I am going to speak up regardless. I look at my reflection in the mirror: ripped jeans and heels, my trusty black M&S suit jacket layered over a white t-shirt.

'I've not seen that jacket for a while.' I stop still on seeing Wolf letting himself into the apartment as I walk into the living room.

'I've not seen *you* in a while.'

He paces across the room to hug me; he feels a bit like a stranger to me now.

'How was your trip?'

'Oh, you know, bit of networking, putting feelers out for new roles.'

'I thought you were in Cannes for the festival with your parents?'

Wolf's jaw drops, his face burning bright red before draining of colour completely. 'How do you know that?' He looks horrified, apologetic, *embarrassed*.

'Turns out we have some mutual contacts in the industry. So much for all your anti-establishment, struggling actor part, eh?'

'I *am* a struggling actor.'

'You're choosing to be.'

'I want to make it on my own, unlike those losers at RADA who just used their connections to get where they needed to in life.'

'*Some* of those people might have connections, but that doesn't mean they don't work really hard, that they don't use those connections to help lift other people up.'

'You've changed your tune,' he grumbles.

'I actually feel like I'm just starting to remember it again.'

'Looks good on you.' He shrugs half-heartedly. 'Bit irritating, but still.'

'So, how come you didn't stay for the full film festival?' I ask, knowing that I need to leave or else risk having Wolf make me late again. Not that I can really blame him or anyone else for the goings-on of these last few weeks.

'What, and witness all the roles I should have got?'

'Take it from me, Wolfgang.' I lean on the back of the sofa, patting him on the shoulder as I do. He physically bristles at the sound of his full name. 'There is no alternative you out there who got those roles: there's only *this* you, the one who is struggling to find parts because he refuses to work the small ones, even though they could be his big break.'

'What are you trying to say?'

I thought I was saying it quite well actually, but then, I know what it's like to listen to someone and not hear what they're really saying.

'Life's too short not to take the opportunities that come your way, whether it's the small roles you get yourself or the big roles your parents get for you. Just do something good.'

'Now who's been ordering the fortune cookies?'

'Oh, and don't piss your parents off,' I say, making my way to the door. 'I may need them to cover the whole rent if I lose my job tonight.'

'Why would you lose your job tonight?' He looks across to me quizzically.

I don't have time to explain; I simply smile back at him. 'Welcome home, Wolf.'

Walking into The Ivy at Covent Garden feels nothing like arriving at the Boo Babes' brunch only seven weeks ago. For starters, I'm not eyeing up everyone in the room like they're my competition, disliking them before they find a reason to dislike me. Still, there is a natural divide between the once-basement staff and the originals from the tenth floor. Blair and co. are congregating on the left side of the restaurant, gathering around the long trestle tables laden with sharing platters and sliders. Amber, Josie-Anne, Teegan and the others are gravitating towards the 'Pimp Your Prosecco' stands and photo-op backdrop brandishing our new microsite name on the right. I can't help but smile at how *obvious* it all is: Poster Girl. I guess some things will take more than a couple of months to change.

I scan the decadently dressed room, mood-lit and humming with conversation. Cally is nowhere to be seen. I double-check my phone and by the time I look up, I can see Harry walking in my direction. My mind flashes to the last time I saw him: he was fuming at me, disappointed in me. And I've been so disappointed with him too; for not fanning the flicker of whatever we felt into flames. My pulse panics, but there is nowhere to hide. Instead, I fix my eyes on him as he approaches, my heart throbbing in my chest and the air seeming to grow thin. He looks handsome in black chinos, trademark turn-ups at the ankle and an ironed black t-shirt. His hair is pushed slightly to the left and I want nothing more than to run my hands through it. His jaw looks less clenched than last time I saw him; I want to take this as a good sign.

'Carter,' he says softly as soon as he's standing in front of me.

'Anderson,' I nod back, my eyes catching on the delicate freckle above his top lip. I want to say something like *Nice of you to make it*, but I know he's got a valid excuse for being scarce this last week. I also want to ask him all about his dad but bite back the words; after everything left unsaid between us, I don't really know where to begin.

'Nice of you to make it.' He steals my first line of questioning.

'Are you *joking*? I've been holding the fort all week whilst you have been—'

'Yes.' His grin sends his dimples deeper. 'I *am* joking.'

Even in the dim lighting, I'm sure he can see my cheeks blush a deeper shade of pink. I want to apologise to him for my part, to tell him about all the things I got wrong. But without saying a single word, it feels like the raging skies are calming between us. Sometimes, all you need is time.

'And thank you for holding the fort,' he goes on. 'You've clearly done a good job.'

'Thanks. Look, I'm sorry for what happened with Cally's photos and—'

'It's okay, I know you've spoken to her. She gave me a bit of context.'

'You've been chatting?' I try to sound unbothered, but I'm sure I fail. I wrack my brain for all the things Cally could have relayed to him, especially after what I did to her.

'Not like that.'

'It's okay. It's none of my business either way.'

He looks back at me, his gaze seeming to drift to my lips before fixing on my eyes. 'What if I want it to be?'

His question comes out so quietly I almost don't hear it over the background noise.

'Look, Kate, I'm sorry too. For not coming clean sooner about meaning to message Cally, for not owning whatever this thing is between us in the office, for fighting you more than fighting *for* you . . .'

The background music almost drowns out the words I've so longed to hear as the room grows more and more crowded. There is so much we need to talk about, so much I know I need to ask him, to tell him, but not here, not now.

'I think we have a lot to catch up on,' I whisper, his body

feeling like a magnet, the way it always has when we're not busy repelling one another.

'I know. I've wanted to message you so many times but—'

'But first . . .'

My words cut across his for the thousandth time and I watch as Harry comes to, scanning the room like he's only just remembering where we are. I want nothing more than to be somewhere else, alone, with him. But I've promised Cally I will make things up to her; I've promised myself I'll go through with this too. I half expect Harry to disappear back into the crowd, to pretend we don't really know one another that well, but he's still standing in front of me, so many things still left unsaid between us. At least, for now.

'How can I help?' he asks.

'I've got the presentation ready to go.' I pull my laptop out of my bag.

'The trusty tote strikes again.'

'You're just jealous. Can you press play when I say?'

'I think my crayoning hands can handle that.'

'But don't look ahead from the first slide,' I warn him.

'But—'

'Please.'

'What part of this dictatorship feels *interdepartmental* to you?'

'The part where you trust me?'

I force a big, hopeful smile to my face. After the mistakes we've both made this last week or so, I wouldn't be surprised if there wasn't any trust surviving between us.

'Okay, Carter.' But still, he smiles softly. 'You win.'

★   ★   ★

336

Harry: Are you sure this laptop is loaded on the right presentation?

Me: Yes.

Harry: But the first slide is surely wrong?

Me: Trust me.

I watch Harry type for the longest time, and then he must delete whatever it was he was going to send. I sip my latest glass of Lavigne red nervously, looking around the room for Cally. Inès catches my eye from across the restaurant; she's busy chatting to Barbie from @BarbieIsReal and I smile back as each of them raises a hand in my direction. I hope they are as proud to be associated with Poster, with *me*, after this launch presentation is through.

Harry: Gareth's saying we should get started?

Me: But Cally isn't here yet.

Harry: I'm not sure we can wait any longer.

Harry: Plus, I'm not sure she's going to want to see this.

Me: Play it.

Harry: Really?

Me: What have we got to lose?

You know, apart from our jobs. The lights lower and the noise dissipates as the projector at the back of the room illuminates the large screen that has been set up at the front of the restaurant. I scan the room, people from both sides mingling into the middle to get a better look but still subconsciously staying beside the colleagues they know the best. I breathe deeply, trying to remember every reason I wanted to break the rules here in the first place. And still, the good girl inside me, the one that has always wanted to conform, to do what is expected of her, is silently screeching for this whole evening to stop. I glance towards the entrance, the light from outside forcing its way into the room through the open door. I could just message Harry, tell him to pull the plug on the presentation, and then we could escape into the evening and finally say all the things to one another that we should have said in the first place. But then, I see her unassuming frame silhouetted in the doorway; Cally is here.

I brush past person after person until I'm there beside her, hooking my arm through hers and leading her further into the fray. I can feel her arm chattering against mine as I pray that this next part goes to plan. Together, we stand there in the middle of the crowd, looking up to the screen. Out of the corner of my eye, I can see that Gareth has managed to make his way to the front of the pack, a Lavigne sister on each arm, a pre-emptively smug smile on his face. I can't wait to wipe it off. I turn behind me to see Harry, bent over my laptop, his now sheet-white face highlighted by the screen. Then I gaze back to the presentation. There on the screen, projected for the entire room to see, is an image of fourteen-year-old Caroline Brown.

The room fills with chatter, some laughter, quietly at first but then louder and louder. I watch as Gareth's lips purse together, embarrassment scaring away his smugness. I feel Cally stiffen beside me, her scared face shooting to mine, her eyes filling with tears and silently screaming back at me: *But you promised.* I grab her arm before she can try to leave.

'There must be some sort of mistake.'

Gareth's imposing voice booms across the crowd at the same moment that Caroline Brown's photo fades to black and I hold my breath for what comes next. There in front of us, fading in slowly, are two photos of me, side by side. The first is one I begged my mum to burn, an image of me as an awkward fifteen-year-old, all greasy skin and puppy fat and a haircut that I don't know how she let me leave the house with. The second is a photo taken just days ago: me, makeup-free in a Meatloaf tour t-shirt, my Art Attack mouse mat suspended proudly in one hand. Cally looks to me, eyes wide, trying to stifle her smile. I look behind me to Harry and see that he's not even trying to hide his.

Gareth is straining to spy Harry at the back of the room, his hand slicing across his neck: he either wants him to pull the plug on the presentation or he's going to decapitate me once he finds out I'm responsible for this. But my image is fading into the next one quickly: this time, two photos of Blair, the first of her dressed head to toe in black, the second of her in her fluffy dressing-gown, tea-towel collection displayed oh-so-proudly in the background. This one gets a big laugh. I try to catch her eye, but she's too busy hooting loudly, Charlie and Toby beside her. Their photos fade in next: Toby with his aquascapes, Charlie as a young boy dressed in his sister's dancing tutu. The entire crowd is laughing now, so much so that Gareth's objections can barely be heard above them.

The images come thick and fast then: awkward teenage photos of Olive and Sebastian, embarrassing images of the rest of the devs team. I howl as the image of Amanda, fag in one hand and slice of pizza in the other, fills the screen, and then Cally descends into giggles as an old school photo of Georgina is displayed: not only has she got the world's most unfortunate bowl-cut I've ever seen, but she's somehow managed to button her cardigan up wrong so that it's gaping on all sides. She looks goofy and uncool and not at all like her, but as I find her frame in the crowd, I can see she's laughing along with the rest of us. Amber and Teegan and Josie-Anne's photos come next, a smorgasbord of Steps t-shirts and Baby-Spice-esque pigtails and proudly displayed stamp collections.

Gareth is storming through the troops now, fists clenched and looking for blood. He knows Harry is controlling the presentation and he's coming for him. Still, the crowd is gathering closer and closer to the screen, jostling and joking, so that it's almost impossible for him to get through.

A photo of Barbie is displayed next, a close-up of her twelve-year-old face filling the screen, her smile broad and beaming and crammed with train-track braces trying and failing to tame her unruly teeth. Photos from Angela, the buyer at Boohoo, and Chloe from *Grazia* come up next, images of them caught behind the scenes at fashion shows in awkward poses and with skirts accidentally tucked into their underwear. It's at this moment that Gareth barges past me, turning to Cally with pure hatred on his face: 'Did you know about this?' She shakes her head, her entire body shaking too. I grab her hand, standing there in solidarity.

'Oh my gosh, it's Rumour Reign.'

A voice from the crowd beckons Gareth's attention back to the screen. There, in front of us, is one of the country's favourite singer-songwriters, displayed as a young woman dressed in multicoloured overalls and playing the fife. It's a really ugly photo, and yet, the way it's causing a joyful laughter to bounce around the once-stuffy room makes it feel like the most beautiful image I've ever seen. I look back to Harry, whose face is a picture, and can't wait to tell him how I managed to wangle my hands onto this image.

Our gaze is pulled back to the screen again as the Caroline Brown image we started with is beamed out proudly once more. This time, Cally doesn't look scared about it. In fact, she smiles. Turns out when everyone isn't pretending to be perfect, we're more similar than we thought. She squeezes my arm tighter in hers as I wait for what comes next.

BECAUSE WE CAN BE MORE THAN JUST ONE THING.

The font pops over Caroline Brown's image as the room falls silent and still. All I can hear is my heart, pounding and pounding, terrified and proud. *More than just one thing.*

POSTER: REAL AND PROUD ...

The images fade so only the words remain; even Gareth's angry eyes are drawn to it. Then, we all watch as some of the words fade, until only 'real' and 'proud' remain. Finally, they merge together to read:

REALLY PROUD TO PRESENT ... POSTER GIRL.

The music cranks as the images from our microsite are displayed on the screen, Cally arching and twisting in different poses across Neal's Yard. Our beautiful It-girl. But a beautiful It-girl who refuses to be put in a box, who will inspire others to step out of it too.

Chapter Thirty

Cally throws her arms around me as soon as the lights go up; she has nothing left to hide.

'Thank you,' she whispers into my hair, the crowd of colleagues still surrounding us.

'No, thank *you*.' I pull away to smile back at her. 'I literally couldn't have done it without you. Any of it.'

'Cally!' A colleague grabs her from behind. 'That was *amazing*.'

'Great job,' another squeals as she's engulfed into a group of women who want to celebrate her now.

Cally attempts to continue our conversation amid the fawning. 'Sorry, Kate, I—'

'Go, enjoy it.' I beam back at her. This microsite is going to be a success; she's going to be a success. And somehow, today, it feels like there's enough to go around.

I walk towards the back of the room as quickly as my legs can carry me, wanting nothing more than to throw my arms around Harry, to celebrate what we've managed to make. But then, as I see him, I remember all the things left unsaid between us. And, as much as I wish we could ignore them, I know that not talking about the things that really matter is what has got us into this mess in the first place.

'Why didn't you tell me?' he asks as soon as I'm standing in front of him. His arms seem to lift beside him, as if he's subconsciously drawn towards me; I feel it too.

'I'm sorry, I . . .' I begin. He's right: despite everything, we were meant to be working together. But then, a grin spreads across his face, his dimples lighting up his pretty face.

'I have some great not-great shots of me,' he continues. 'And you know Colin the Lion would have *loved* to have made an appearance.'

I laugh, the loud chatter surrounding us making me feel like it's only the two of us in the room. Either that, or that these people have better things to talk about than us. 'I thought you'd try to stop me.'

'Because I like to object to everything you do?' He stares down to his feet.

'No.' I inhale sharply. 'Because I'm about five minutes away from being fired and I know you wouldn't want to see me – or anyone – punished for a presentation.'

'Well, I loved it,' he grins. 'I always loved your real woman campaign – I should have fought for it harder, but turns out you were right.'

'I was?'

'Just the mention of a promotion was enough to make me back out, because I guess I never really did feel like what I was doing was enough. I did feel like a disappointment . . .'

'I never should have said that; I didn't mean it.'

'Yes, you did.' He smiles sadly. 'I felt it too. But I finally

344

plucked up the courage to talk to my dad about it, about his expectations, my missing them . . .'

He breaks away, and I can't speak for the lump in my throat.

'Is he . . .?' I croak the only words I can manage.

'He's not better, no, but things *between us* are. And that's enough, for now.'

'I'm so sorry.'

'It's not your fault.'

'No, I'm sorry for everything,' I go on. 'For going in on you like I did for messaging Cally. I have spent so long protecting myself from people like you and then—'

'People like me?'

'I know, it's stupid.' I look around the room, at those from the upstairs office finally merging with those downstairs, no barriers left between us.

'It's not stupid. I've been trying to protect myself from people like you too. I didn't think I was "smart" enough for you.'

'And I didn't feel "cool" enough for you.'

'I guess that's why we've spent so much time trying to push each other away.'

'I thought we were enemies and then lovers and then,' I pause, studying his soft smile, the way his eyes are drifting to my lips. 'I didn't really know how to be your—'

'Friend?'

'Yeah.' I grin back at him.

'Maybe we should work on that?'

He's smiling back at me, and all I want to do is kiss him. I don't want to be *just friends*. I'm not sure he wants to be either. But I know that if we're going to have any sort of relationship that is built to last, we're going to have to be friends too; that in between the high moments and the low moments, the black and the white of life, we're going to need a friendship that sustains us through all those grey days.

'I'd like that,' I say, and the fact that he reaches for my hand, twisting his fingers through mine, gives me hope that this friendship could be so much more. And the way he clings on to me even tighter as Gareth approaches us makes me know it for sure.

'What the hell was that?' Poster's CEO thrusts his way into our conversation.

'Our presentation?' I play the fool.

'Of course your fucking presentation.' He spits the words.

Harry holds me tighter. 'We wanted to blend the It-girl and the real woman ideas,' he tells Gareth.

'Without running it past me? I was completely blindsided back there.'

'We thought you wanted us to work together?' I ask innocently.

'I wanted you to work for *me*.' Gareth looks down at Harry's hand in mine, fuming. 'Thanks to you, we almost lost the Lavigne investment.'

Neither one of us apologises.

'And you embarrassed our It-girl before we could even launch her on the world.'

'I'm not embarrassed.'

I whip around to see that Cally has returned to my side; she's looking to Gareth with confidence in her eyes. She knows what the future of Poster is going to look like, and there is no space left in it for entitled men like him.

'And this microsite isn't launching me into the world,' she continues. 'If I remember correctly, I had two million followers before you even asked me to work at Poster.'

Gareth stands there silently simmering. All we can do is wait for him to blow.

'Who did this?' he demands.

'We did,' Cally says.

'Me too.' Blair has come across to join us now, standing side by side with Cally. Two women who have been blamed and blackmailed by the men of Poster for far too long.

I look from Cally and Blair, beaming back at me, to Harry's hand held firmly in mine. Maybe this could be the moment where we all take the fall together, where we call Gareth's bluff and see if he's brave enough to fire so many of us in one fell swoop. But this isn't a movie, this is real life. And I vowed I'd take the blame, be a woman of my word.

'Guys,' I say, taking a step closer to Gareth but looking back to Harry and Cally, my teammates – my mates, full stop. 'Let me take the credit for something for once.'

Gareth looks me up and down with disgust. I don't even care.

'It was me.'

'Well, bravo, Cath.' He grins sarcastically. 'You're fired.'

I look around the busy room, at the aftermath of the beautiful truth bomb I've managed to detonate tonight, the effects of which can be seen in Amber laughing with Toby, Barbie chatting with Charlie, and the expanding group of friends surrounding me now. The It-girl campaign will be filling up newsfeeds the world over this weekend, our real images remaining safely behind closed doors, for now. Gareth is still calling the shots, for now. And for now, lighting the fuse that might one day turn into fireworks feels like enough.

I gaze back at Gareth, not scared of him anymore; not scared of who I really am.

'It's Kate,' I say for the thousandth time, before turning to leave him and Poster behind. I don't need to glance back to know that Blair is following in my wake, that Toby and Charlie will soon come looking for us too. To know that Cally is leaving the launch party with her head held high. That Harry is tracing my footsteps, having my back. That I may have just lost my job, that I may have to leave London too, but that I haven't lost everything. That I've found a strength in numbers, in vulnerability. A power in our differences that has always been there, that we were just too stubborn to see. Until now.

Epilogue

Six Months Later

I slow at the decadent doorway into Poster House for the countless time, looking up towards the tenth floor as it towers over me. I am surprised to find I'm smiling as I make my way across the once-intimidating ground-floor lobby, even more so that the previously automatic draw towards the basement hasn't even crossed my mind until now.

'Poster, right?' a guy in the lift presumes when I step inside, pressing the button for the tenth floor on my behalf. I'm not sure why what I'm wearing today – an old band shirt tucked into high-waisted, tailored trousers – identifies me as part of the team, but as the lift ascends, I can't help but hope that the perceptions around Poster are finally changing. I know the vibe in the office certainly is.

Amber is the first person I see as I walk across the upstairs lobby; she lifts her hand to wave at me as Josie-Anne does the same. Blair is sitting in the same spot she took on the first day of our office merger, but she barely notices me approaching as she laughs at something the woman next to her is showing her on the screen. It's the same person that used to drive Blair crazy by flirting with the guy on the other side of her, who I notice is now nowhere to be seen. I wonder if they ever eventually got together. Maybe he's moved on to a new job? Perhaps he'll be back in another five years to pick up their flirtation all over again.

'What time do you call this?' she grins as soon as I'm by her side.

'Fashionably late?' I ask, hopefully; I had to make a detour for a decent coffee.

'Amanda's waiting for you in Gareth's office.'

'Are we still calling it that?' I kiss my teeth at the thought.

'Until they've found a suitable replacement and someone makes it their own.'

The news about Gareth Grey broke just a couple of weeks ago and it's been chaos ever since, but I can tell from the energised faces and conversations of the colleagues I pass that it's chaos in the best way; that although everything is up in the air right now, it feels a lot more like confetti than shrapnel. As I walk ever closer to Gareth's corner office, to see Amanda sitting behind his big, masculine-looking desk, I can't help but think she looks good there, like she belongs; only time will tell if the management team risks a woman on top.

'Kate!' she beams as soon as I give a courtesy knock on the frame of the open door.

'This place suits you,' I say, as she leans back in her chair, accentuating my point. 'Reckon you could handle the role of CEO at Poster one day?'

'If Georgina doesn't beat me to it.'

'May the best woman win.'

Amanda shines back at me; we both know either of them would make a fantastic CEO, that they could compete with one another in a way that means everybody wins. We also know there's every chance the company directors could hire another old, stale male, but it would have to be a good one, a kind one otherwise I'm not sure they'd last long, now that the staff are finally looking out for one another.

I turn to see Cally standing in the doorway to the office. Her face is a bit fresher than it was when she first started working here, her posture more relaxed, but her hair is still impeccably, impossibly bouncy. Some things never change.

'If it isn't our favourite freelancer,' she says.

'Hey! She's not freelancing for us yet,' Amanda says.

'Well, she's *my* favourite freelancer then.'

After Gareth fired me for my performance at the microsite launch, Amanda and Georgina both tried to fight for my role. But it was too late. Gareth was still in charge. Thank God that I had a couple more weeks left with Wolf and Boner and their impossibly cheap rent – and that @CallyforniaDreamin could hire me as a freelancer to work on her own real woman campaign whilst I figured out my next steps. And now, though returning to Poster House feels like some sort of homecoming, I know there's no going back. I like freelance life, doing bits for Do Good, things for Cally. But maybe I could enjoy picking up little bits of work for Poster on the side, too.

'Thanks, Cal.' I grin back at her as she takes a seat in front of Gareth's old desk. I know working here, with him, has been hard, but I also know she's had no end of good people around her, championing her until the truth came out. Not to mention that I have it on good authority that she's just one good campaign away from being promoted to Innovation Director. I'm still not entirely sure that's a job, but if anyone can do it, it's her.

'Sorry I'm late.'

My heart skips a beat as Harry walks into the office, hair ruffled and smile broad. He pulls out a seat beside Cally as I try to regulate my unruly heartbeat. This is *too* weird.

'Great, now that we're all here, let's talk Phase Two of the microsite,' Amanda says as I take a seat on the other side of Cally. 'Everybody ready?'

'Not quite,' he says, and I have no idea why my heart still races around him. 'Can I stop "acting professional" and kiss my girlfriend hello, please?'

My face warms as he leans across Cally, smiling broadly in my direction.

'Not whilst I'm *right* here,' she objects.

'Didn't stop us the first time.' Harry laughs.

'What?' She crinkles her button nose, the other three of us laughing as she does.

'No, Anderson,' Amanda says sternly. 'You can kiss her when you both get home.'

The smile spreads across my face. On the one hand, moving in with Harry after being together for a matter of weeks was absolute madness, never part of my plan. On the other hand, when Wolf's housemate returned from tour, everything kind of just fell into place.

'And you guys working together again . . .' Amanda looks from him to me, eyes narrowed in suspicion. 'It's not going to be a problem, is it? It'll be fun, yes?'

'No.'

'Yes.' My answer argues with Harry's, the way it so often does.

'It'd better *not* be,' Cally chips in.

'No, it won't be a problem.' Harry turns to face me fully, grinning from ear to ear.

'Yes,' I say, smiling back at the one man I still love to hate. 'This is going to be fun.'

Acknowledgements

It's hard to believe that I wrote my first acknowledgements page for my debut novel in 2020 and here I am writing my *seventh* one in 2023. To everyone who has championed me and cheered me on along this wild publishing ride, thank you.

Particular thanks must go to the publishing professionals who make the dreams of us writers become a reality. To my agent Sallyanne Sweeney, my editor Bea Grabowska, and the entire team at Headline Review, thank you for supporting this story from start to finish.

And now closer to home: thank you to the friends and family who have put up with me missing things to write my books – and listening to me bang on about them when I do make it. To Mum, Dad, Tom and Rachel for being the original fanbase. And to Nick for loving me as well as you do – and for a particularly well-timed birthday trip to Bordeaux!

It's impossible to thank God without me thinking of an overly emotional Oscar's acceptance speech, but I truly believe none of this would be possible without Him. I am beyond grateful.

And to you, reader, you have no idea how much it means to me that in a world of so many extraordinary books, you decided to spend your time with this one.

Eve doesn't have time for dating, but having watched her best friend and flatmate have her heart broken one too many times, she reluctantly volunteers to play her Cupid.

Max is too much of a hopeless romantic to find the algorithms of online dating anything other than clinical, but he lives with his romantically challenged best friend who desperately needs his advice.

And after all, what are friends for?

As Eve and Max become more involved in their best friends' relationship, they quickly realise there is a fine line between instruction and imitation.

Especially when they find they can't stop thinking about their best friend's date . . .

Available now

REVIEW

KEEP IN TOUCH WITH
LIZZIE O'HAGAN

© Juliet Trickey

 @LizzieOHagan1

 @lizzie_ohagan